BOTTOM BRACKET

A MYSTERY BY

Vivian Meyer

SUMACH
PRESS

LIBRARY AND ARCHIVES CANADA CATALOGUING IN PUBLICATION

Meyer, Vivian, 1958-
Bottom bracket : a Sumach mystery / Vivian Meyer.

ISBN-13: 978-1-894549-58-5
ISBN-10: 1-894549-58-9

I. Title.

PS8626.E945B68 2006   C813'.6   C2006-904346-9

Edited by Jennifer Day
Designed by Liz Martin
Cover photography by Jerzy Smokey Dymny

Sumach Press acknowledges the support of the Canada Council
for the Arts and the Ontario Arts Council for our publishing program.
We acknowledge the financial support of the Government of Canada
through the Book Publishing Industry Development Program (BPIDP)
for our publishing activities.

ONTARIO ARTS COUNCIL
CONSEIL DES ARTS DE L'ONTARIO

Printed and bound in Canada.

Published by

SUMACH PRESS
1415 Bathurst Street #202
Toronto ON Canada M5R 3H8

sumachpress@on.aibn.com
www.sumachpress.com

To all the people who work tirelessly
in the struggle for justice
and equality.

Acknowledgements

Although the act of writing can be solitary, to publish a book is truly a collaborative affair. I would like to offer a general thank-you to all my family, friends and colleagues who helped to nurse me and the book along. In particular, I would like to thank the women at Sumach Press for having the faith to publish *Bottom Bracket*. Of course, I am most grateful for the patience, creative ideas and continued encouragement from my editor, Jennifer Day. This book would not be in the form it is today without Jennifer's sage advice. I would like to thank my children for sharing their mother's time and special thanks goes to my partner, Jerzy, who offered excellent bicycle advice and a non-judgemental ear throughout the book's conception. I have learned a great deal from start to finish in this endeavour and I am thrilled to have the opportunity to share *Bottom Bracket* with all of you.

The warm spring air wafted through my window along with the Saturday bustle in Kensington Market. The mellow rhythms of reggae competed with some spine-tingling sitar as shopkeepers vied for people's attention on the street. This, together with the familiar bleachy-fish odour of the store below, reassured me that all was well in the Market; I felt a wave of satisfaction as I stared proudly at the front page of the newspaper.

"Hey, Andy," I exclaimed as my friend sauntered into the room towelling his hair, buff in his tight bike shorts and bare chest. "Take a look at this." Excitedly I pointed to the headlines. "The trial is actually set to start. For once, the big boys are going to have to pay," I crowed gleefully. "Can you believe it?"

"Good going, Abby," he said as he snuggled in next to me on my small white wicker couch. "And how about today? Is Ms. Big Shot Investigator still going to try to smoke me on the Lakeshore trail?"

"Absolutely, Doctor. Gotta get back in shape for the Alley Cat Courier Race. 'Motion is lotion,' as you always say ... Hey, cut that out!" I laughed, swatting the hand that was creeping up my thigh. "Go get dressed, or I'll be forced to help you and we'll never get out of here."

"Hmm," he said, obviously considering his options, but I poked him in the ribs and he reluctantly got up and finished dressing without any interference. We grabbed our helmets and bikes from my array of multicoloured bike hooks. I was feeling confident that, with the day's headlines and, of course, the doctor's help, I could put the past behind me and finally ride away from the disturbing memory of last autumn's violent murder in Kensington Market.

CHAPTER 1

SIRENS WAILED AND, FOR A THIRD TIME, O'CASEY'S FINE SPEECH ON the problems of gentrification in Kensington Market was interrupted by yet another police car trying to speed the wrong way down Augusta Avenue. We waited patiently for the noise to recede and O'Casey, up at the podium, gracefully shrugged aside the interruption and wrapped up: "I will continue to do whatever I can to help. We must preserve this unique Kensington community!" The small crowd of about fifty people applauded politely as the silver-haired, left-leaning lawyer stepped back down into the group.

As people gathered around the speaker, my friend Beano leaned over and said dryly, "Nice speech but where does *he* live? That guy's got the big bucks."

"Oh I don't know, Beano. He's okay. O'Casey's in this for the long haul. He was the one who tried to help keep my dad out of jail back when he was doing all those anti-development demos. O'Casey did the whole bit pro bono as well."

"Whatever you say, Ab." Beano didn't sound convinced.

As we headed towards the door our conversation was cut short by an ambulance blaring as it, too, navigated against the flow down the one-way street. As I uncovered my ears, another friend, Sparky, burst breathlessly into the hall, her arms loaded with pamphlets and posters.

"What a racket," she said. "Big doings down near your place, Abby. Police cars everywhere, and the street's cordoned off. I had to go the long way round — lucky I got here in time. Can you help me out with these?" she asked as she handed us each a stack of pamphlets and a roll of posters. "Just post them up or pass them out wherever you can in the Market. We want to get as many people as we can out to the big demo at the hospital. Did Janet say her bit about the toxins spewing from the smokestack?"

"Yeah, but no one from the hospital showed up. Maybe they're just trying to ensure future business, Sparks," Beano said, winking. "I did mention the demo though and I'll put these on the counter at the store." Beano runs the coolest bike shop in Toronto, just up the street with his partner Alice. "Want to go grab a beer at Stan's? I need to pick your brains about the computer set-up at the centre." Sparky is a computer whiz who usually works by night and sleeps by day.

She shook her head. "Sorry, Beano. Not today. I've got a deadline. I just wanted to unload some of these." She piled the remaining pamphlets on a ledge by the door and turned to leave. "See you, guys."

"Wait, Sparky!" Beano said. "I'll walk you up to College Street and pick your brains as we go. Maybe I can get Alice to go with me to The Free Times instead. Are you coming, Abby?"

I smiled. "Nah, Beano, I want to speak to O'Casey before he leaves and then I'm kind of anxious to see what's going on out there."

"Ah yes, the insatiably curious Abby." He grimaced. "I guess it's right next door to you, so you have to check it out. I'm keeping out of it though. I hate gawking at other people's business. Besides, I get enough gossip at the shop. See you."

I nodded to the departing pair, my attention already centred on O'Casey as he drew away from the handshaking crowd and headed towards the door. As he approached, clearly focussed on a quick escape, I stepped up, holding out my hand.

"Hello Mr. O'Casey. I'm not sure you remember me." The distinguished-looking lawyer looked at me questioningly. "My name is Abby Faria. I knew you when I was a little girl. You were a bit of a hero to me back then, defending my father in court like that." His eyes brightened in recognition and he shook my hand again in a much friendlier way.

"Ah yes, Joe Faria's daughter. Not little Abby any more, I see. Are you following in your father's footsteps, my dear? Is that why you're here? Be careful, this is still a pretty dirty business, you know." My smile wavered. I don't really take kindly to being told what to do.

But I decided to relax: this was an old-world gentleman, just being protective. He didn't seem to notice my momentary consternation and continued affably, "Well, well. And how is the old man? I always felt badly about not being able to keep him out of the courts."

"He's okay as far as I know," I said. "But he's never been the same since that stint in jail."

He nodded. "I know — your mother told me the sorry details when I helped her with the divorce. At least that went amicably. She's quite a woman, your mother."

"Yes," I said. "She's doing pretty well now."

"I'm glad to hear that, my dear. And what is your father up to anyway? Still fighting the good fight?"

"As far as I know. Last I heard he was either helping tree spikers out West or doing some underground railroad work with conscientious objectors from the US. Probably both, knowing him."

"I hope he's careful," he frowned. "The Americans aren't fooling around when it comes to security. Well, at least he's not blockading development sites anymore. I admire the guy's commitment, but he does play a little recklessly."

"I know," I said, as O'Casey stood a little straighter and looked at his watch.

"And what do you do Abby? Still live in the old neighbourhood?" He meant the Portuguese enclave just west of the Market along Dundas Street. I shook my head.

"Well, actually, I live in the Market now and I mostly courier in the downtown core."

"Yes, I seem to remember you racing around the block on your little bike when you were a wee, wild thing. But you be careful, young lady, with all this activism stuff. I'm too old to be defending the second generation." He laughed at his joke as he shook my hand. He was obviously still hale and hearty, well coiffed, and very dashing in his full-length cashmere coat, jingling the keys to the Mercedes sports car outside the door. He had a thriving practice in Yorkville, old money, and obviously enjoyed using his time and prestige to help us folk down in the bottom bracket occasionally. I suppose that's why he was a hero to me — one of the few privileged people who actually deigned to be concerned about social issues.

As I mused, O'Casey glanced again at his Rolex. "Well, Abby. I must say that this has been a pleasure. Here's my card if, by chance, you don't take my advice and you ever need my help. I suspect you are a bit of a chip off the old block," he smiled. "Give my regards to your parents."

"I'll do that sir," I said, stuffing the card in a pocket of my bike jacket. We shook hands again and he swept away.

Most people had filed out while O'Casey and I were talking. I wondered again about the earlier commotion down the road. It had remained quiet since the ambulance had threaded its way by, so maybe things had calmed down on Kensington Avenue too. I set down the pamphlets I was still holding, realizing that I hadn't even given one to O'Casey, and helped the organizers stack chairs and tidy up. I spoke briefly with Janet, a local activist who was helping organize the next rally and the demo at the hospital, and got her to take some of the posters from my bundle. With that load slightly lighter I stepped out into the cool autumn air to see what was up.

It was pretty quiet as I walked down Augusta Avenue. The shops were closed and there was rarely much street action on a Tuesday night anyway. The police cars with flashing red lights sitting at each intersection probably didn't do much to encourage regulars to stick around either. But the usual ragtag bunch of anarchist punks was milling about outside Stan's, a local hangout.

"Hey Abby — did you hear about the murder down by your place? Rumour is someone got hacked to pieces."

My stomach churned at the thought of a bloody, dismembered body. Good news travels fast in our neighbourhood, I thought grimly.

"Jesus, Jeff! I can't believe it. Chopped up? Where the hell did you hear that? And who was it?"

"Uh, some crackheads on Spadina told me — they heard it from their dealer. They said the body was in bits and pieces, blood all over the place! Word has it it's Dan Burnett. It was at his house on Kensington Place."

I knew which house Jeff meant. I had always thought it was a crack house with all the comings and goings. But I reserved a sliver or two of doubt about the accuracy of the report, considering that the news came from such reputable founts of info.

"Any idea what was going down?"

"Don't ask me," Jeff shrugged evasively.

"Well, I guess I better see for myself what I can find out." I took a few steps down the street, warily skirting the pair of Rottweilers that sat fairly docilely by the group.

"Good luck," said Jeff, "but I don't think you'll get much out of the cops, Ab. They've taped the crime scene, haven't let anyone by. Ruined our night; Stan's had to cancel the Open Mic. We're heading over to Spadina. See ya later." He turned to go, grabbing one of the fiercer looking dogs by its studded collar and gesturing to a small sharp-faced woman in loose ragged army gear, cinched tightly at the waist. His latest lady love, I guessed.

As I turned down Baldwin towards Kensington Avenue, I could see red flashing lights reflected at weird angles through store windows. It had a garish funhouse effect but didn't prepare me for the full scene as I rounded the corner onto Kensington Avenue.

I am not a stranger to emergency scenes; there have been a few too many mysterious fires in our neighbourhood recently and I do live in the downtown core of a large city. But even by Market standards, this looked like a big deal. Beyond a noisy crowd of onlookers I could see at least six police cars, as well as a fire engine and an ambulance, all parked with their lights flashing. Their radios emitted loud unintelligible bursts of sound, adding to the general cacophony of voices. But it looked like I'd missed most of the action. A few cops lolled against their cars and some walked up and down past yellow tape strung across the street, but most of them must have been inside the house beyond. I wondered briefly what would happen in the morning when the Market woke up. Would it all be business as usual by then? But my immediate concern was whether the police would let me cross the yellow tape to go home.

My humble abode is located above Neptune's Nook Fish Shop, which is owned by friends. The shop is on the north side of Kensington Avenue, a couple of stores up from the corner. To get into my apartment I enter through the back from a side lane. As I started down Kensington, a very young officer stepped out of his car, which was blocking the street.

"Excuse me, ma'am — no one is allowed down there."

"Yes," I said. "I can see that something is going on but I live on this street." I pointed in the direction of the shop. "Can't I just go to my apartment?"

"Sorry, no exceptions I'm afraid"

"You mean I can't go home?" I was becoming exasperated. "You can watch me. I really just want to go home."

Fortunately, just then another officer approached us. I recognized him as a veteran who had once helped my father and who often worked overtime at demos. He was a pretty easygoing guy for a cop.

"Is there a problem, Chuck?" he asked affably.

The younger cop stood a little more to attention. "I don't know, Frank. This lady says she lives down the street but I'm not supposed to let anyone past the tape."

"I know her, Chuck. It's okay."

"Hi, Officer Berrigan. I'm glad to see you here. I live just over there above the fish shop," I said pointing toward Neptune's Nook.

"Okay Chuck, I'll take it from here," Berrigan said. The younger officer nodded and happily got back into the warmth of his car. Berrigan started walking with me down the road. "I'll just see you to the laneway, Abby. Stay home tonight, will you? We're pretty busy."

"Okay," I agreed. I stopped as we reached the lane, figuring I would try to pump him a bit. "Hey, Berrigan, what's happening? I heard there was a murder."

"That's true," he said nodding, "and it's a messy one. But that's all I can tell you."

"Some kind of bad drug deal go down?" I said, ignoring his comment.

"You know better than to ask me that," he admonished. "But I'll tell you this: there is likely to be more to this than meets the eye, so don't try to get in the way of the police investigation. As you just saw, some of our young guys are going to do this by the book and I don't think the bad guys are playing around either. Go home, be a good girl and relax. Let us get our job done so people can go to work tomorrow."

I listened and nodded contritely, but inside I was annoyed at his paternal tone. However, I knew better than to argue just then. I would bide my time; maybe I could sneak out to take a look later.

"Okay Berrigan. I hear you. Thanks for the help tonight. Good luck with the case."

He smiled in his kindly papa-knows-best way and said, "Good girl. Actually I'm heading off for tonight, and only too glad to. This was a tough one. I'm happy to let forensics and the detectives take over. 'Night Abby." He nodded again and strolled away. With little immediate choice, I turned down the lane and headed for my door.

It was nice to have my little lane to myself. Sometimes I get a little nervous entering it alone at night, but with all the cops around I figured I didn't have much to worry about. I guess I was still a little hyped by my tête-a-tête with the police because I just about jumped out of my skin when a stray cat leapt out from behind a row of garbage cans. But if it weren't for the cat I may very well have passed right by what looked, at first, like a bundle of blankets piled next to the cans. Instead, my pace was arrested by the sight of a pale white face turned towards me, eyes wide with fear.

CHAPTER 2

"WHOA!" I SAID SHAKILY AS THE SLIGHT FIGURE HUDDLED A LITTLE tighter against the garbage cans. "What are you doing here?"

She remained mute, shaking her head; I crouched down to get a better look.

She looked terrified. "Are you okay?" She was trembling uncontrollably. I took a deep breath and, praying she wasn't a violent junkie, said, "You'd better come into my place, just back here, and we'll see what we can do." I helped her up. As the young thing unfolded her thin frame to her full height, I felt a jolt of recognition. It had been hard to miss her the few times I had seen her in the Market — really tall, slim and unusually striking. But tonight she was haggard and tense, little of her beauty shining through. Of course I had only ever seen her from a distance. Perhaps even then some of the beauty had been on the surface, for tonight her white cakey makeup was streaked with black blotchy mascara.

"I've seen you before," I said as I fumbled for my keys. "Don't you live near here?" She didn't answer, shooting nervous glances over her shoulder, so I continued. "My name's Abby. Come in and tell me what's the matter." I was beginning to think it was going to be quite a one-sided chat if she kept up the silent treatment.

I ushered her in and led her to my main-floor room. Even though most of my simple apartment is above, I have this one special room downstairs, a converted storeroom at the back of the fish shop. It is my little retreat from the hubbub of the Market, well soundproofed and equipped with a Hepa filter to blot out the stink of fish, bleach and sundry Market smells.

I chattered on as I led her to my Salvation Army couch, grabbing a blanket for her as she was still shivering uncontrollably. It was then that I noticed the patches of brown on her jeans and sweatshirt. I had a pretty good idea what it was, but in as controlled a voice as I could muster I asked her, "What's that on your sleeve?" She stared at her clothes. Mouth opening soundlessly, her eyes rolled and she crumpled into a dead faint.

"Oh shit," I muttered catching her by the shoulders and laying her carefully on the couch. "Now what?" I shook her gently, calling out, "Hey, hello! Wake up! Please wake up. What's going on?" Her eyes fluttered open and focussed, and she tensed up again.

"It's okay," I said softly. "You're safe. Do you remember coming in here? Do you know where you are?" She nodded.

"Okay, listen, just lie here quietly for a minute while I get you some tea. All right? Will you be okay alone for a few minutes?"

She nodded again and closed her eyes.

I shut the door behind me and started up the stairs to the kitchen. I don't need much; I live simply with one or two exceptions. Rent is low, the landlords are my friends and food, if a little repetitive, is readily available. But I have a habit to support. Many women cherish handbags and shoes, but me, I am the Imelda Marcos of bicycles. I reached the top of the stairs and flicked on the light: there hung my impressive fleet, all in a row in my combined living room, kitchen, bike showroom. This is where I tinker with my bikes, lovingly keeping all ten in good shape and gleaming.

Unfortunately, I had no time to linger. I blew them a kiss and headed for my little kitchen corner where I have a hotplate, bar fridge, kettle, blender, toaster oven, small counter and sink. It serves me well because I usually just whip up a noxious but healthy brew in the blender when I'm not partaking of something already prepared in the Market.

I quickly filled the kettle and found some mint tea and a jar of honey. Hot tea with lots of sweetener helps soothe someone in shock and this girl was surely there, if not on something as well. While I waited for the kettle, I took stock of the situation. What had I gotten myself into, taking in someone with blood on her clothes just around the corner from a murder scene? Did she come from that house? I wondered as I poured the water into the teapot. It was getting a little late and I knew I would probably have to courier the next day. There was no way I was going to get enough rest to deal with insane city traffic tomorrow.

Oh well, I shrugged. I would have to find a way. Funds were running low.

With teapot, mugs, spoons, honey and a plate of stale cookies balanced on a tray, I made my way back downstairs. I wanted to know what was going on and see what I could do to help her, but I didn't want to press her too hard, as she looked pretty spooked and might just take off. At the very least, I had to find out how that blood got on her clothes, make sure she wasn't a vicious murderer in disguise. I knocked to announce my return.

"Here we go," I said, sounding a little like a jolly nurse. She sat up as I came in, and pushed her dark curls away from her face. "Oh shit, I was going to bring some water and a cloth," I said. "Oh well, never mind. You can have a shower later."

This was no mild gesture. I have a pint-sized water heater and treasure my showers above all else. I pulled up my little garage-sale coffee table, and my favourite chair, a plush wingback deal that I actually bought new, perfect for curling up in with a good book.

As I moved the tea tray from my desk to the table I asked, "Do you think you can talk to me a little now?" I look at her inquisitively as I poured her tea and stirred in copious amounts of honey. Her hands shook as she took it, but she did offer me a very small salutary smile of thanks.

"I'm Abby," I said, returning her smile.

Peeking over the rim of her cup, she took a deep breath and whispered, "I'm Anita." She paused, and I nodded encouragingly. "Something terrible has happened to my boyfriend. I think he's ... dead. I saw ... I saw him ..." her voice trailed off.

I knew it! I leaned forward and touched her shoulder gently. "Can you tell me what happened?" I asked softly.

Huge scared eyes staring heartbreakingly into mine, she began to tell her story, haltingly at first, but I didn't dare interrupt her.

Her boyfriend's name was Dan. She had lived with him in the house on Kensington Place. She'd been out working until about seven, and when she got home, Dan was there with some guys she didn't know. He had shooed her straight upstairs to take a nap before she went out later in the evening. She didn't know how long she slept but was awoken by yelling from downstairs.

"I was scared. There was the sound of arguing." She took another small sip of her tea and the shaking started again. I waited; the words came in a rush.

"I couldn't make out what they were saying, so I went to the top of the stairs and looked down into the living room. There was no one there but I saw the yellow blanket from the couch covering something on the floor. It looked like there was blood on it."

"I guess that was your friend under there," I said, putting my hand consolingly on her shoulder. She nodded.

"People were still arguing in the kitchen so I wanted to get out of there. I snuck downstairs and would have run past the blanket except I saw ..." She swallowed hard and set down the cup shakily. "I saw Dan's arm. I thought I recognized his shirt, but I just had to make sure ... I lifted the blanket and it *was* him. His eyes were open — staring — and there was blood everywhere." She looked down at her clothes and gestured at the brown stains on her pants wordlessly.

"Oh my God!" I said, horrified as I remembered Jeff's comments about the chopped up body. I asked hesitantly, "Did you see any ... wounds?"

She looked at me blankly and shuddered. "No! No ... I ... someone came in from the kitchen, and I was terrified they were going to catch me and kill me, too. I ran out and down the lane and hid near the parking garage behind a car. I heard some running and talking but then — they were gone. When I heard all the police sirens, I snuck up to hide where you found me. But, Abby, those people in the house saw me and they know I saw them. If they find me ... I don't know what to do."

"No wonder you're scared. But why didn't you go to the police and tell them what you saw?"

She tensed up, looked at me sideways and said vehemently, "No! I can't. I am not legal here — I'm from the Czech Republic. I don't trust the police and I don't think they will believe me anyway."

This complicated things considerably. She was definitely in trouble: an illegal female living in what appeared to be a crack house, blood on her clothes and absent without leave from the scene. It didn't augur well for her chances with the police.

"Okay, I see your point. Tell you what — why don't you stay here for the night while we try and figure out what to do. Can you think of anyone nearby who you trust or who could help you? Maybe I could go get them."

"No." She shook her head slowly. "No one."

What a position to be in, I thought. And she had nobody. I was beginning to feel protective.

"Come on upstairs. I'll show you where things are and then you can have a shower. Sorry, but there isn't too much hot water. It lasts about ten or fifteen minutes max."

We went upstairs and Anita gazed with silent wonder at my bikes. I couldn't help but feel a moment of pride at my assembled beauties, but this was no time for bike talk. Instead, I showed her into my messy bedroom. I dug up an old sweatsuit for her and a couple of clean towels.

"Once you're done in the shower, just go back downstairs. I'll have the couch set up for you. I'm just going out for a quick look around, but I won't be long, okay?"

She nodded, somewhat wearily.

"Thank you," she said. "You have been very kind even though you don't know me." She was still shaking slightly. "I am very grateful."

"No sweat. You've been through quite an ordeal. Try to relax if you can. I'll see you in a bit."

I grabbed a jacket against the cool night air and ran back downstairs. The couch, a comfy monstrosity, would fit Anita's long frame no problem. As I unrolled a sleeping bag and plumped up a pillow I wondered about the girl. What was she doing in that house and how did she get here if she was illegal? Was she even telling me the truth? The couple of times I'd noticed her before in the neighbourhood she'd seemed like a tough little number. I wondered how she would be when she was more herself.

I locked the back door as I left. One night visitor was enough.

Chapter 3

About an hour had passed since nice Officer Berrigan had seen me off, and I hoped he truly had left the crime scene. Otherwise, I was in for another lecture right away. The emergency vehicles were still there with lights flashing but now, alongside the ambulance, there was a long black limo — a coroner's car? I quickened my pace.

Quietly, I ducked the yellow police tape at the corner, aiming to get a look down the lane at the offending house on Kensington Place. As I turned the corner and checked up St. Andrew towards Spadina Avenue I saw media trucks and cars parked up to the tape. I guess they had done their big stories for the evening news and were waiting to do another live feed at eleven, because there wasn't too much human action on the street just then. The extendable satellites were up on the trucks and bright lights were trained toward the house down the street. I strolled up St. Andrew trying to look like I belonged there, and noticed that my friend Mario was being his enterprising self and serving his famous locally roasted coffee to the media folk and the cops.

Crafty devil, I thought. He would simultaneously garner goodwill and good business for his coffee shop, being the only show in town besides the Chinese takeout around the corner. I gave Mario's place a wide berth, not wanting to draw too much attention to myself.

There was a sudden buzz of activity as a young woman, this one looking a little more self-possessed than Anita, was led handcuffed from the house to a waiting police car. Even though it was really too far away for them to get a good look, the alert media types rushed to the yellow tape only to be intercepted by equally alert policemen. I joined the reporters at the line, trying to blend in as they waved their microphones and began yelling questions at the handcuffed woman, whom they seemed to recognize.

"Any comment, Ms. Blair? What was your part in Mr. Burnett's murder? Do you have a lawyer?" They kept on shouting questions at the unresponsive woman until the car sped off with sirens wailing, probably purely for effect since there was no longer any urgency. The media settled back to wait for the next bit of excitement.

They didn't have long to wait. Within minutes ambulance attendants wheeled out a sealed plastic body bag, which garnered more film footage and loud questions. I guessed this was the late Dan Burnett.

Just as I was about to ask a reporter who Ms. Blair was, another bored looking young officer sauntered over.

"This is a police investigation. Please move along."

I didn't want to draw any further attention, and there was nothing to see other than Tyvek-suited and masked police workers scurrying in and out of the house with various bits of equipment and plastic bags. I decided to heed my weary body and go home. I could just as easily wait for the Kensington grapevine and the media reports tomorrow.

"Of course, officer," I answered sweetly. "I live above that fish shop. Can I just scoot around to get there?"

"Okay but be quick. Please go straight to your home."

I had no problem with that. I was eager to speak once more with Anita and then to hit my bed.

She was already dozing and looked so cozy and relaxed that I didn't have the heart to quiz her further, but I did want to let her know I was home. I crept up and shook her gently. She looked much younger and more vulnerable wrapped in the sleeping bag, all traces of makeup removed from her waxy skin; young, but not particularly healthy.

"Hey, Anita," I said gently. "It's me, Abby. Can you wake up for just a moment?"

She started awake and blinked her eyes, momentarily wary. Then, realizing where she was, she relaxed again.

"Hi Abby."

"I'm going to bed now too, but I just wanted to let you know I have to work tomorrow during the day. You can stay here if you like.

My friend, Maria, runs the shop, and you can trust her."

She gave me a wan smile. "Thanks. Can we talk tomorrow?"

"Okay, sure. I'll get something for us from the café in the morning and then we'll have a chat before I go to work. Try to go back to sleep. I'll be right upstairs."

I hesitated at the door. "If you need me in the night just come up and get me."

She nodded. As she closed her eyes again, I turned off the light and shut the door on my way out. I tried to imagine how I would feel if I came across someone dead and covered in blood; I hoped I wouldn't find out anytime soon.

The front room upstairs was filled with eerie red light flashing from the various vehicles on the corner. Fortunately I could close the door to my bedroom and enjoy relative peace, but one thing I desperately wanted before I fell into my bed was a shower. I prayed that enough time had passed that the little water heater could have warmed the water, and I was in luck.

There's no better place to think and relax than in the shower. As the water poured over my head, I thought about the evening's events. I couldn't even remember what I had done with the flyers — I hoped I hadn't left them in the alley. But more intriguing was the question of who this Ms. Blair was. Anita hadn't mentioned any other woman. But Ms. Blair had seemed very self-assured and not particularly worried about the scene in the house. I shrugged to myself as the heat seeped into my bones, and decided that it could all wait until the morning.

I beat the shower to the punch and got out before it cooled down on me. It's a fine art to second-guess my unpredictable water heater. Satisfied, I quickly dried off, threw on a long flannel shirt, set the alarm for an ungodly six o'clock and hopped into bed. Sleep was immediate and dreamless, but all too short.

Chapter 4

Most days I seem to have this unwanted tendency to wake myself up about fifteen minutes before the alarm goes off, which is a royal nuisance because I lose precious minutes of sleep. I unset the alarm so I wouldn't have to hear its jarring noise and dragged myself out of bed. Stumbling into the shower, I tortured myself with chilly water so that I might be frozen awake.

Once suitably wide-eyed, I turned the water to my usual scald and began to plot my day. After getting dressed I would say good morning to my bikes, peek in on Anita and run around the corner to Overdrive, Mario's coffee shop. There, I could get the local gossip, scan someone's paper and grab some carbs and coffee to start the day. After that I would come home to call my preferred courier company to see what they had for me.

Plan in place, I thanked the shower and hopped out.

In the closed bathroom all I could see in the steamy mirror was a shadow of my thirty-something body — way past adolescence and the carefree freedom that comes with it. Don't get me wrong. I'm in good shape and work at it. I will only settle now for a partner whose mind has developed past ogling prepubescent girls and who appreciates a high-spirited, independent, tough-minded, mature woman; a man who believes in pursuing the mystery of the body and soul hiding beneath the outer wrapping.

Today I had to be colourful because a bike courier must be not only wind resistant but visible too. When we make what are admittedly risky manoeuvres for the sake of speed, we are fast, and for double insurance we make sure we're visibly avoidable. I eschewed the latest styles in lime green and stuck to my rainbow leggings and close-fitting sweater and my trusty, still-sort-of-yellow, still-sort-of-holding-together bike jacket. A mix of panache and down-at-the-heel seems to engender good tips.

Suitably attired, I ventured out of the bedroom to commune with my bicycles: two gleaming new beauties not yet fully paid for, three semi-dismantled antiques, two serviceable standbys and three nicely preserved museum pieces. Apart from my collection of bikes, my apartment is a study in minimalism. Formica kitchen table, two bargain-shop-special chairs, a wicker Sally Ann couch, clock radio and my one extravagance (other than the ten-minute shower): a new double bed and shelf unit. I didn't have time to linger so I did my little ritual hello to my bikes, grabbed my jacket, made sure Anita was still asleep and slipped out to get revved up at Overdrive.

Entering the coffee shop, I saw Mario's sister Veronica behind the counter.

"Hey, Abby. How ya doin' … the regular?" As she began to make me a frothy cappuccino she tossed conversationally over her shoulder, "I guess you know about the big hullabaloo here last night?"

"Yeah, Veronica. I had a hard time getting into my place without getting the third degree. The buzz is that someone was murdered. Hey, I noticed that Mario had the place open for business. Was he trying to get in good with the cops? Where is he anyway? I wanted to talk with him."

"Sorry, Ab. He's sleeping. He kept the shop open until three in the morning. That's when most of the cops finally cleared out although there are some still at the house, I think."

"Yeah, I saw one standing guard on Kensington Place. So, have you heard the scoop?" I asked, feigning indifference.

"Not much," she said, handing me my coffee. "All I've heard is that this guy, Dan Burnett, was murdered." She turned back to wipe the counter. "They say his girlfriend Sonya Blair found his body, all cut up on the living room floor. The cops took her in for questioning."

I almost choked on the foam in my coffee. Girlfriend? So much for Anita's story. Still trying to seem my simple, nosy, gossipy self, I kept digging. "Who was this Burnett guy? I always thought that place was a crack house."

"You're close, Ab. He was a dealer but he sold mostly weed, coke and heroin. Rumour has it that he thought of himself as a big shot dealer. He was a pimp too. There were one or two girls around who called him their boyfriend. They didn't hang here though. Usually down the corner of Dundas at the doughnut shops."

This was just getting worse and worse. But at least I could see why Anita would call him her boyfriend. It sounded way better than pimp. I was desperate for more info from Veronica but just at that moment a police officer came in and ordered three double espressos to go so I clammed up and took my glass mug off to a nearby table. There were no newspapers lying about so I would have to wait until later to check out the headlines. When the officer finally left, I went back to the counter with my empty mug.

"I should have made it a double too," I said. "Can you make me another, to go? I'm calling in to see if I can work today ... otherwise I'm going to have to ask you for credit soon," I added with a quick laugh.

"That wouldn't be a problem, you know that Abby."

"Yes, but I have my pride. While you're at it, can I have two choc- olate croissants as well? I might as well load up on carbs so I'll have fuel for the morning. It's starting to get a bit cool out."

"Sure," she said, depositing two luscious pastries in a paper bag and handing me my extra coffee. "These just came in an hour ago. The media hounds and police cleaned us out of everything last night. Mario said the murder was very good for business." She laughed wryly.

On that note I left the café. As I rounded the corner, I saw that the yellow police tape was gone from the street but still cordoned off the house of the murdered man. A rather portly officer stood kitty- corner from me sipping a coffee. I recognized him as one of the two who had escorted Sonya to the car the night before. They work long hours, I thought. No wonder they're drinking doubles. A police car stood in front of the house, but otherwise there was little evidence of the previous night's excitement.

I was eager to get back to my place to find out what Anita had to say about this Sonya Blair. I had a pretty good idea why they both seemed to be calling themselves his girlfriend. And then there was the inescapable fact that I had to go to work, which meant that I had to call the Arbuthnot brothers who, ironically enough, ran the "Call Girls Courier Service."

The food stores in the Market were starting to wake up; delivery vehicles were filling the street. The owner of the corner vegetable store was stacking boxes for display and next door they were unloading huge crates of apples by forklift. The clothing and sundry other stores stayed quiet, as they would open nearer to noon. Four or five oblong styrofoam boxes of seafood stood piled up on the street in front of the fish shop where I live. My old school friend Maria, and Irene, her mother, ran the shop together. Irene was already inside hacking chips from a block of ice to serve as a bed for the waiting fish. I went in the front way.

"*Bom dia*, Irene," I said. Irene, like many first generation immigrants, has remained most comfortable in her mother tongue. We, the progeny, usually speak a form of Portuguese liberally sprinkled with English words.

"There was quite a bit of excitement here last night. Did you hear about the murder?"

"I saw it on the news," she said excitedly. "I am worried for the store. Such a dangerous neighbourhood now. I'm so glad Maria and Frank live away from here. You should move to Mississauga near Maria, then your mother, poor Arabella, would feel much better."

I rolled my eyes. Irene could sound like a broken record sometimes.

"Come on, Irene," I said. "This is a great community — you should know that, so many years at the shop."

"Maybe so, maybe so," she said. "But, murder, Abby! This is not good. And too many drugs."

I nodded. We'd had this same conversation a hundred times. "Uhh, I'm in a bit of a rush today," I said, edging around her. "Could you do me a favour and let Maria know that I need to speak to her before I go to work?"

She waved me through in acknowledgement and turned back to her arduous task. I always wondered why they don't just get crushed ice. Must be some traditional thing from the old country. Maybe this kind of attention to tradition is part of what makes the Market so appealing.

I peeked in on Anita when I got to the back of the shop. She opened one eye sleepily when she heard me at the door.

"Good morning, Anita," I said brightly, the coffee now kicking in to wire my neurons. "Here's an early morning treat." I set her coffee and the croissants on the little side table and looked at her sideways, continuing the one-sided conversation.

"Take your time waking up, I'll just leave these here for you. Feel free to use the staff washroom across the hall. Maria, the shop owner, keeps it in good shape. Oh, and you'll probably see her or her mom working up front. Don't worry; I told them you were here." I stopped for a second, thinking. "They don't know you, do they?"

She shook her head. "I don't think so. We mostly ate takeout, or Dan ..." her voice wavered, "ordered groceries. I didn't go out unless I had to, um, work."

"Okay, that's probably just as well. Listen, I've got a couple of calls to make before I go to work but I'll be right back." She nodded.

As I was leaving the room, I saw the pile of pamphlets and posters on my desk. I would have to deal with those soon — one more thing to do. Preoccupied, I closed the door and headed up the stairs.

The upstairs living room began to fill with light from the bright fall morning. A few reflected beams of sun played over my bikes, creating a kaleidoscope of light around the room. It was quite lovely actually, a bit of promise after the previous night's horror. I savoured the effect for a brief moment and then turned to the serious task of ensuring my next paycheque.

The message light was blinking anxiously on my antique answering machine, a reminder that I do have a few friends and a social life that still ticks along. I decided to take a few seconds of my precious time to listen — anything to put off calling the Arbuthnots. I couldn't help but keep my fingers crossed as I pressed the play button. Maybe I had won the lottery.

"Abby!" My mother's excited voice sang across the wires. She has moved up to the northern part of the city, and now looks down her nose at us inner-city dwellers. We have a good telephone relationship, but things tense up if we spend too much time together.

"Abby dear, I need to change our Thursday lunch date. My reiki master was sick yesterday and has rescheduled, and I just can't miss that class. I know you'll understand."

I smiled. Despite our challenging relationship I still find my mother amazing. She is always trying new things and exploring new alternative health paths. If I have half her energy at her age I'll be happy, if not dead from exhaustion. I scratched our date off my desk calendar while the next message started.

A familiar, well-modulated male voice floated up from the speaker. "Abby, do you have time for dinner Thursday? Haven't heard from you for a while, babe. Give me a call."

Roger, a too-young, too-handsome lawyer I met while couriering, was my current sometime bedmate. Despite the "babe" reference, I tolerated Roger for important reasons. He adored me, we were great together in bed and, most importantly, he fed my second largest appetite (after bikes of course): the desire for good food. Roger wined and dined me lavishly and, while I did not like to abuse his good nature, I do believe in the sliding scale method of meal payment. But neither of us has illusions about the permanence of our relationship. Although he is very sweet, I knew I was not going to fit into his upwardly mobile life for long. In the meantime, we kept each other satisfied.

Salivating at the thought of another gourmet meal, I pencilled in Thursday night. The third message was just background noise and I was about to give up in disgust, my finger hovering over the skip button, when I heard a barely audible, "Hey Ab ... It's me, Beano." He cleared his throat.

Of course, it was the bike shop. That had been the sound of bike tools clinking and a truing stand being moved around. Music to my ears.

"Just checking in," he said. "How'd you do last night? I read some stuff in the paper this morning. Sounds gruesome." He must have called when I was out for coffee. Beano was up awfully early. I listened with interest as he continued. "I heard they're searching for suspects and want to find some girl named Anita who lived in that house — she's gone missing. Not much detail about her but there is a picture in the paper. I thought you might know her, Ab. Not that I care particularly, I told you I'm not into other people's business, but Alice said she's met this girl a few times and she's worried about her, so call us if you've seen her. Oh, and you should see what just came in from Shimano. Drop by later and we can talk bikes." He hung up.

"Shit," I said to the machine. Now I had another reason to be worrying about Anita. Worrying is not good for work. I have to be clear-headed when dodging big hunks of metal on the road. I realized the good side of not having any flesh-and-blood kids. The kind of anxiety I would have about my own child would not be healthy for either of us. I thought about Beano's message. It was unusual for him to take such an interest in other people's affairs, but maybe he was doing it to please Alice.

Since that was the last message there was no more putting it off: I knew I would have to bite the bullet and become a Call Girl. I picked up the phone to report myself available for business.

Chapter 5

Jerry and Louis Arbuthnot run a very successful courier agency with the dubious name of Call Girls Courier and Escort Service. I am pretty sure that they don't supply escorts, but what some of the women do on their own time is considered to be their own business. It's a reflection on the mentality of most businessmen that this name nets them such a large volume of calls.

Jerry and Louis are sleazy at best and pride themselves on their stable of women couriers. I tolerate them because: one, they hire women; two, they are up front with the sleaze; three, I can get work whenever I like because they say they recognize my "talent"; four, I like most of the other women who work for them; and five, Jerry and Louis are true characters. I tend to gravitate towards unusual people.

An additional advantage to working for this firm is that, because of the name, many clients get the idea that our services extend beyond delivering items; sometimes they offer generous tips in the fruitless hope that they might be able to acquire other services. With some difficulty I can usually pocket my sharp tongue and my feminism and generate a tolerable income.

While waiting for the dispatcher to pick up the phone, I pawed through my kitchen drawer for my pager and my Call Girls ID — two indispensable items while on the move.

To my surprise, Jerry himself answered with a long, drawled, "Call Girls Couriers, can I help you?"

"Hi Jerry, this is Abby. I am at your mercy. Do you have any extra work today?"

"Abby, angel of my dreams." I winced. "You must have ESP, we are *so* short-handed. Why girl, I have been relegated to the *phones*." I know that Jerry actually loves the phones but it is true that they usually have a very efficient dispatcher, while the two kings have other fish to fry. Wily investors, those two.

"Yeah, so I see — well, should I come in or do you have a pickup somewhere I can go to straight?"

"Straight ... why girl, that's no fun." Jerry is completely gay, and much more fun than Louis. "But as a matter of fact I do have a pickup at the theatre in the Manulife Centre. Pick up from Personnel, deliver to Bay Street Twin Towers, you know, the black monstrosities." Although he makes his living off this business, Jerry never tires of commenting on the uglification of the city. "Then, if you're quick you can hop over to the Gold Robbers' Tower and get a little package from the Foreign Loans Department and ride it over to the Heineken downtown business office. Call in after that."

"Thanks, Jerry," I said. "Say hi to Louis for me. How is your other half anyway?"

Louis, Jerry's younger brother, is his diametric opposite. The two carry on a loving relationship well disguised behind insults, jibes and sneers. It seems to work. Jerry is tall, Louis is short. Jerry gay, Louis uptight hetero. Jerry drawls sweetly while Louis is sour and staccato. Like I said, I was happy to speak with Jerry. Louis would have been more inclined to call me "angel of the damned," as I am strong on independence, which he professes to consider an unattractive trait in a female. Of course most of the women in their stable were variations on my theme.

I looked at the clock. It was eight-thirty. "Can you give me a half-hour before that first pickup? I have a couple of things to do before I am completely at your disposal."

"No sweat, Abby."

With no possible way of delaying further, I bumped my couriering bike, a nice little Trek aluminum baby, down the stairs. Maria had arrived for work and was helping her mother lay out the day's offerings. As I approached she had just finished setting up a rectangular pile of about thirty shiny red snapper.

"Hi Maria." Impeccably put together, as always, she turned to me with a look of concern on her face. Her dark hair curled softly around her lovely warm face. She has this ability to slow me down, to make me breathe easy and relax. We are a study in contrasts. Although we have been friends since grade school and we have chosen very different paths, she has remained steadfastly uncritical of my choices. She shares the suburban lifestyle of many second-generation Portuguese Canadians and yet Maria is one of the few members of my generation who still retains some of the Old World Portuguese charm. She seems happy raising her family and selling fish, following on in the family business.

"Oh Abby, that horrific murder! Are you okay? Did you see anything? Were the police interviewing door-to-door?"

"No problem, Maria," I lied, omitting reference to Anita's blood-stained appearance at my doorstep. "The police weren't very friendly but I wasn't even home when the body was found. By the time I got in they were just investigating the scene, I guess." I didn't want to worry Maria. She can be a bit of a mother hen at times.

"Mother said you wanted to talk to me," she went on. "I see by your, er, outfit, that you're probably working today. Is there something you need me to do?"

"Probably not. I just wanted to let you know I have a guest. Her name is ... Mary," I lied again, which I don't like to do with Maria. But I went on gamely, "She's a friend from down the way and she's a little freaked out by last night so I said she could stay with me. Listen, I've got to go, but I'll fill you in later."

"Okay," Maria said doubtfully, that worried look still on her face. "But no sneaking past me when you get back from work. I can tell there's more to this than you're saying, Abby. I've known you too long for you to get away with lying to me."

Apologetic but relieved, I said, "Thanks Maria, you're a doll. I'll tell all, I promise, if there's time tonight. I have to do grease monkey duty with the kids at the community centre later on."

She shook her head. "Not *if* there's time — you'll *have* to find time."

"You win," I said smiling. "I've got to go. I'll just let Mary know you're around and then I have to run or I'll be late for my pickup. See you later."

"Okay Abby. Be careful." Maria turned back to her fishy friends while I headed back to speak to "Mary."

She was up and flipping through a bike magazine when I peered around the door.

"Hi Anita. I've got to go to work, but I'll be back around noon to check on how you're doing. I don't have a television but you can listen to the radio if you get bored." I looked at the sweatsuit, baggy but too short for her. "I'll try to pick you up some clothes later from Exile." I took a breath before giving her the real scoop.

"Anita, you really do have to stay put. The police are looking for you — it was in the news."

She began to shake again. "Oh God! What if they find me?"

"Listen, no one knows you're here but my friends in the shop, and they just think that you came over because you were frightened by the murder. If you stay inside and keep a low profile until tonight, we'll talk and try to figure out what to do then. Okay?"

She nodded. "I don't think I have any choice. Don't think I'm ungrateful. I just don't know what to do. It's hard to sit still." She did look antsy as she got up and started to pace.

I stopped her and held her at arm's length, looking up into her anxious gaze. "Trust me, Anita. I'm going to try to help you. You've just got to stay put for now."

She relaxed a bit and shrugged off my hands. "Okay Abby, and thanks. Maybe I'll try to sleep again. I'm still pretty tired."

"Good idea. See you later. I'm sorry I have to leave you but you'll be safe here I think."

"Bye Abby." She looked so young and forlorn just standing there the sight tugged at my heart, but I gave her a quick hug and headed out the door.

Buckling up my helmet, I walked my bike out the back door. As I rode past the front, I rang my bell and waved at Maria and her mom busily chipping ice and hauling in fish for the day's business.

I zipped down the side streets, which were pretty quiet at eight forty-five in the morning. Occasionally I'd get a honk from someone who thought it outrageous that I would be going the wrong way on a one way street.

At Queen and Jarvis I stopped for a quick coffee at the Redeye, my second-favourite courier stop. Sort of like a truck stop but instead of trucks lined up three deep, bikes occupy every available inch and then some of bike parking. It was there that I finally caught up with the morning paper and read that the hunt had started for Dan Burnett's murderers.

Burnett was described as a small-time dealer and pimp. One possible motive put forth by police was a turf war between rival gangs. And there was, indeed, a picture of Anita, but my concern that she would be recognized was immediately dispelled. In the grainy picture she looked much younger, like a sweet young thirteen-year-old instead of the worldly young woman I had just met. I wondered where they got that picture. It won't help much, I said to myself.

I was a bit surprised that the news had made the front page. Death in the bottom bracket didn't usually get that much attention. It must have been the gory nature of the crime, or maybe it had been a slow night for news. But the article didn't even mention exactly where the murder took place. It wouldn't be long, I was sure, before the murder would move to the back pages and then into oblivion. I looked at my watch and reluctantly left my half-finished coffee, a true sacrifice, to begin my day's work.

Things had heated up on the streets and my adrenalin began to flow as I dodged traffic. The morning passed as uneventfully as it could for a thirty-something courier in colourful garb. I received my quota of catcalls, car horns, propositions and jeers, the main reason I hated this job despite the obvious perks of good tips, independence and speed.

It was the usual, delivering documents or cheques as fast as I could while dodging cars and the ever-unpredictable pedestrians, who gave no thought to the possibility of bicycles when stepping off a curb or quickly changing direction. The most interesting delivery was a bottle of chilled champagne with a double plastic bag of ice and a metal bucket from a gift basket company, which I had to rush to a hopping early office luncheon party on the 25th floor of the Royal Bank Tower. For my pains I received a shrimp roll and a hefty tip. I wished I could have stayed around to see if the entire contents had erupted upon opening after the shake-up of the bicycle ride.

That was the last of my morning pickups and deliveries, and as it was only about eleven forty-five, I decided not to call in to dispatch but rather to head back towards the Market. I wanted to make sure Anita was okay and I figured she could use some company for a few minutes before I had to get back on the road.

Some locals describe Kensington Market as alien territory. I'm not sure if that's a comment on the use of drugs in the area or the alien nature of the place compared with much of the rest of the city. Numerous developers have tried to make inroads in the Market, conveniently located near Toronto's downtown, but few have had any success. Originally a Jewish stronghold, Kensington stores now reflect a mixed bag — Jamaican foods, Asian foods and goods, age-old cheese stores and numerous inexpensive, funky used or new clothing establishments.

The locals are friendly and colourful. Those who actually live in the Market are often poor, eccentric, gang-connected or university students who think they are roughing it in the inner city. No regular would admit to considering moving out of the area, despite cockroaches, termites, rats and pressure from human versions of the aforementioned. But recently, a local community college campus was converted to condos, a portent of possible changes in the future. Hence our neighbourhood meeting of the night before.

I am known well enough in the Market to be considered acceptable, a semi-regular, a stable tourist. As I was locking my bike to the nearest parking meter Maria poked her head out of the shop.

"Hey, Abby," she said, waving her hand. "Mary left. She said she was going to Stan's. I tried to tell her to wait for you but she insisted. I guess she isn't so nervous any more."

Maria didn't know the whole story; I couldn't very well blame her.

"It's okay Maria. I'll go find her at Stan's. You were right this morning — there's some heavy stuff going on." I gave her a quick hug. "Don't worry, I'll tell you everything when I get back."

Anita was sitting alone, an empty coffee cup in front of her and the hood of the sweatshirt she had borrowed pulled up well over her head. I prayed no one would recognize her, worried that her height might give her away.

While one hand held up her head, the other substituted for food. She looked pretty wound up as she chewed away at her fingers. I pulled over a chair to her small table and a quick hush spread over the place. The locals were interested in what we semi-outsiders were up to. I looked around belligerently, plainly letting everyone know we did not welcome the extra ears, and a regretful hum resumed. I gave Anita a brief hug. Her rigid body received it and seemed to let go a little. By now I was sure that real trouble existed.

"What's up?" I hissed at her. "I thought we agreed that it's not safe for you to be out today."

"Uhh ..." she said hesitantly, "I don't know. Everything is so confused. I know you're trying to help but I don't know if I should even talk to you. I don't know who to trust. So many different people could be after me."

"Come on! It can't be that bad," I said hopefully. "After what you've been through, you can deal with anything."

She responded with silence and then her eyes brimmed with tears.

"Oh Abby, I can't put you in danger unless you know everything. There's more to this than just murder."

Here it comes, I thought. "I already suspected that, Anita," I said quietly. "I'm glad you want to open up — it will help me figure out what we can do. But if you stay out here you could get picked up before I can do anything at all." I looked at her seriously. "Let's get you back to my place and then we'll talk."

Anita stood up with me but, unfortunately, just as I was rummaging for cash, my pager beeped. "Damn," I said, as she drew back. "Should have turned this off."

"No, Abby, it's okay. You must be busy." She scurried off towards the door. I plunked down a couple of dollars from the morning's tips for her coffee, cursing the timing of my pager, and raced after her.

"Wait!" I called out. The locals were all ears.

"Really Anita," I said as I caught up with her. "Don't worry. Come on, let's go home." I was feeling a little exasperated by this dance, and with myself. Anita was right. I did have to go to work. She took control and solved my dilemma.

"Okay, Abby," she said resolutely. "I'll go back to your place but I'll talk with you only after you finish work." Although she sounded calm, she still looked jumpy. I hoped she would stay in for the afternoon. As we walked back to my place, I hooked my arm in hers.

"I'll be back by five-ish for an hour or so. I'll make us some food and we can talk while we eat. I have a stint with kids at the community centre on Wednesday evenings, but I'll be back again afterwards, so you won't be alone long. Does that sound okay?"

She seemed almost too agreeable as she said meekly, "That's fine, Abby. I understand." I gave her a studied look.

"You can go upstairs too, Anita; check out my CDs if you want, and look through my closet to see if there's anything else that fits you. Oh, and I'll try to pick up some clothes for you later. Help yourself to anything you want from the fridge."

She nodded. "Thanks for everything, Abby. I'm sorry I worried you, and don't worry about food. Your Maria keeps offering me buns and drinks. She is very nice."

"Yes, Maria is a good friend. I'll let her know you're back on my way out. See you." She closed the door to the downstairs room and I walked through to the front of the store. When I told Maria that Mary was back, she looked at me archly and said, "I hope you know what you're doing but I know it's useless to give you advice unless you ask for it." That Maria never misses a beat.

I gave her a hug. "Thanks Maria. I'll talk to you soon. I promise."

As I fumbled with my bike lock I felt frustrated and increasingly curious about Anita. I quietly cursed Kensington locals, phone pagers and the necessity of work.

I rushed through the afternoon, preoccupied and putting myself in immense danger as I ducked around the innumerable large trucks on the road. I was behaving fairly politely on my way home but I finally lost it after being cut off three times, and the next car that came too close got kicked in the door by my boot: "Keep your bloody car out of my lane," I yelled. "You don't own the road!" For this behaviour I received the finger, which wasn't bad, considering.

Chapter 6

WHEN I FINALLY GOT BACK HOME, THE FISH BUSINESS WAS IN FULL swing. I leaned my bike against the wall in the back hall and walked to the front, where I watched Maria lifting two-thirds of a remaining eel out of the ice for a customer's inspection. The choice tongue and eyes were already gone. Other sea creatures remained, staring blindly at passers-by, not that people noticed as they sailed on, immersed in their own thoughts.

I usually hang out in the shop to chat with my fishmonger friends, especially after a day of riding. I'm so speedy from the adrenalin required to keep me alert that I need to talk myself down. I get an olfactory workout too, as the morning's bleach has generally subsided by that time of day and the fish odour has supremacy. After the evening cleanup, bleach once again triumphs in the odiferous battle.

But today, I had little time to chat. While watching the brief and undignified end to the eel, I fidgeted impatiently as I waited to speak to Maria. Finally she got rid of the customer, but there were several more waiting.

"Hey Abby, it's been so busy I haven't had time to think. Can't talk right now, after all, so you're off the hook. But I'll catch up with you tomorrow."

I breathed a sigh of relief at not having to be the one disappoint. "Just quickly then — how did it go this afternoon? Any peep from our guest?"

Maria took on her worried look again.

"Actually, I haven't heard a thing. I went to the door a while after you left to see if she wanted anything else to eat. She wouldn't open the door. I knocked again later and she answered kind of groggily that she was okay and I haven't heard from her since. I hope she's alright."

"Probably just resting. She's had a pretty stressful time."

She shook her head slowly. "Seems to me she's all drugged up. How well do you know this girl anyway? I know how you are about picking up lost souls."

I smiled ruefully, "I know, I know. I hope she's straight, Maria. But I'm honestly not sure." I looked at my watch. "I'm sorry, I've got to get going. Can I grab those?" I pointed at three remaining Portuguese buns looking lonely on the counter.

"Sure, go ahead," said Maria. "I've got to get back to work." With that she turned to her customers, and I took the buns and hightailed it to the back of the store. Assuming Anita was still holed up in my downstairs room I knocked on the door and without waiting for a response called out, "Hey, Anita. I'm back. Just going for a quick shower and then I'll check in." That done, I grabbed my bike and dashed upstairs.

I snapped on the radio and got ready for the shower. The CBC regional news had just begun. Usually I only half-listen and talk back to the announcers, but today the words "body," and "Kensington Market" jumped out at me. I turned up the volume and gave my full attention to the rest of the broadcast.

… Investigators continue to hunt for suspects in the horrific murder. They say they have a number of leads and that the victim was known to police. Evidence is being collected at the scene and the chief has assured the public that it is only a matter of time before the murderers are apprehended. It is assumed that the killing is connected to a rapidly escalating drug war between rival gangs.

"Police are asking for assistance from the public. Anyone with information should call Crime Stoppers or contact the nearest detachment. Of particular concern is the disappearance of a young woman, Anita Wallach, who lived in the house. She may have been a witness to the murder. Police fear foul play and would like any information as to Ms. Wallach's whereabouts.

I frowned, thinking that it was unlikely that too many people in Kensington Market would volunteer info to the cops. I wondered if Sonya Blair had been the one who told the police about Anita. As I stepped into the shower for a second time that day, I hoped fervently that Anita would come clean to me about her situation. I already knew she was illegal and that she had witnessed the murder. What else could she be hiding?

As the water revived me, I went over all the unknowns in my head. What was her real relationship with Dan Burnett and how was she connected to Sonya? What had been going on in that house? She was definitely very spooked and it didn't look like she had many options. If she went to the police, she would likely be deported. There had been a rash of deportations lately as the government was in the middle of a general crackdown on illegal immigrants. No matter what she did, someone was going to catch her sooner or later, be it the police or the murderers. It was obvious that she wouldn't be safe for long at my place. For one thing she didn't seem able to stay put; she was very restless. And, on that note, was Maria right about Anita using some kind of drug? She was restless, jittery and sniffling: typical symptoms of heroin withdrawal.

Wide awake and anxious, I cut short my usual ten-minute shower and hurriedly dried off. The mirror wasn't even fully steamed up, and I caught a glimpse of my face in transit to the closet. It's amazing what anxiety can do to one's appearance. Worry lines etched my taut features, aging me a decade. I hoped Anita was willing to talk — I was ready for the whole truth.

I threw on my grungiest bike gear, as this was the night for my bike maintenance workshop for street kids at the local community centre. My rusty no-name bike from the rack would suffice for the short commute. Once I had it propped by the door in readiness, I mixed a quick yogurt-banana-kiwi-ginseng concoction in my trusty blender and poured it into two tall glasses. Then, balancing glasses, bike and the buns, no mean feat, I bumped back down the steps.

Maria rescued the bike at the bottom of the stairs. "Whoa Abby, slow down," she said, leaning it against the wall next to the office door. She looked at my choice of outfit disapprovingly. Although Maria had just spent her day scaling and gutting fish, she was still impeccably put together, relaxed and friendly. Maria even smelled good, like lilacs on a spring day — no scent of fish or bleach. I don't know how she does it. It's as if her saintly nature lulls the seafood into obedience.

"Oh, come on Maria," I said defensively, "Tonight's my night with the kids at the centre. I get all greasy and grungy. You want me to go there all dressed up?"

She grinned reluctantly. "Well no," she conceded. "I guess I can't argue with that logic. But listen," she continued, lowering her voice to a whisper. We were right outside my downstairs room and she obviously didn't want Anita to hear us. "Your visitor finally surfaced. You were right; she must have been resting. I said hi to her when she went across to the washroom. She looked like she had just woken up, but she was very pleasant. Maybe I was wrong about the drugs."

"I hope so," I said with a smile as she opened the door for me. Glasses in hand I entered my little sanctum, and Maria closed the door gently behind me. Anita was sitting in the chair in front of my desk, looking much more relaxed.

While setting down the glasses, I considered how to approach her. As I flipped through my mental Rolodex of options, none seemed likely to work, so finally I settled for honest curiosity and concern. It's the only one I do well, anyway. Usually curiosity supersedes concern, but this time they were equally matched as I sat near her on the edge of my desk.

"Hi there! How are you feeling? Maria said you were quiet all afternoon. I hope you weren't too bored, or were you able to take that nap?"

She smiled very pleasantly and stretched but didn't look me in the eye. In fact she looked down and picked at her pant leg as she said serenely, "Mmm. Yes, I slept for quite a while. It was very nice. I'm sorry I caused you all the anxiety earlier."

Her general air of evasiveness and nonchalant calm after so much anxiety was activating my warning bells.

"Hey!" I said, a little more harshly than I intended. "Are you on something? You're a little too relaxed, if you know what I mean. I wasn't born yesterday you know."

Her smile stretched thin as she shrugged, avoiding my eyes.

"You're right, Abby," she admitted. "But I was so tight from the events last night. Dan was supposed to give me some stuff yesterday but then … I had to run. Oh, this is all coming out backwards. I'm sorry." She finally looked at me, a little shamefaced.

"I had a fix this afternoon. That's why I had to go out. There's this one guy I know of who hangs out at Stan's. I had to get some stuff." She looked at me pleadingly. "I couldn't help it. I never did that stuff until Dan got me on to it. But now … I need it, Abby, you don't know what it's like."

A series of emotions vied for my attention as I considered Anita. Disappointment at being used and played for a fool, anger at Burnett for doing this to her, depression about the way society works and fear that this fellow Anita had dealt with would betray her whereabouts to the wrong people. I decided to start with the last thing first.

"This fellow you got your drugs from — was he still at Stan's when I got there?" She shook her head. "Did you tell him where you were staying?" She shook her head again. I took another deep breath. "Okay, we'll have to hope for the best."

She looked at me again. "Abby, I want to stop using. I know I can but this is just such a bad time … I hadn't had a fix for a couple of days and I was really feeling it. I know I can stop. I know I can. Don't give up on me. Please, I need your help."

"How long can you go between fixes?"

"I think two to three days. It depends on what else is going on and how stressed I am."

I thought for a minute or two and then, even without conducive water from a shower on my head, I had an idea.

"Okay, I have a friend up the road who volunteers at a rehab centre. He's pretty smart. He might know how to deal with this whole illegal status thing too. I'll see him tomorrow and suss out how much I can tell him. Maybe he can set you up in a safe place to get clean."

"Really? I'll do anything," she said fervently as she seemed to relax a little more, although I had, as yet, learned little that I couldn't tell from body language. I still had no idea how much I could trust her. In my experience, addicts say whatever they think you want to hear. Only time would tell whether she was on the level with me, and I had no idea how much time we had.

"You're safe here but if I'm to help you at all, you have to explain what has you so spooked. But first do me a favour. Take a deep breath, count to five and have an Abby Faria Special." I handed her one of the glasses, which she took willingly. The mix might clear her head, or then again could make her gag; I eyed her as we both downed our brew.

"Do you think you can fill me in a little more about your life with Dan?"

A hopeful look crept over her face. "You probably think I can't be trusted, but you'll see Abby. I'll prove you wrong. If I can get out of this mess, I'll prove you wrong."

"I hope so. Because I think we're both taking a big risk here."

She nodded seriously and then began her story, speaking a little softly; the mellowing effects of the drug, I presumed.

"You don't know what you're getting into, Abby. It's much worse than it looks and I don't know how to get out. I know they are saying gangs are involved but it's not just local kids. There are big players here and Dan was just a middleman. I didn't even know the guys he was hanging with last night, but I think it was a kind of hit. I think they were enforcers. I just don't know why they were out for Dan." It was as if once she had decided to let go of all the pent-up anxiety, the floodgate was released, but then her voice trailed off as she organized her thoughts. After a moment of silence, she continued. "I know I told you Dan was my boyfriend and he was — at least I thought so for a while — but, lately, I think he just saw me as a source of income. There was this other woman, Sonya, who showed up. I'm not sure who worked for who at that point. I thought I liked her at first, but now I'm not so sure. She started to get bossy and acted like she owned Dan and me. Oh, I don't know ..." Anita looked at me again and took a deep breath, suddenly looking like she was out of steam.

"Abby, there's more. But you know, I'm feeling so tired. How about I finish after you come back? I guess I need to rest now."

I didn't argue. "It's okay Anita. I've got to go anyway. Just rest." I motioned to the buns, picking one up for myself. "Here are some more carbs if you like. The shake should give you nutrition but these might fill you up if you feel hungry." She nodded, but went over and lay back down on the couch. I noticed she still had on my sweatpants and hoodie — I really had to get her some other clothes. I pulled the sleeping bag over her, tucking her in gently. "I'll be back soon. You might hear Maria out there closing up the shop, but she won't bother you. And, Anita," I said softly, "thanks for trusting me. It doesn't sound like you have been having a very easy time. You deserve to rest."

She said, half asleep already, "Thanks Abby. I'll be fine. I'll have a fair bit of energy after this sleepiness wears off. The junk is a mixed blessing, I guess. It always helped me get through the night when I was working."

I was pretty sure she meant when she was out hooking. I could see that drugs might help dull the senses in that line of work unless someone truly chose the profession. "Okay, see you later Anita," I whispered to the dozing girl as I turned out the light.

I closed my office door and had a hurried consultation with Maria, who promised to look in on Anita/Mary before she left. Reasonably sure that Anita would be safe at my place, I hopped on my bike and zipped over to the centre.

Chapter 7

I HAVE BEEN RUNNING THIS WORKSHOP FOR SO MANY YEARS THAT I have a regular space at the community centre and my own closet for tools and parts. The room is littered with stripped bikes and frames and I try to avoid asking where they came from. Sometimes I wonder if I am simply training kids to alter bikes to sell after they steal them, but I prefer to believe I am providing them with an employable skill.

I first met Beano when he joined the group a number of years back. I suspect this was just before he had hooked up with his gang. He had been a tough little guy. I knew him then as Dylan, a smart talker, always ready with a sassy greeting or a quick quip. Once he became actively involved and on the ascent in the gang, however, he left the bike workshop. I would see him from time to time on the street; he was always friendly but I knew he was walking a dangerous line.

A few years later, he told me how glamorous it had all seemed until he actually started seeing people dying. He had been dealing and after a year or so of being hooked on heroin himself, he had a sort of epiphany and decided that a different life might be better. The police also had a hand in this decision by arresting most of the gang. Of course those who were put away were just supplanted by others, but Beano benefitted by getting out the easy way. As he put it, usually you only get out of a gang in a body bag. He was lucky.

Beano got into rehab and, after recovering, decided to become a reputable coffee addict instead. He was a courier until he was hit one too many times and damaged his hips. He gets around on good days with a cane. On bad days he sticks to his walker or his wheelchair, which he handles like a pro. He says things are getting better with continued physio. Even on bad days though, nothing stops him. He also has a special modified wheelchair-trike that he rides "pedalling" with his hands. His is a true good news story. He used the insurance money he got from his accident to open the bike shop. Now he works on bikes full time, constantly chewing on espresso beans — hence the moniker Beano. His chocolate skin accentuates his shining bald head and broad smile.

Now he's my main source when it comes to bike supplies, and sometimes I help out around the shop, opening up for them on days when they're running late or working after hours in the winter assembling bikes.

I hoped Beano might be able to use his experience to help Anita, though I wasn't sure how far gone she was. Things do not often turn out rosy in the real world of hard knocks.

As I straightened things up getting ready for the workshop, I thought angrily about how Anita had been used. I might have clunked some tools down with a little too much vehemence because as Orlando, a cute little ten-year-old, walked in, he said, "Whoa Abby, did your date stand you up?"

"What? Oh, I'm sorry Orlando. I'm a little annoyed, that's all. I'll be all right."

"Well baby, you know I can always take his place. I'm always here for you."

Orlando was a little too worldly-wise for ten. Unless he's lucky, he'll end up on the path Beano first took. I know what sponges kids are; they squeeze out what they've absorbed.

"That will be quite enough of that," I said, sounding like Mary Poppins. For the time being we would concentrate on our shared love — taking apart and putting together bikes. As the rest of the kids trickled in and I started the workshop, I took a break from my worries about Anita.

They all flooded back on my way home. What else did Anita have to tell me and what did she want me to do? Most importantly, what *could* I do for her? I wheeled my rusty bike cautiously up the back way. In the autumn, darkness comes early and I'm more careful. All this business of murder and cut-up bodies made me a little nervous, but things seemed reasonably peaceful tonight.

The light bulb at my door was chronically smashed out, but tonight it gleamed a welcoming pale yellow. I had long since given up replacing the bulb but Maria must have done it this time. I usually rely on my very powerful bike light to fill in the shadows and I hold my nice heavy U-lock in readiness. It's wise to look tough when you're living on your own and have chosen a profession like mine. And I take precautions whenever possible.

Once inside, I leaned my bike against the wall in its customary spot. Black handlebar marks have formed an artistic border as evidence of the continual presence of my bikes in the back hall.

"Anita! It's me!" I called out so as not to startle her with my bumping around. No answer. I figured she was still asleep.

"Just give me a moment to change," I said, as I opened the door.

She wasn't there. The blanket was folded neatly over the arm of the couch, the sleeping bag was rolled up and the dirty glasses were gone. Oh no! I thought. I ran upstairs to my apartment; same old mess but no Anita. "Shit!" I said to the empty room. "Now what?" I had been so sure that she had been ready to tell me the rest of her story. I sank down into a rickety chair. What next?

Across from me in the dish rack were two gleaming glasses. At least she wasn't panicked when she left, or she wouldn't have washed the glasses. I wondered if I should walk over to her old house. But surely she wouldn't have gone there. Casting about, I noticed that the answering machine was blinking. Maybe it was a message from Anita; I hurriedly hit the button.

"Abby, it's me," said Maria's warm voice. "I just wanted to let you know that I brought your friend here for the night. She was awake when I was leaving and still looked a little scared. She seemed happy when I suggested she come home with me. We all had supper and she is upstairs playing with the kids." Maria has two children, eight and five. "She seems relaxed enough here; she's going to sleep over. I'll bring her back in the morning. Oh, and she left you a note on your desk." I hadn't even noticed it in the mess. Relieved, I ran downstairs and fished Anita's note from amongst the scattered papers.

Abby, thanks for listening before. I want to tell you the rest of my story but I am scared to stay here alone. Maria is taking me to her house. I guess it will be nice to be away from downtown for the night and I love children. I used to take care of my younger brothers. Don't worry about me. I'll see you tomorrow.

I breathed a sigh of relief as I headed back upstairs. Still, tomorrow was Thursday and I had committed to couriering. I also had a date with Roger but, hopefully, I could sort things out to satisfy all my needs. I had my employment, desire to help the underdog and curiosity, not to mention two big appetites, to consider. I grabbed the phone and punched in a familiar number. When Maria answered I started right in.

"Hello, Maria? Is there any way you could keep Anita, I mean Mary, up there until tomorrow evening? I have to work all day and I don't want her to be alone." Anita would be safer out of the Market.

"For goodness sake, Abby, slow down. For a start, you can stop calling her Mary. Anita has filled me in and I'm happy to help her out for a little while. She seems to have had a rough time. As for her staying here tomorrow, I have already asked her to. Thomas isn't feeling well, so Frank is staying home with him, but he's sick too. Anita said she'd be glad to help. I'm happy if that suits you too!"

"Hold on Maria," I said abruptly. "How much did Anita tell you? I'm not sure you are aware of the potential risks."

"What, you think that you're the only one who knows things? She has told me about the murder, and her addiction. She can't handle this by herself. Look, nobody saw us leave, I'm sure of it, and she seems relieved and happy to be here. Frank will be around in case she gets weird, and she is wonderful with the children, full of ideas for crafts."

"Okay Maria," I said gratefully, but I was still doubtful. "I'm glad you know that much anyway. She seems to have more to tell me so I want to talk to her soon. Look, she may get a bit antsy as she comes down although she told me she'd be okay for a couple of days. I was just a little worried about her being around the kids. I don't want to export any trouble. But if Frank's going to be there ..." I paused.

"Frankly, Maria, I didn't know you had all this intrigue in you," I added.

"See, you don't know your old friend as well as you thought you did. Don't you remember I used to go to those demos with you and your dad? I always thought it was fun even though I drove Mamãe mad."

"Yeah, I remember. I just thought you'd grown out of all that now that you're a respectable adult. Anyway, tell Anita to call me if there are any problems. She can get me through my pager anytime."

"Okay, will do."

"Thanks again Maria. You are a saint. See you tomorrow."

Even though I was relieved to know that Anita was safe, I was restless. I had been all geared up to hear her story and now had to wait. Thinking about my upcoming dinner with Roger was the best diversion. He had mentioned that the venue would be special, which meant that I had to come up with suitable attire. Since I normally specialize in dressing down I realized that I was going to need some help working in the opposite direction. I could think of no one better than my fashion design student niece Arabella Jr., or Bell, as we affectionately called her. She had always said that she'd like the challenge of dressing me up.

Keeping my fingers crossed, I dialled her number, only to get her voice mail.

"Hey Bell, it's me, Abby. I know it's short notice but can you come by my place around five tomorrow and help me find something presentable for a big date with Roger? I need a fairy godmother with a big magic wand. I'll be working during the day so just leave a message on my pager with a yes or no. That way I'll know whether I can count on you for a miracle."

I hung up the phone and tried to decide what to do next. In frustration, I put on my favourite Annie Lennox CD and headed over to my bikes.

Sometimes I find the best way to take my mind off things is working on my bikes. It did the trick for a while. I became so engrossed in cleaning and oiling chains, tightening brake cables and adjusting gears, that all thoughts of Anita and the Market murder were banished. Of course Annie Lennox belting out her twisted tunes helped too. It's useful having no immediate neighbours to bother at night.

An hour later I had completed most of the minor tune-up work on my two recent favourites — a glossy Trek road bike and a lovely Cervello — and was toying with the idea of riding one of them the next day. I sadly reminded myself that neither was fully paid for and that they were just too nice and new to put through the torture of being ridden when I was on the job.

So I safety-checked my older Trek standby, a nice aluminum model. I had stripped it last year of any brand names and now it had a lovely unique paint job that consisted of skulls on a splotchy red and black background. It clearly gave off the message: "This bike is ridden by a tough babe and you had better not mess with it" — an important statement in the world of crazy bike couriers. I daydreamed idly about a fantasy world where I radiated an unbreakable force field as I rode all day, untouched by comments, weather, cars or customers. Ms. Super Bike Courier, lofty, supercilious and kind.

Finishing off my bike and all ready for the next day's workout, I realized that I was too tired for another shower. As I hastily washed away the accumulated grease, it mixed with soap and water in the sink and created an iridescent muddy spiral which swirled with a sucking sound into the drain. A suitable comment on the day. No need to worry about getting grease in the bed — who would know but me? Not many bedmates were ever exposed to my little haven. The fish odour from downstairs and the bike paraphernalia upstairs didn't exactly set a romantic scene.

Despite worrying about my finances and Anita's predicament I fell asleep quickly. The smell of bike grease and metal polish in my hair were all the soporific I needed.

The only dream I remember was of racing along a country road, trees flashing by. I felt free and fast, and woke up quite refreshed at six-fifteen, but was still startled by the shrilling alarm at six-thirty.

Chapter 8

Before my much-needed shower I grabbed the phone and called Maria's house. She was an early riser so there was no fear of waking her up. True to form, she answered the phone more brightly than I felt.

"Good morning, Abby!"

"Hi Maria. Any problems last night? How is Anita doing?"

"That's my Abby, straight to business and still short on pleasantries, I see. Well, here's the report: Anita's fine. I told her to sleep as long as she can. Thomas was coughing a lot last night, and Anita let me sleep while she took care of him."

"That's great. It sounds like it's working out just fine."

"Oh yes, it's amazing. The kids took to her immediately. Usually when they are sick they have to have their mama but not this time. So don't worry. Anita will be too busy today to think much. Shall I tell her you'll call her this evening?"

"Sure, and thanks Maria. Now I can relax while I'm out working. See you later."

"Bye, Abby."

Reassured, I was able to luxuriate in the steamy bliss of my ritual shower. I was actually looking forward to dodging cars and delivering high cost mail. After a delectable blender concoction, I felt ready to battle the streets. I was about to call for my assignments when I noticed the message light blinking. Thinking it might be Anita, I pressed play.

My mother's voice rang out, "Where are you at this time in the morning? Well, anyway, how about Saturday for our lunch? I've been feeling guilty about cancelling today's date. If you're busy let me know; otherwise, I'll assume that you can come unless I hear from you."

If I called I would interrupt her reiki so I decided to call later. Always put off until later what you don't want to do is one of my mottoes.

I rang Call Girls. Jan, the dispatcher, was back, friendly and efficient. "Oh, hi Abby. How ya doin?" she asked rhetorically. "Got a pen ready?" I wrote down a list of five pickups and times. She told me to call back after those were done, and said she wouldn't page me unless there was a change or an emergency.

"Thanks Jan, I'll talk to you later."

I took one last longing look at my super deluxe bikes, then grabbed my trustworthy Trek and bumped my way down the stairs. Maria's mother was already in the shop chipping away at the block of ice as usual. I wasn't in the mood for a long conversation so I ducked out the back way while her back was still turned. I almost crashed into Maria as I was heading out the door.

"Abby, watch out! In a hurry, as usual!"

"Sorry," I said.

"Haven't you forgotten something?"

I looked at her questioningly.

"Your helmet, girl!" It was a comment on my state of mind that I had forgotten my indispensable helmet. I know that helmets save brains. I grabbed it from a hook on the wall and gave Maria a grin as I walked my better-behaved and dependable bicycle out.

My first pickup was not for a half an hour, so I zipped over to Overdrive.

With a proprietor who loves cycling, the place is often full of whatever bike couriers can find an excuse to detour through the Market. Mario sponsors many local underground cycling events and in return receives a loyal clientele. That early in the morning the place was tolerable, not too crowded. Most of the youngsters who habituate the place like to sleep in. Having already consumed my health beverage for the day, I figured a double espresso would be suitable additional fuel.

Mario can be quite taciturn with the crowds, but I usually just ignore his rough edges and enjoy a little banter. Mario, like me, remains pretty *au courant* fashion-wise, with his short spiky hairstyle, nose ring and tight, glamorously-patterned bike shorts. We flirt unabashedly with no fear of true romance, having long ago figured out that we weren't each other's type. Like the early morning coffee, the exchange gets the adrenalin going.

"Hey Abby, you in the business again? You can call my house anytime."

"It's just temporary. I need to pay the bills, but you couldn't afford me anyway."

"That's true. I know your taste in food and men."

"I do like them luscious and lean, with good taste. You fit the bill on one count, so don't give up, handsome."

"Whenever you're ready, I'm here. You know Abby, you could always work for me instead of the Arbuthnot boys."

"Thanks Mario, but I like the freedom of the road and, besides, your crowd are lousy tippers."

"I'll give you one tip for the road Abby," he said, turning serious. "Watch your ass out there. It's bad enough here what with murder on our doorstep but out there, those drivers are crazy. Murderers in metal boxes, I call them. Cyclists are getting hurt all the time. There's a vigil tonight at Queen and Jarvis for a commuter who was squashed last week."

"I heard," I said. "I have no intention of becoming road trash, and you know I'm careful, but thanks for the warning. Wouldn't want to miss out on our future date. Thanks for the tank-up, Mario." I downed the last of my espresso and stood up. "Got to get going. I'm a working girl now."

Mario should know about danger on the road. He saw enough biker friends get mashed to make him decide to get out of couriering while he was still in one piece. Mario, like me, was a loud proponent of taking the city's bike safety course. We are both careful, if a little crazy, and we both believe in staying alive.

With these sober thoughts, I nonetheless began my day's work. For up to eight hours I was at the mercy of the Call Girls Courier Service. The first pickups and drops were uneventful. The fourth pickup was for Johnson Developers, famous for taking rundown sections of downtown Toronto and converting them to condos with street-level coffee shops and chi-chi boutiques.

The city is coming of age, I suppose, as downtown areas become gentrified. The problem, from my perspective, is that these "rundown" areas are neighbourhoods for real people who couldn't possibly afford condos. As a result many low-rent tenants get booted and have a hard time finding a new place to live. Needless to say, I was not terribly impressed by the likes of Johnson. He was one in particular who we had decided to keep an eye on when we held the meeting on preserving the Kensington community — where O'Casey had given his great speech. I hoped to get in and out of Johnson's fast and prayed that I wasn't contributing to the end of another squat or low-rent spot as I played carrier pigeon.

It turned out I was to deliver the package to the law firm Roger worked for. I guessed that some kind of deal was going through because the instructions were to wait for papers to be signed and bring them on back. From previous experience I knew this might go on for a while as offers and counter-offers were shuttled to and fro. So much for my hope to be quit of Johnson's quickly. I zoomed over to the lawyers, package in my bag.

Smythe, Blondin & Associates is located in the thick of Bay Street's "Cutthroat Row." The receptionists are friendly and the front lobby decor is a mix of warm tropical style and sterile glass and mirrors. It's a large firm with loads of hardworking junior lawyers in cubicles in the centre of the floor while the partners' offices are strategically arranged around the outer edges, sporting windows and snazzy furniture.

Roger was a comfortable junior lawyer, seemingly on the way up. It wouldn't do to advertise that he had a grubby Call Girl Courier for a sometime girlfriend, so I didn't inquire after him. I dropped off the parcel, agreeing to be back in thirty minutes, and placed a call to the Arbuthnots to explain my new assignment as go-between for some nasty development deal. With half an hour to spare I dashed into the nearest underground mall food court and grabbed a stir-fry, reckoning that this was the least likely to be an abomination to the word "food."

For a few minutes I watched all the well-dressed folks rushing in for a speed-lunch, stepping over or around the homeless person who sat cross-legged on the ground at the entrance to the mall. Most people avoided looking at the man as he proffered his hat hoping for change. I'm no saint and don't have the money for all the homeless in Toronto, but today my pockets jingled with tips, so I figured I could spread the wealth, such as it was.

When I got back to Smythe & Co. the package awaited, so I headed back to Johnson's with it. Their lobby is not nearly so lovely. You would think that a company that builds yuppie condos would be more inviting. It was stark and tasteless with a black and white checkered tile floor, white reception desk, a hard and unwelcoming lobby couch, the requisite two potted plastic plants and a cheap coffee table laden with a multitude of promotional pamphlets. The picture was topped off with a cardboard glam couple smiling in front of a photo of a living room with a view, all under a huge banner saying "Watch Us Grow."

Maybe there was a warmer inner sanctum for more important personages but I obviously didn't rate as the receptionist looked down her nose and told me coldly I could wait in the lobby until the package was ready for its next shuttle across town. Icy reception tends to spark rebellion in me, so I plunked myself on the edge of her desk and said, "I'll wait here if you don't mind."

She shrugged. "Suit yourself, but the couch is probably more comfortable."

No doubt she was right, but sheer perversity kept me perched where I was. She minced her way through a door to a dark, panelled office. After a few minutes I began to glance idly around her desk and computer. I am naturally nosy, so when I saw the words "Augusta" and "Kensington" on a manila file folder, my curiosity was piqued. Was this a hint that the Johnson group was setting their sights on Kensington? I looked around and, still abandoned, I lifted the cover of the file. The first page was headed "239 Augusta," which was interesting because that place had been burned in a spectacular fire a year ago. It had been boarded up ever since. It seemed that the file was due to go out. It sat on a large envelope beside a sealable courier package.

Oh well, I thought. Other developers have tried to make inroads into Kensington without much success. Johnson might as well waste his money trying too. We were on to him.

Not wanting to sully the reputation of Call Girls by getting caught snooping, I closed the intriguing file and looked over at the PC. I'm the only person I know who doesn't have a computer, and the little experience I've had is with Macs. If I need anything more complicated than basic word processing or e-mail, I go to my favourite expert, Sparky.

I stared, intrigued, at the receptionist's screen-saver, which was an interlocking, constantly changing puzzle of her latest screen. With the ever-shifting blocks of words it developed into a series of Picasso-esque images. From what I could make out it was just some boring memo to building with no reference to Kensington, so I gave up on that too. An attention-getting ache in my leg forced me to get off the edge of the desk in favour of the couch, so I was sitting demurely counting the minutes when she finally returned.

"You might as well take this package with you, too," she said slipping the file I'd snooped and a computer disc into the large envelope, which then went into the sealable package. I noted that both items were headed for the same law firm. They seemed to be getting a lot of business from Johnson today.

"No chance to peek," I said, although, in fact, I know the tricks of the trade. If I had really wanted to get into it, I could. I smiled sweetly, which is something I find difficult to do so it probably looked as false as it felt.

"All right then. I'll be off," I said, shoving the package into my bag. "See you later." I varied my route back, a little bored with this routine. Traffic was light as it was the lull between lunch and the end of the workday so I wasn't overly challenged in any direction. I hoped this back-and-forthing was not to go on for too long, because I wanted to suss out the Market scene for more info about the murder, and call Anita before getting ready for my date with Roger. So much for this girl to do.

When I arrived back at Smythe & Co., Sherri L. the receptionist took the two items from the package, placed the Kensington file on her desk and whisked the other to the inner sanctum. Fortunately, they were much more efficient and the wait was short. Sherri was also much more forthcoming than Ms. Hoity-Toity at Johnson's.

"This will be the last trip today for this deal," she said brightly. "Does that mean you're done for the day?"

"I think so," I said. "I'll just carrier pigeon this back and hopefully be on my way home. It's a bit late in the day for any new pickups. The other courier girls will probably have it all sewn up. Seems like a big deal what with all this back and forth ..." I said leadingly.

"Yeah," said Sherry. "The buzz is that some hotshot is cementing a partnership with Johnson." She shrugged her shoulders as if it wasn't a big thing to her. "Have a great day," she said, turning her attention back to her computer.

"You too," I said as I picked up my satchel.

As I waited for the elevator with half a dozen other folks, all much better put together than I, Roger emerged from the office, nodded surreptitiously to me and headed for the stairway. His furtive manner was more compelling than the green light creeping up and down the floor indicator so I nonchalantly headed that way too. There was hope for Roger, I thought. He is usually not that quick off the mark.

"Hi Rog!" I said as I clattered down the first flight behind him.

"Abby," he said warmly, "It's nice to see you."

"Mmm, just doing my day job Rog," I said. I am such a gifted conversationalist. One floor down he stopped, drew me to him in a comfortable embrace and an enthusiastic kiss. I could almost hear him panting like a puppy dog. This was definitely a fun departure from the day's business plan.

"I can't wait to see you at dinner tonight Abby."

"I'm looking forward to it myself," I answered, a little breathless. It was true — my appetite for an amorous interlude and a decent meal were now more than whetted. Our furtive little tête-à-tête was brought to an abrupt end, however, when we heard a door open a little higher up the stairs. So we guiltily hurried on down the stairs, businesslike again. We agreed that he would pick me up at my place at six-thirty. I was counting the hours, all four and a half of them.

I squeezed his hand at the bottom of the stairs and rushed off to unload the last set of papers. I hoped Johnson's was turning over a new leaf, planning, say, to build low-rent housing subsidized by their ill-gotten gains. An unlikely scenario but a distracting fantasy.

I was released from couriering after I dropped the package with the snooty receptionist at Johnson's, a bit pissed at receiving no tip after all the waiting around. Call Girls should charge a fifteen percent gratuity for shuttle service, just like restaurants do for large parties.

As I travelled the few blocks west home, I was almost blinded by the autumn sun. As I knew this would be the case for car drivers too, I exercised extra caution. I was rewarded with my life when a car cut me off not once, but twice! I managed a good kick at the passenger door the first time and was ready with lock in hand the next time to give a whack at the car, a feat I would not recommend to the novice biker, especially one who isn't quick enough to avoid an irate swerving driver. As it was, I had to deke up a side street while the driver screamed obscenities after me. It never crossed his mind that he had almost killed me.

Reaching home unscathed and hyped, I decided to use the overdose of adrenalin to pass those pamphlets around the Market, and make my way up to Beano's to see whether he was ripe for helping Anita. I left my bike propped up in the downstairs hall, sure to incur Maria's wrath, but hey, I was on a schedule. I grabbed the pamphlets and a couple of posters and snuck out the back way.

CHAPTER 9

THE MARKET WAS MELLOW. IT WAS THURSDAY AFTERNOON AND the proprietors were just beginning to think about the rush hour ahead. The clothing store across the street from Neptune's had some easy rock blaring from a speaker sitting next to a uniquely dressed mannequin done up in cowboy boots, pink fishnet stockings, a green tutu and an army jacket, topped off with a leather flying cap and pink goggles.

Next door, my friend Sarah leaned against her cheese shop smoking a cigarette. She perked up as I approached, "Hi Abby," she said. "How's things? You done couriering for the day or just taking a break?"

"Hey, Sarah. Yeah, I had a string of runs back and forth between two places and then they let me off. Good thing too, I needed to find some time to get this stuff distributed." I handed her some pamphlets and a poster. "I know your place is crammed but could you find some room for these?"

"No sweat. If you have time, come by on Saturday. We're having a special on your favourite, the spiced Gouda. And I'll fill you up with some other samples."

"I'm having lunch with my mom Saturday so I don't know what kind of time I'll have, but it sounds enticing. Maybe if I get up early enough ... you know it's the best way to breakfast in the Market, a sample here, a sample there."

"Yeah, you're not great for business, Ab. But when you get moaning over some cheese, it does sometimes get other people interested in buying the stuff." We laughed.

"Okay, Sarah, gotta go. I'll talk to you later."

A little further along, I crossed the street and handed some flyers to the local Rastas, their dreadlocks hanging out of brightly-coloured caps.

"Hey guys, can you spread these around?" I turned to a young woman with a child in a sling.

"I know you're concerned about the smokestack being so close to the playground, Angie. We're staging a demo next week. Do you want some of these to hand out to the other mothers who take their kids there?"

Angie nodded, taking a handful of pamphlets. She was grooving to the reggae that emanated from their tiny speaker on the table where she was selling brightly knit hats like the ones the Rasta dudes were wearing.

"Cool," she said. "We'll be there in full force, Abby."

I wondered if, indeed, the papers would get passed out. She seemed mellow from the large pipe of hash she was puffing on. She was totally unconcerned about smoking it openly on the street. I politely declined an offer to share — my lungs get enough crap while I'm pedalling through the downtown smog — and moved on.

Down Baldwin, Harry the street person was selling the local homeless newspaper in front of the large European butcher shop, huge hunks of meat hanging in its picture windows. Averting my eyes from the carnage, I exchanged a pamphlet and a dollar for Harry's newspaper. "Thanks, Abby. That was my last one," he said, pocketing the pamphlet. "Now I can go get a coffee." Before continuing down the street I contemplated the Market scene. I do love the place — it's such a rich mix of people from all walks and cultures and we all seem to get along. I have never seen people fight in the Market — murder aside. Occasionally a vegan extremist may look askance at some fur-wearing tourist whose coat risks a coffee stain, but that's it.

I ambled along down the road, feeling pretty good. I had already unloaded half of the flyers and I wasn't even finished with Baldwin Street. I stopped at Neptune's competition and got the go-ahead to put up two posters. Crossing the street, I gave a nosy peek through the door to Roach-a-Rama and The Hot Box Café, the only openly pothead restaurant in Toronto. It looked cosy, all couches and low tables. The menu included foods to please vegan and carnivore alike, though clients suffering from the munchies might not be picky about their food anyway. It was a crafty way to ensure business. Seeing no one around, I dropped a few pamphlets on the nearest couch and made my way to Stan's, a little further down the road.

It was dark and loud inside, as punk rock throbbed from the group tuning up in the back. While most of the clientele are in their twenties and thirties, some of the regulars have been hanging out and getting old in the Market for almost two decades. As the rest of their generation graduated to more mellow music with the odd foray back into the punk scene, these guys have become the granddaddies of pitbull owners and heavy metal music.

Peering through the gloom, I recognized Jeff from the other night hanging with the band at the back. He saw me and waved, then said something to the guitarist and slouched across the room towards me.

"Hey, Abby. How'd it go the other night? Cops hassle you?"

"Big time, you were right. They didn't want anyone around. I had to be awful nice before they would let me go home."

"Knowing you, Abby, that must have been tough. D'you find out anything?"

"Nuh-uh." I wasn't about to tell Jeff, one of the town criers, any details. It was one thing to listen to gossip but I'm careful about sharing it. I shrugged and looked at the grungy poster board. "Oh good, thanks for putting up the demo notice."

Jeff looked around guiltily. "Oh, that wasn't me ... I forgot, sorry. Someone else must have put it up."

I wasn't surprised. " S'okay. Maybe I'll just drop a few flyers on the counter as well."

"Suit yourself," he said. "Jan's cool." Jan, the manager of the bar, was indeed cool and tended to let things be as long as folks weren't too aggressive or drunk. Despite the intimidating look of Stan's, the most dangerous thing that ever happened there was the occasional dogfight.

"Well Jeff, I'm off. I want to check out Beano's place, 'scope what's new. Take it easy." He nodded, his attention already back with the band. As the din continued I was glad to return to the fresh fishy-veggie air of the Market.

Passing the Bed, Bath and Camouflage clothing shop, white table-cloths fluttering next to flak jackets, I chuckled at the variety of the Market. I hated the thought of anyone coming in and trying to sanitize it.

I wanted to stay revved so I headed for the next decent coffee place: the candy, dried fruit and nut shop at the corner of Augusta and Baldwin. It was still warm enough for jacketed locals to sit on the bench outside the shop to sip and smoke. I'm not a fan of smoking, but I keep my mouth shut. So I said a general "Hi" to the folks and went inside. The tiny shop has two stools and floor space for one or two other people. You can't really linger or chat unless you're prepared to brave the elements outside. I grabbed three cappuccinos to go and continued my way up the street. The empanadas next door looked tempting but I knew I had a promising dinner ahead so I refrained.

I dropped the remaining flyers with Harvey, Beano's competition. Harvey runs a very small, recycled bike shop down a gravel lane off Augusta. He seems content to work in his grubby, unheated space throughout the year. He's not really competition. Beano often sends Harvey people who can't afford his high end stuff or whose bikes are in too awful a state of disrepair. Harvey's is a gold mine if you're looking for a used bike or a discontinued model. He's totally honest, which is more than I can say for some bike shops I know, which the police visit on a regular basis.

"Hi Harv. How's business?" I asked, once my eyes had adjusted to the dimness of his shop — actually more of a garage, with a small window and a filthy skylight for illumination.

"Oh, hi Abby," he said, adjusting the bent glasses on his nose. A thick black line on the side of his nose indicated that he had repeated this action many times with his oily fingers. One does not visit Harvey looking for a clean, organized looking business. He seems to know exactly where to find his parts, though.

"Can I leave these on your windowsill?"

"Go ahead. I already have a poster up," he said indicating the poster pasted in his one window. "Are you going to be at the demo?"

"I hope so," I said. "Depends whether I have to work. Sparky will be there though. These posters are her handiwork."

I knew that Harvey had a crush on Sparky, which she thought was sweet but did not really reciprocate. She's mostly into those who speak in binary code. I'm sure she'd be happy to chat with him at the demo, though, one of the few times she would be out in daylight.

His eyes lit up. "Well, I'll be there for sure. Maybe I'll see you guys then."

"Great, Harvey. Try to talk it up. If there's a big crowd we might even get some media attention this time." I reached for the door. "I've got to go now, my coffees are getting cold. See ya."

"See you Ab," he said, turning back to tuning a decrepit wheel.

That was my last stop. I hurriedly navigated my way up the rest of Augusta to The Squeaky Wheel.

"Hi guys," I said as I walked into the store. Beano and Alice run a clean, orderly place. They take turns staffing the repair area and the front desk. A row of gorgeous new bikes lines one side of the spacious store. New wheels and tires hang from the ceiling, filling the place with a heady rubber aroma, while parts and accessories line all the other available wall space. On the wall beside the front counter is a large bulletin board, which displays pictures and ads for bikes and assorted community events.

"Hey, look what the cat dragged in, and with coffee yet," said Alice. "Thank you very much m'dear," she said as she took two cups from the little tray and handed one to Beano. Alice's heavy head of dreadlocks created a wide frame for her petite face. A misleading package, Alice may be tiny but she is fit and powerful and an amazing bike racer. When she was a little younger she was into some fantastic freestyling on her custom BMX.

Beano took a gulp. "Ahh, definitely needed a jolt of java, Abby. Great timing, the evening rush hasn't started yet so we can relax a bit and shoot the shit."

"Precisely why I'm here Beano," I replied. "But I can't stay too long. I have a date with Roger tonight and, as you can see, I'll need some time to transform. You remember my niece, Bell? She's going to help me out."

"The Cinderella routine, is it? I know the guy is good for your dietary needs but don't you think it's time to find someone a little more you, someone you can introduce to your friends, Ab?"

"Not that it's any of your business, Beano," Alice interjected. "Don't listen to him, Abby, he's just jealous. He wishes I could wine and dine him like that." Alice gave Beano an affectionate tweak.

I laughed, refusing to be offended by Beano's banter. "Don't worry, Beano. I don't think Roger and I harbour any illusions of permanence. But we have fun. He's sweet and we like each other so I'm going to just go along for the ride right now."

Alice smiled broadly, "You go, girl! It's about time women stand up and take what they want. Men have been doing it for centuries. You're my hero, Abby."

"Thanks Alice, but let's not get carried away. I envy you and Beano you know — you're so good together. I wouldn't mind finding someone to I could share more stuff with. Anyway, you guys — I came bearing gifts but I have an ulterior motive. I need your advice."

"What is it, Ab? Your new Market cruiser giving you problems?" Beano asked.

"No, nothing like that. Although, come to think of it, the bottom bracket on my Trek is starting to creak. Do you have another in stock?"

Beano shook his head as he put down the wheel he was working on.

" 'Fraid not, but I think there's one in the order coming in on Monday. I'll put it aside for you to pick up. But what's this advice you need?"

"Well, I need some help for a friend."

Beano looked mildly interested, "That reminds me, did you find anything out about that girl, Anita?"

I feigned disinterest. "Oh, you mean the one Alice wanted to know about?"

Alice looked confusedly up from the counter? "Huh, what's that? Beano?"

He blushed and looked a little sheepish. "Okay, I'm the one who wanted to know. You remember Artie, Alice?"

She bit her lip and said a little hesitantly. "That guy you used to hang with?"

"Um, yeah, I know you don't like him Alice, but he's not so bad. Anyway, it turns out he met this Anita on the street and developed a soft spot for her. He's been calling everyone trying to find out if she's okay. I told him I'd check around. I didn't want to get into long explanations, so I just told Abby it was for you."

"Well it's not, and don't use me like that," she said angrily. "You know I hate that, especially when it's totally unnecessary." She shook herself and looked at me sheepishly. "Sorry, no need to air dirty laundry. You see? We're not perfect either. But anyway, what was it you wanted, Abby?"

I was feeling pretty confused by this little interchange. Something strange was going on here. My protective instincts warned me to step carefully. "Oh, it's okay. Nothing that can't wait," I said evasively.

Alice looked gentle daggers at Beano. "I'm sorry, Abby." She looked like she wanted to say more but just then someone entered the shop so she stopped herself. Then she said, "Beano, why don't I watch the front here, and you two go out to the back to hash things over. You'd better work things out with Abby."

"Okay boss," said Beano, grabbing his cane. "The master has spoken. C'mon Ab."

"I think we're making too much of this," I said. "It's not a big deal."

"It is to me, Ab," said Alice in her usual determined fashion. "Now go, please."

We walked to the back workroom where Beano settled down in front of a bike on his workstand, saying "I'll just tweak this baby while we talk."

I looked at my watch; it was already three-thirty. "Okay Beano, but I am going to have to keep this short. I have to go soon. I'm expecting Bell over in a while to help me."

"I'm all ears, Ab," he said.

"Beano, please don't tell your friend Artie."

His eyes widened. "So you do know about Anita. I thought that, if anyone did, you would. You seem to attach yourself to stuff. Okay, sure Ab, I promise but I will probably have to tell Alice."

"That's all right. I trust her," I said, ignoring his comment about me and my attachments. I decided to keep most of the details to myself.

"I haven't actually met Anita yet but I told a friend that I might be able to find out where to get her some help with her drug problem."

"Whoa, that's big time, Abby. There are a lot of people looking for that girl. Where is she now? You could be in big trouble if anyone finds out that you know."

I nodded. "Yeah, not that I really know much. She's somewhere safe but it's complicated, Beano. She can't go the police. She's sure they won't protect her and she's in the country illegally. I haven't got the whole story yet, but of course she's afraid of the guys who killed Burnett too and she seems to think that there is someone else behind all this. The little bit I got from the police seems to confirm this too. I think this is bigger than a simple territorial slaying."

Beano raised his eyebrows at me. "So what do you think I can do? You know my history, she can't hole up here. The police are always looking for something to hang on me."

"Well, she's hooked on heroin too, although apparently she wants to get clean. I wanted to know if you can help." He looked at me questioningly as I continued.

"I know it's a lot to ask Beano, but you're the only person I could think of who might know about some kind of safe-house type rehab. Can you think of anywhere?"

Beano looked doubtful. "I don't know, Ab. I have to think about how to do this best." He seemed to come to a decision. "I tell you what. I'll make a few discreet enquiries at the centre. Call me later tonight or early tomorrow morning."

"You're a pal, Beano," I said carefully.

"No sweat," he said, turning his attention to the bike. "Can you do me a favour on the way out, and let Alice know we're at peace? Otherwise I'll still be in trouble. I've got to keep working on this bike. Dude wanted to pick it up on the way home from work."

"For sure Beano. I'll tell Alice and I'll call you tomorrow morning. Thanks again."

I flew through the shop and hastily reassured Alice all was well, keeping my reservations to myself. I told her that Beano would explain things and hurried out of the shop.

It was almost four o'clock. I needed to get cleaned up, confirm that Bell was still coming by and check in with Anita, so I negotiated my way as quickly as I could back through the Market. It's impossible to run with all the obstructions: cars on the sidewalk and cars on the road, people navigating strollers and shopping carts around vegetable stands and racks of clothing and through the crowds. It's hard to even walk purposefully through the Market so I had to make a conscious effort to switch myself into slow Market mode as I made my way through the obstacle course.

Maria was busy with the late afternoon shoppers; I waved briefly and made my way to the back. She waved back cheerfully enough but I noticed a note taped to my bike in the hall. It simply said, "Again?" I smiled and detached the note. We had a continuous battle going over where I leave my bikes. Fishing a pen from my jacket pocket, I wrote in, "Sorry!" and stuck the tape on the wall before grabbing my bike and making my way up the stairs.

I decided to make a little peace offering for Maria and quickly cut up a banana, mango and pear and threw them in the blender. Adding some water, yogurt and powdered greens I blended the whole concoction smooth. Putting aside a small glass for myself I then filled my most beautiful tall blue glass with the rest and descended the stairs with the brew.

Bev, the high school part-timer, was working in the store so I was sure I could take Maria away for a minute or two. I beckoned to her from the back of the store and motioned to the glass. She saw me and after speaking briefly to Bev, Maria made her way to the back. I handed her the blue glass as I said, "Hi, I'm sorry about the bike. I was in an awful hurry."

"What else is new?" she shot back, but she accepted my peace offering gracefully. "Mmm, this one's pretty good, Abby. Thanks," she said as she sipped.

"Maria, I think I might have a lead on where I could take Anita for help. Thanks again by the way for taking her in."

"That's okay. I called home a while back to check on them. They're doing just fine. She's such a sweet girl. I hope you can help her."

"I hope so too, but listen, can you keep her another night? She told me yesterday she should be okay for two or three days and I need at least until tomorrow to set something up for her up."

"Sure, sure," said Maria. "The kids will be happy. They already adore her and I know Frank won't mind. It gives him more time with me."

"Fantastic, Maria. Thanks. I was planning to go out with Roger tonight but I was worried about leaving Anita alone. Now it's all cool. You truly are my best friend." I gave her a hug and a kiss. Maria laughed and handed me the empty glass.

"I hope you're not going out like that. Isn't Roger the one who likes fine dining?"

I laughed too. "It's okay Maria. Bell is coming to the rescue. I'm going to get in the shower before she gets here. She might come through the front if that's okay."

"I'll keep an eye out for her and send her up," Maria said. "Now, I'd better go rescue Bev." The customers were piling up.

"Thanks Maria, I'll talk to you later," I said. I made my way happily up the stairs.

Chapter 10

The phone call was first. I dialled Maria's number and was rewarded by the sound of Thomas's sweet, slightly hoarse voice.

"Hello," he chirped, "Alvarado residence."

"Hi Thomas," I said. "It's Abby. Are you feeling better?"

"Oh hi Abby," he said. "I'm okay. I've been playing with Anita."

"Can I speak to her please?"

"Sure," he said, "hold on." A few seconds later, Anita came on the line.

"Hello? Abby?" Her voice sounded stronger and clearer. Maybe her time with a normal family had been good for her.

"Hi Anita, how's it going? Are you okay up there in nosebleed country?"

"Yes, I'm good. They have all been so nice to me."

"How about the drug thing? Are you still cool? Do you think you'll be able to handle another day?"

"I'm pretty sure," she said. "I'm feeling much better. Right now I feel like I can do anything. Of course," she lowered her voice, "I'm usually good for two or three days anyway, but I might not be so hot when I start needing a fix. These people are so nice Abby. I don't want them to see me that way — but I think I'm okay for at least another day."

"Fantastic," I said relieved. "I'm working on something for you here so I might be able to get you away by tomorrow. I've talked to Maria; she's happy for you to hang out there until then. From what I hear, you've been a great help."

"It has been fun, Abby. It makes me miss my family, but I almost feel like I can be normal some day."

"That reminds me — I still want to talk with you, you know, and hear your story."

"I would like that," she said quietly. "Tomorrow, maybe?"

"For sure."

Just then I heard the supposedly sick Thomas yelling, "Come on, Anita."

"Whoops," she laughed, "Thomas wants to play another game of checkers. I'd better go. Bye Abby."

It was wonderful to hear Anita feeling well. I had no idea where this was going or whether her euphoria was related to the drug, but at least there was a hint of promise.

With Anita taken care of I began my shower ritual. Before immersing myself, I checked my pager. No message from my niece. We had arranged earlier that she would call only if she couldn't make it. I breathed a sigh of relief as I stepped in, surrendering to the heat. I finally turned off the taps as the water cooled down and stepped out of the steamy sanctuary to the sound of music.

Securely swathed in two large towels to ward off the cold, I peered into the bedroom. There was Bell, rifling through my closet humming and bopping to some metal tune. She turned to me and pursed her lips.

"Really, Auntie Abby, you expect me to dress you with these clothes?"

I shrugged my shoulders. "You're the expert, Bell." She made a face.

"What are these?" she said wrinkling her nose and holding up two conservative suits in plastic dry-cleaning bags.

"Oh, those are from Arabella Sr. I figured they might come in useful if I ever need a disguise."

She put them back in the bags. "Gross. Anyway Abby, I brought some stuff over. I've been working on a line of more lively evening clothes at the college. Wait till you see. It's pretty good if I say so myself."

She went out to the living room and returned with four suit bags and a shopping bag. "You'll have to give these back when you're finished, unless of course you can afford to buy them." She smiled ironically. "Okay, let's see what we can do."

We giggled and chatted like girly-girls, trying different combinations of brightly coloured full skirts and tight velvety tops. There was a wild fairy-like feel to the pieces — light, lyrical and lively. Finally we decided on a red and black number with a layered knee-length skirt riddled with gold threads that would pick up light. A crimson jacket complemented the tight black velvet top. Bell pawed through my jewellery tin and found two gold hoops and an amber pendant that set off the ensemble nicely. With the air of a professional, she tied back my dark curly hair. She stepped back and eyed me critically.

"Looking good, Abby. Do you have any shoes other than those?" She poked at my well-worn, trusty cycling shoes.

"I think so," I said, ignoring her sarcasm. I rummaged in the back of my closet and pulled out a pair of black flats.

"Those will do," she said. "Here, I brought you these." She handed me a new pack of pantyhose. The things I go through for a good meal! The ensemble complete, I admired my transformation in the mirror.

"Thanks Bell. I owe you one."

"You look pretty good, Auntie Abby. What fun! I don't often get such raw material."

"How'd you get here with all that stuff anyway?"

"Monica drove me on the back of her motorcycle. Not the easiest feat, I'll have you know. At least the rain had stopped, but we had to bag everything carefully, in case of muddy splashes."

Monica is Bell's girlfriend. She is described as a roommate to my sister, who's not yet aware of her daughter's sexual orientation. I'm hoping that the family will support her when she comes out to them, but I'm not so sure.

"It's almost time for Roger to pick me up. You want a ride home? I'm sure he won't mind."

"Okay, that would be great. Where are you going, anyway?"

"I don't know — he just said it would be somewhere special."

"Ooooh — sounds exciting. You sure this isn't Mr. Right?"

"I don't think so, but he's fun to be with. I'm not sure I'm looking for Mr. Right anyway. More like Mr. Left."

"Whatever you say, Abby. Hey, how would you like to come over to our place for dinner next week? It's been a while."

"Sounds good, Bell. I'm working on something right now, but I'll call you when it's finished."

"Suits me, but don't forget. Monica loves to cook for you. I've gotta say you're more appreciative than most people when it comes to food."

Monica is a great cook. She is presently at college aiming to be a chef, and if I'm any judge she'll be very successful. I love her food.

"It's too bad I don't go crazy over food like you do Abby."

"Hey — you and Monica seem to appreciate each other anyway. You're a fabulous pair."

After we packed away the discarded clothes, we sat chatting at the kitchen table for a few minutes, waiting for Roger. At the sound of a horn honking, I looked out the window to see Roger's sporty little Jeep outside on Kensington Street.

"Come on Bell, let's not keep Prince Charming waiting. We wouldn't want him to turn into a frog!"

Like two young teenagers, we traipsed out of my apartment giggling and jostling each other. Roger was at the front door of the shop peering in.

"Wow!" he said, when I opened the door. I laughed and introduced him to Bell.

"You can give her all the credit for this transformation. Can we drop Bell at College and Clinton, Rog?"

"Sure thing, babe."

I really had to speak to him sometime about that whole babe thing.

"Thanks Roger," Bell said as she folded herself into the jeep. "Where are you taking Abby tonight?"

"We're going to The Scarlet Pimpernel up at St. Clair and Avenue Road."

"Mmm, fancy place! Abby, I'm glad we dressed you up. It'll be great exposure for my designs. Monica says that the food is fantastic there and it's supposed to be very romantic."

"Stop, Bell. I'm salivating already."

Roger laughed. "I started salivating when I saw you at the door."

I blushed as Bell laughed but by then we had reached her place. We dropped her off and drove on. A few blocks further on Roger pulled over to the side of the road. I looked at him questioningly.

"What's up?"

"Nothing. I just wanted to say hello properly before we got to the restaurant. You look so damn good — and I've missed you."

"You're sweet Roger, but we just saw each other a few hours ago."

He took my hand and leaned over to kiss me, at first gently, then intensely. I must say I gave as good as I got. The car, the rain and our unanticipated early loving were raising my temperature immoderately; the windows steamed up and I felt like an impetuous teenager.

I decided to slow things down when I came up for air. First things first, and I had my eye on dinner.

"Whoa Roger. I need to breathe," I said, my heart racing in my ears, my cheeks hot and every breath adding to the cloud on the windows. "Roger, this is more than nice," I said, trying to keep my eyes off his lap, "but I think we should wait, don't you?" I opened my window a bit.

Now it was his turn to blush. "Of course, Abby. I wasn't actually going to ... here ..."

Flustered, he opened his window too, drops of rain pattering in, the closest thing to a cold shower available at the moment.

"Hey Rog, you don't want to ruin your suit. You know, you're looking pretty dashing yourself," I said, giving him the once-over.

He was. He had on a stylish pinstripe suit with a casual red silk shirt, no tie. His sandy brown hair shone and his blue eyes did their usual heart-piercing thing. And he smelled good — not all perfumed with colognes like some guys, but just clean and soap fresh. Maybe a few pheromones were filling the air too after our little encounter.

Once the windows cleared we drove on, holding hands when he wasn't changing gears. I plunked in my Annie Lennox CD and relaxed, anticipating a great meal.

The Scarlet Pimpernel is on a quiet cul-de-sac on the street level floor of an old apartment building where mostly wealthy seniors live. The exterior is extremely understated and you wouldn't know one of the best restaurants in the city was in there. The first clue is the cluster of Jags, BMWs and Mercedes in the small parking area. The second clue is the carhop who materializes as you pull into the circular driveway, giving royal treatment to every patron — however clad or groomed.

They do, however, have X-rays for people's wallets as they enter. If your plastic count is high enough, they don't blink. Roger must have had some pull or made it worth someone's while, for we were shown to a choice candlelit table by the windows. We looked down the hill at the twinkling city to the south. One fun thing about this kind of place is people-watching. Another is the food. I couldn't decide which to do first, so I talked to Roger instead.

"Perfect choice, Rog. Here I can be nosy and eat good food at the same time. Pretty good company, too. Thanks for the treat."

"You deserve to be spoiled, my intrepid cyclist," Roger replied lightly.

Really, he was hard to believe: young, good looking, bright, attracted to me — for my sparkling wit perhaps? Hmm. Maybe my friends are right. I don't know what I want.

Having agreed to go slow earlier, Roger had relaxed. We chatted amicably over a nice bottle of Chardonnay — dry and fruity. No one hurried us while we planned our meal. For starters we chose cold smoked salmon and goat cheese, served with capers, olives, onions and a watercress garnish. Our salad was described as organic greens with slivers of Parmesan and garlic roasted pine nuts with basil tossed with a light raspberry lemon dressing. We decided to share each course so that we could sample more delicacies. For the main course we settled on fresh hand-made pasta medallions filled with crab and chanterelle mushrooms, accompanied by a creamy tomato sauce and Asiago cheese. Next we would have a morsel of black Alaska cod in a teriyaki sauce, served Japanese style on a bed of sticky rice.

That done, we settled back to some serious people-watching. I pointed out a relatively famous local actress who was dining with the city budget chief, and started identifying as many other diners as I could. Roger humoured me for a while but finally shushed me.

"I'm not really into this, Abby. None of these people can hold a candle to you."

I squirmed. The words were more than right, but too close to overkill. Luckily the food arrived just then.

We ate, drank and generally made merry as the night waxed. The food was superb, sating part of my appetite. I pointed out two more celebrities I recognized from magazines in the dentist's office. They were sitting at out-of-the-way tables and dressed low-key, obviously attempting to remain as inconspicuous as possible.

I turned to look as a new foursome were being seated near us, and I almost gagged as I recognized condo king Johnson and his wife from the society pages. The couple accompanying them seemed singularly out of place: they were brash and loud, drawing a lot of attention to themselves as they gushed all over the Johnsons, who seemed very uncomfortable. I kept glancing over at them, wondering who they were. On a long shot, I decided to ask Roger.

"Hey, Rog, do you know that guy?"

He looked up reluctantly from his fish, "Still people-watching, Abby? Who do you mean this time?"

"The man sitting next to Johnson … the loudmouth with the overblown wife."

"Oh, him," Roger said with mild disinterest. "He's one of Smythe's new clients, some fellow named Andersen. They're working on a big deal just now. I've seen him with the boss a few times. Not that they have any time for me," he muttered, "I'm too low in the corporate lawyer echelon."

It was obviously time for some positive strokes. I took his hand and said, "Don't worry Roger. I know you'll move up. Your … um … creativity and silver tongue won't go unnoticed for long."

I was rewarded with one of his heart-melting smiles.

"Thank you, Abby."

I was already off on another mental tangent as I patted his hand absently. If Andersen was working on a deal and Johnson was having dinner with him, perhaps there was some connection between the Market property I had seen referred to in the Johnson file and

Andersen's business. Roger's firm is well known for brokering some development partnerships and Johnson specialized in condos. Could Johnson and this Andersen fellow be planning to build something in the Market?

The thought was not too appetizing and it was distracting me from the delectable meal in front of me. Anyone who comes between good food and myself is not my friend. I was equally unhappy with the idea of someone taking that wonderful, grubby bit of community and turning it into a sanitized mall. Not a pretty picture in my mind.

I was brought out of my gloomy thoughts by a tickle on my elbow. I looked up as Roger ran his fingers up and down my arm sending corresponding shivers up my spine. He smiled.

"Welcome back."

What was I doing? Here I was with an attentive gentleman, a fantastic dinner, and all I could do was obsess about developers. I gave myself a shake and smiled back, determined to focus on my date and ignore the bad taste in my mouth from the sleazy party next to us.

"Sorry Rog. Sometimes I can't turn my over-active brain off." I looked at our empty plates as I took a sip of wine, "Time for dessert?"

After a smooth cappuccino and a nice mix of blackberries, raspberries, huckleberries and mangos served with crème fraiche, we moved to the bar for a nightcap. We were sharing a Courvoisier and waiting for our temporary chauffer to arrive when O'Casey and a beautiful young woman entered the restaurant.

Pleased at the happy coincidence, I had one of my instant brainwaves: maybe he could help Anita with her legal problems. Even if he couldn't himself, surely he could recommend someone else. I wondered briefly if it would be uncool for me to approach him here but decided to go for it. I'm not really known for either my tact or my sensitivity. Nice people call me "dogged" when I'm stuck on something, and it's true. So, when his companion walked off in the direction of the washroom, I slipped down from the tall stool to take advantage of the opportunity.

"I'll be right back, Rog. I'm just going over to have a word with Mr. O'Casey, there. He's sort of an old friend of the family."

"Oh, really," he said, his mellow manner and roaming hands indicating his pleasantly pickled state. "He's a bit too old guard for me but suit yourself. Just don't be too long. I'll miss you."

I gave him a quick peck on the cheek and made my way to O'Casey's side. O'Casey looked at me appraisingly as I first walked up. It was pretty obvious that he didn't recognize me, probably because of my fashionable getup and the atypical setting, but it was also pretty clear that he was assessing me in an alpha male way. Despite his reputation as a progressive lawyer he was also known for his wandering eye, which partly explained his succession of wives. In fact, if I remembered my gossip correctly, he'd only just gotten hitched to his latest two months ago. That must be her in the washroom. And here he was giving me the eye. Gross! I tried to ignore his look as I walked up and re-introduced myself.

"Hi again, Mr. O'Casey. I guess you're surprised to see me here." I shook his hand. "I'm having dinner with a friend."

I gestured to Roger waiting at the bar, realizing ruefully that he was younger than me too so maybe I had something in common with O'Casey.

At least the older lawyer had the grace to look flustered. "Oh, hello, Abby. I didn't recognize you all dressed up." He regained his composure and relaxed, "Lovely evening, isn't it?"

"Why yes, sir. We just finished a great meal." I wanted to change tack quickly because I knew his wife would be back soon. "Um, Mr. O'Casey ..."

"Call me Liam, dear."

"Okay, um, Liam. I'm sorry to bother you here tonight. I just wanted to let you know that Johnson, you know, the developer, is having dinner over there with a man called Andersen. Don't ask me how I know but I think they're doing some kind of deal that involves condos in Kensington. I'm wondering if you can find anything out that will help us stop them?"

He raised his eyebrows. "You are a crafty young lady but you know what I said before, Abby. These developer types are not fooling around these days." He looked at me warmly and patted my hand. "It's a good tip, though, and I'm glad you are telling me instead of running off half-cocked like your dad used to. That's using your head. I tell you what I'll do. I know Johnson a little from way back with your father. I'll chat with him tonight and see what I can find out informally. Let me take care of things."

I felt a mixture of annoyance and relief at his paternalism.

"Thanks, Liam. Can I call you in a few days to see what you have found out? Maybe I can get the neighbourhood association to help out. I also wanted to see if you could help a friend of mine from the Market. She's illegal here and she needs some advice."

"Of course, of course," he said, seeming a little preoccupied as he looked up and straightened a little. "Ah, here comes my wife." The stunning blonde woman, just slightly older than me, approached with a feline possessiveness — understandable, I guess, given the man's history. She quietly slid her arm in his as she purred, "And who is this, Liam darling?"

"Ah, Simone, this is Abby Faria, the daughter of an old acquaintance. I used to do some work for her parents. Abby was just saying hello, isn't that right, my dear?"

"Hello," I said. Simone O'Casey and I shook hands. She seemed to relax a little once she'd learned who I was. "It's a pleasure to meet you." I turned to O'Casey and shook his hand again. "It was nice to see you again, Mr. O'Casey."

He nodded. "Thank you for the tip. Now, if you'll excuse me, we need to get seated."

"Have a nice dinner," I said. I left the couple as the hostess approached to escort them to their table.

Roger was still happily mellow when I returned. "That O'Casey seems to have it made," he said as he slid his arm around my waist. "I don't know how the old fart does it; fast cars, beautiful women and a thriving practice too. Of course, he started with money, which might have helped."

"Are you sucking sour grapes, Rog?" I asked, squeezing his well-manicured but insecure hand. "He's a good guy, despite his lifestyle. He helped my dad many years ago — there's more to him than just money grubbing. He takes on lots of human rights cases too."

He looked surprised, "Really? I didn't know that about him." He brightened. "Let's forget about him and all these celebrities. The night is still young my dear, and I have a little treat waiting at my apartment."

"Other than the one I'm expecting?" I asked archly.

"You'll see," he grinned.

"Now you have me intrigued. You clever man, you know I love a mystery."

As he slid me off the stool and started edging me toward the door, I couldn't help thinking he was a little over-eager. A sudden puppy-dog image of him panting at my feet and licking my hand cooled my heated response a notch as I imagined patting his handsome head. Happily oblivious of my unfortunate train of thought, Roger took my hand and gave it a tug.

"C'mon then, the car is ready. Let's go."

Chapter 11

Roger's condo has beautiful views of the city and the lake, which today were sparkling, washed clean by the rain. I sank into the luxury of his living-room couch while he opened a little bottle of ice wine to top off the evening.

"What a great dinner! I feel utterly and deliciously spoiled," I purred. He snuggled up to me and agreed that the meal and the company were rather pleasant. After an intense kiss, his hands started to roam. I knew nature was not to be put off any longer.

"Hey Rog," I murmured heatedly, "These pantyhose are way too uncomfortable. Would you mind helping me out of them?"

"I think I could manage that," he murmured suggestively, maneuvering me off the couch and toward the bedroom door as he began to undo my bejewelled vest.

"It goes both ways, big boy," I laughed, starting to undo his shirt. By the time we reached the bed, all that was left were the offending pantyhose; Roger made short work of those.

When I came to, we were tangled in a sweaty pile of sheets and pillows on the floor. I nudged Roger, who was likewise spaced out. I hated to leave his warm side after such a fabulous evening but there was something else that just couldn't wait.

Even though I had alerted O'Casey to the possible link between Andersen, Johnson and Kensington Market, the discovery had taken hold of me. I was more like my father than I cared for O'Casey to know; I had to see for myself what I could find out about those Kensington properties.

I was so determined that I was willing to forgo one of the best perks of Roger's apartment: unlimited hot water in the shower. I leaned over Roger's dozing form.

"Hey, Rog," I whispered. He grunted softly, eyes still closed. "I'm sorry, but I've got to go work early tomorrow morning and I still have to fix a brake cable on my bike," I lied.

This got his attention. I expected him to protest vigorously but he must really have worn himself out because all he said was, "Oh, do you really have to?"

I gave him a nod and a reassuring kiss. "Okay," he said groggily. "I'll let you go on one condition — that you come over for pizza on Saturday night."

"I think I can handle that," I said, glad to be let off so easily. "Tell you what. I'll leave these fancy clothes hostage here if you lend me a sweatsuit. Then I'll have to come back to make the exchange."

"Sure, Ab," he said, pushing himself up on one elbow. "You know where everything is. I'm beat. I don't know where you get your energy — must be from all the bike riding in the great outdoors." He fell back on the pillow. I leaned over and gave him a chaste kiss.

"Good night, Prince Charming. Have a good sleep. I'll call you soon." I grabbed a dark sweatsuit from the drawer. We are of a similar size and sweats are very forgiving, so I looked reasonably respectable for the short trip home. Once I was ready, I carefully placed Arabella Jr.'s lovely ensemble on his dresser, gave the now-sleeping Roger one last kiss and crept out into the cusp between night and morning.

I caught a cab on Yonge Street and was home in ten minutes. I quickly assembled what I needed for my next foray into the night: bike pants and a dark jacket, a blank computer disk, a flashlight and some lock picks I had confiscated from an enterprising youth in my bike repair workshop.

I travelled cautiously in the dark. It was pretty quiet considering it was only one in the morning. Of course, I was heading into the warehouse district where the nightlife is more subdued. I locked my bike in an out-of-the-way spot a few blocks from Johnson's office. Adrenalin pumped blood into my ears and kept me warm even though I shivered with excitement as I cased the area for security guards or any other activity.

Feeling around in my pack for the set of picks, I remembered their previous owner's surprise when I caught him working his way into my tool locker in the community centre. In return for absolution, he contritely surrendered them to me. I don't harbour any illusions that he went straight at that point, but at least my locker stayed secure. One night, for a lark, I got Beano to show me how to use the picks, a skill he had gained in his former incarnation as a juvenile delinquent. Now I'm pretty good at it, if I say so myself.

Even so, breaking and entering isn't my favourite pastime, so my fingers were a little shaky at Johnson's door, but my confidence swelled as the lock yielded. I slipped into the building. I pulled out the flashlight and, after carefully shutting the door, turned it on.

It turned out I didn't need it yet; the stark little foyer was fairly well lit by the exit lights and the glow from the fish tank in the corner. Remembering the layout, I stole across the floor and entered the sacred inner sanctum. Here I needed my flashlight. I turned it on again and found myself in what I guessed was Johnson's office; panelled wood walls, soft carpet, big oak desk flanked by comfortable chairs. Four filing cabinets stood against one wall; framed pictures of various developments adorned the other. Curtained windows filled the wall behind the desk. To my left as I faced the desk was a sitting area with a couch, a rectangular coffee table and two easy chairs.

On another small square table to the side of the couch stood a computer monitor and more brochures. I guessed that this was a virtual display of Johnson's various condos around town. Moving towards the desk, I had to remind myself that no one could hear the blood pumping through my body. I took a deep breath, touched the mouse and held my breath. Nothing. I jiggled the mouse and pressed the space bar and was met with a brightening screen but, alas, a request for a password. Shit!

As I sat there moping, his screen saver reverted to a lovely tropical beach scene. I was utterly stumped. Then I had a flash of insight: call the expert. Knowing Sparky for an extreme night owl, I resolved to head for her place immediately. I wanted to get out of Johnson's office fast.

I had just hit the sidewalk of the quiet street and was about to pat myself on the back for a clean escape when a police car rounded the corner. Controlling the impulse to run, I walked along nonchalantly.

The car slowed down as it approached and the officer rolled down his passenger window.

Please don't let it be anyone I know, I prayed to myself.

"Evening ma'am," said a young, hunky, square-jawed police officer from the car window, his partner eyeing me from the driver's seat. "It's awfully late to be out alone on the street."

"Good evening, officers," I said as calmly as I could. For some reason police always make me nervous or angry, or both. I bit my tongue on any wayward retort waiting to bubble up. "I'm just heading for my bike that I left locked here earlier. I was couriering and lost my key. Had to get a replacement from home and now I'm going to pick it up."

Lame excuse and probably way too much information, but it was the only thing I could come up with at short notice.

"Not the best time to be about. Maybe we should escort you to your bike just to make sure you'll be safe."

Sure, I thought to myself. What gallantry in the police. They must be having a slow night; either that or they want to check out my story. I hoped my bike's recent arrival had escaped their notice.

"That's not really necessary," I said brightly. "I'm sure you're busy. I hate to trouble you, and it's only two blocks."

"No trouble at all, ma'am. Hop in. We'll drive you there," he said, climbing out and opening the back door for me.

I hoped that I seemed mature and responsible enough to lack persecution appeal. Too many of my young friends had a history of police harassment and the number of strip searches reported in the news was increasing. I did my best to behave, entering as demurely as possible. No point drawing more attention to myself out here in the middle of the night. I was lucky these guys seemed cool.

Acceding with grace, I said, "Thanks, Officer. My bike is parked at the corner of Spadina and Wellington."

I was thankful I had parked somewhere legal and that I had my light in my pack. With my incriminating B&E equipment on me, I did not want to rock the boat. We travelled the two blocks in relative silence. Their radio beeped in and out. This is kind of like a taxi, I thought, except for the wire cage between us.

"That's my bike there," I said when we reached the corner. "Thanks again for the ride."

"Our pleasure, ma'am." He got out and opened the door for me again, keeping his fingers a shade too long on my elbow after he handed me out.

Slipping out of his grasp, I said, "That was good of you. You have renewed my faith in the police force."

"Any time, ma'am. Name's Bob Jones and this here is my partner, Albert Frost. If you ever need —"

Fortunately for me, Bob was cut off because voices began bleating urgently from the police radio. The driver responded to the radio while his gallant partner made some effort to apologize for not being able to drive me home. Thank God, I thought. I thanked Bob again as I edged toward my bike and wondered why unlikely young men are interested in me, especially when I look the worse for wear, tired and all dressed in sweats. Maybe he'd caught a subconscious whiff of my evening's activities. The police car sped off as I unlocked my bike.

As soon as I was sure that my police escort had found better things to do, I headed my bike to Sparky's. She operates from a converted double garage in a back lane just on the edge of the Market. About halfway there I spotted a pay phone. I'd better call ahead, I said to myself. I didn't want to catch her with her pants down, so to speak. I fished out a quarter and dialled her place. Sparky answered on the first ring.

"Hi Sparky, it's me, Abby. How're things?"

"Not bad, Abby. I just finished setting up a web page for Avtech Industries, so I'm free to play for a while." When Sparky refers to play, she means the work she does for non-profit groups. Although she is a computer nerd, her social conscience is what first drew me to her. I met Sparky while she was helping set up a computer lab at the community centre where I run the bike workshop. Sparky has a big heart, especially when she can find its beat through a computer. She and I hit it off right away. At that time I was more of a night person, hanging around the punk scene and some of the underground clubs, so our paths crossed more often. She knows me well.

"What kind of trouble are you in Abby?"

"Am I that transparent?" I laughed.

"Let's just say that both of us have singular addictions — you for excitement and me for digital data. I can only guess that this call links the two. That, and the fact that you are calling me at two in the morning. You're not much of a night person anymore."

"Can't fool you, Sparks. Can I prevail upon you to put your expertise into action since you have time to 'play'?"

"You can try," she said.

"I should warn you, Sparky, it might involve stirring up a nest of vipers. Utmost secrecy is required," I said dramatically.

"Whatever you say, Abby. I am always careful — don't want to lose my anonymous cracker status."

"Hacker, you mean?"

"No, m'dear, we in the upper echelons of computer derring-do now call ourselves crackers. Y'know, 'cause we crack codes like safecrackers — it's more of an art form for us. Anyway Abby, aren't you the computer-phobe? Are you finally getting turned on to binary beauty?"

"Oh, nothing as serious as that. I just want to know how to access a computer's files if you don't have the password."

"Well, bypassing a password is child's play. In fact, I have a pretty little trick you can do remotely. If you tell me what you want, I could bust in for you from here." I sighed in relief at not having to go through that nerve-wracking break-and-enter routine again.

"Gee Abby, you're breathing awfully hard! Computer lingo never seemed to excite you before."

"Well Sparky, it's your stimulating conversational skills," I grinned over the phone. "Listen, do you think I can come over to discuss your devious tactics?"

"I have some time right now if you want or is it past your bedtime?"

"I'll see you in ten minutes," I said. "You're a lifesaver."

"See if you can stay out of trouble until you get here," she laughed.

I decided to make a pit stop for the usual late night snack —

doughnuts and sugary beverage from the closest all-night doughnut joint. I needed some basic fuel.

Despite the sugar fix, when I got to Sparky's I was on my way to catatonic and I worried about the day of dodging cars ahead of me. I hoped we could be done quickly and I could be on my way, without seeming rude, to a much-needed rest.

I was lucky. Sparky had just received a rush e-mail from an anarchist collective so she didn't have much time to chat. She gratefully received the late-night snack food I delivered, but kept me at the door with instructions as she handed me a CD.

"Sorry, Ab," she said. "I was looking forward to a chat, but these guys need some help fast."

"No sweat, Sparky, I'm exhausted. And you're right, it's past my bedtime." I safely stowed the disk and made it home to bed without further incident.

CHAPTER 12

OFFICER BOB AND ROGER WERE SHOWING ME AROUND A GLAMOROUS condominium apartment. How did they know each other? The building shook as a wrecking ball bashed through the walls of the condo, almost knocking us over. As Roger and Bob scattered like two bowling pins, the scene faded and my wits slowly collected themselves.

I was still in my apartment but the wrecking ball hadn't stopped. I held my head and allowed consciousness to slowly seep in as the noise continued. My head was reverberating with the effects of last night's high-class drink, fantastic sex, very early morning bike ride, failed break and enter and too little sleep, but what was that noise?

The banging stopped only to be replaced with an urgent voice yelling, "Abby! Open the door, it's me."

"Stop. I'm coming," I yelled back, which hurt but did stop the banging.

I unlocked the door and stepped back holding my head to let an anxious-looking Maria in. "Uh, hi Maria."

"Abby!" she exclaimed. "I saw your bike downstairs. I thought you were staying at Roger's. Is anything wrong? What happened on your date?"

Too many questions. "It's okay, Maria. Everything is fine. I had a good time with Roger. I just had to run an errand after, that's all. I'm a little hungover though." I sat down on the wicker couch. "Where's Anita? What time is it, anyway?"

Maria sat down on the old kitchen chair. "It's seven. I came to work early. Mother has an appointment this morning so Frank said he'd drop her and Anita off here later. Thomas is better but Anita is getting a little restless. I think she's going into withdrawal."

I nodded carefully as she continued. "I'm sorry I freaked, Abby. With the murder in the Market, I got worried that something had happened to you."

I smiled, touched by her concern. "It's okay. You've been so wonderful. It's probably good that Anita is coming back if she's getting jumpy. Hopefully Beano will have set something up and she can go into some kind of drug rehab today. Do you think she's still up for that?"

Maria nodded. "She says so but who knows how she will act when the withdrawal really starts to kick in."

"Yeah, I hope Beano comes through before it gets too bad."

Maria continued, "Anita wants to talk to you today too. She says she remembered something that might help. She told me more of her story. What a nightmare life she's had, Abby. She says she wants to be honest with you, to tell you everything."

"Can you keep her here until I'm back, Maria? I have to do some more Call Girl deliveries today," I said, thinking of my little present for Johnson. "In fact, I'm glad you woke me up. I must've slept right through my alarm. I have to get going. I'm supposed to start at nine o'clock and I desperately need a shower and my morning shake. And I'll never make it without at least one coffee."

Maria got to her feet. "Well, I'll get to work. Do you want Anita to hang out in the downstairs room again?"

"Please, Maria. Tell her I'll be as quick as I can. I think I'll be able to knock off sometime around noon seeing as it's Friday."

On Fridays everyone in the office world tries to get things out of the way in the morning so they can start the weekend early. The delivery business usually slows down on Friday afternoon and then the girls start competing for the remaining jobs. I don't like to get in the way of the regulars so I usually quit at that point.

As Maria headed for the door I asked her, "Would you like me to make some extra green shake for you? I bet you didn't bother to have breakfast this morning if you left so early."

"That would be wonderful, Abby. It will tide me over. Just do me a favour, go easy on the brewer's yeast. I can never get used to that stuff."

"Me neither," I chuckled. "It was a gift from Mother. I'll bring the shake down for you on my way out," I said, closing the door behind her. Given the time, I knew I would have to get into Overdrive soon, in more ways than one.

I dressed in my usual biker garb after a sadly perfunctory shower and then whizzed up a somewhat palatable concoction for Maria and me. As I rushed headlong down the stairs with the two glasses, I almost bumped into two heaping hulks of blue waiting at the bottom.

I recognized them both but neither cop looked terribly friendly at the moment. One was the portly fellow I had seen hanging around Burnett's house and the other was my old friend, Frank Berrigan. I was mentally thanking my lucky stars that Anita wasn't around at the moment. Given that I had a lot to hide I decided to take the innocent, friendly tone.

"Howdy boys. What can I do for you? Thanks for the help the other night, Berrigan," I addressed the older fellow.

"Cut the crap, Faria," the beefier one blustered. While he launched into a tirade about interfering in an investigation, I idly wondered how he'd managed to pass the physical tests for police work. "Are you listening to me, Faria? Faria?"

"Huh?" I tend to tune out when a person starts raising his voice — years of long practice when my mother'd get going. I made an effort to pay attention.

His neck turned red, as his frustration grew more intense. "Keep your nose out of our business."

Well this was just bizarre. What was he going on about? What pebble had I kicked up to generate such a storm? I did my best to assume a mollified expression. "I don't know what you are talking about. Perhaps if you told me what you are referring to, then I could help you out." Not likely, but I was dying to find out what they thought I was up to.

"You've been stirring things up in the Market, asking questions about an ongoing investigation. You know better than that," Berrigan piped in, trying to get an edge on old pudgy-face.

"What questions, what investigation? I didn't know that it was illegal to speak to friends in the Market. Come on boys, what's with the harassment? I've got to get to work," I said, patting my pager. "I'm riding today."

Pudge-face, who obviously considered my choice of career unfeminine, looked at me with distaste. I could just imagine his interactions with the city's mouthy squeegee kids. I hoped my sense of disgust was not as apparent as his was. Berrigan turned to him.

"Give me a minute here, Joe."

Pudge turned and stalked out through the fish shop while Berrigan turned back to me. I was still holding the two shake glasses. Maria was wisely staying out of it all as she worked hacking away at the usual morning block of ice.

"Listen, Abby," Berrigan said kindly. He still seemed to think of me as a wayward child. "While Joe can be an ass, he's right. There's more to this than you know, and things are kind of delicate right now. I shouldn't be telling you this but I want you to understand that there's a lot at stake." Obviously Berrigan was the 'good cop' in this scenario.

"Well, I appreciate the advice. You were always fair with Dad. I'll do what I can to stay out of your way," I said, mentally crossing my fingers behind my back.

"If I were you Abby, I'd drop the whole thing. This could be downright dangerous."

"Thanks Berrigan. I'm mystified really. I don't know what I could have done to get such a reaction. Help me out here," I said as I put Maria's glass down on the stairs and began to drink from the other. He shook his head and then shrugged as he started past me towards the front of the store.

"You've heard my warning. Back off. I don't think you want trouble with the police. Have a good day, Abby."

The other officer was already sitting in the driver's seat of the car idling outside the door. I finished my drink, watching as Berrigan joined him. They had a brief discussion, heated by the look of it, and then good old Joe accelerated with a squeal as he drove away. I guess he wasn't happy.

Maybe I should have heeded their warning. Instead I gave the speechless Maria her drink, stalked to the back, plunked on my helmet and mounted my street bike. I sped down the alley, angry at being told what to do and in a hurry to catch up on my job. Of course I was also curious. They hadn't told me much, but I hadn't told them anything either, so we were even.

The police visit had delayed me enough that I had to forgo the gossip at Overdrive. Instead I grabbed a coffee to go in my bike-friendly thermos and went straight to Johnson's, my first pickup. I was looking forward to my morning discussion with his assistant. She didn't know how much she was going to help me out.

Chapter 13

By day, Johnson's office was less intimidating. As I approached the snooty receptionist I put on my most pleasant demeanour.

"Hi there, um, Natasha. I see that the package is ready to go." In my usual subtle fashion, I then added, "Oh, by the way, the courier company has received these promotional packages from Microsoft." I pulled out the CD, very professionally packaged thanks to Sparky's ingenuity. "This free CD will give you an immediate Windows upgrade. Perhaps you would like to show it to your employer."

I could see the wheels turning in her tiny little head; she would take all the credit for our little gift. That was just fine, as Johnson was a lot more likely to trust her than me. She reached out to accept my gift, slightly less frosty than usual.

"Well, thank you. Do you know if we can use it on more than one computer?"

"Sure," I smiled. "Uh, I've got to get going. The dispatcher told me that this is the only delivery scheduled for you today?"

"Yes, but I believe the deal will be completed on Monday," she said, more forthcoming than usual.

"Maybe I'll see you then. Have a great day," I said, smiling as I left.

It was true about the disk. They would receive a Windows upgrade and they would be very happy with it. What they didn't know was that there was a worm going along for the ride. Sparky had explained that it would self-activate after five hours of computer idle time, at which point all the files on Johnson's computer would be transferred to a web server. From there, Sparky and I could sort through the material at our leisure. Very elegant, and a whole lot easier than last night's break-and-enter fiasco.

The morning passed at a snail's pace. I was a little slower than usual, trying to be more careful given my combined fatigue and hangover. By noon, I was home and desperate for a long sleep that would, unfortunately, have to wait. Since I didn't see Maria's mother I assumed that she and Anita had not yet arrived. Maria was busy with a customer so I signalled to her that I was going upstairs.

I dropped everything in the downstairs room, too tired to drag my bike upstairs. As I pried my eyes open with toothpicks, I noticed that my answering machine was winking its little red light, its solitary eye signalling a message.

Maybe it's Roger or Beano, I thought, pressing play.

The first clue that it wasn't them was a loud buzzing sound on the line. A few seconds later I was jarred to attention by the sound of a strangely flat, mechanical and menacing male voice.

"When you meddle in affairs that don't concern you, you can run into trouble, bitch. Back off or your little friend might not return from her next trip. You know how drug addicts are. You can't trust them to stay clean." A distorted laugh ended the message.

Stunned, I groped for the back of my chair and slowly lowered myself down. It took a few deep breaths to kick-start my numbed brain. This was way out of my league! First the mysterious visit from the police in the morning, and now this. Somebody had obviously found out that I was in touch with Anita, and given the attention I was receiving, that somebody was involved in the murder. But who could have tipped them off? Nobody but Maria knew Anita had been staying with me. Except Beano ... I shook my head. How could that be possible? I've known him so long and I've always been able to trust him. Besides, he knows how hard it is to get clean and he, of all people, appreciates the struggle it takes to get out of the clutches of the underworld. Could he be under someone else's control? Had he or Alice let something slip?

I wracked my brain trying to remember who else I had spoken to about the murder. Veronica? The idea of her being in league with murderers was laughable. I mentally crossed off Jeff since I hadn't even met Anita when I first spoke to him. Had anyone seen us together when we were at Stan's? Or perhaps Beano's friend Artie had got wind of it and had a more nefarious motive for finding Anita than he had let on. And what was the role of the police in the whole thing? This put a whole new angle on their attempt at intimidating me earlier on in the morning.

The mental exercise helped me settle down but didn't throw any light on the mystery. I stood up in disgust and began to pace.

Well, if whoever it was thought that an ugly phone message was going to stop me, they were mistaken. If anything, I felt more determined to figure things out. I was just going to have to be very careful in the meantime. Maybe Anita would provide clues to throw some light on this. I had to find a safe place for her soon. I was obviously becoming dangerous company.

As if on cue, there was a timid knock on my door. Anita peeked in, looking a little more fragile then she had sounded yesterday.

"Hi Abby. Maria said I should come up to find you."

"Hey Anita, how're you doing? Are you feeling okay?"

"I wasn't too bad this morning, a little shaky, but it's gotten worse since then. I think it's being back in the Market. It's creeping me out and I'm starting to feel sick and jumpy."

"That's not good," I said, watching her hands twitching and clutching at her sleeves. "You'd better sit down. I'll fix you something to eat. I haven't heard back from my friend yet but I think he can get us help. Are you up for the rehab?"

"I think so," she stuck her chin up determinedly. "I definitely don't think I can do it on my own but I'm serious about trying to get clean."

"Good for you, Anita. And I think you need a new place to hole up, anyway. I'm beginning to think here isn't so safe. I had a visit from the police this morning. Not about you," I added quickly, to reassure her. "They just warned me off about sticking my nose in where it didn't belong."

"Oh, I'm so sorry Abby," Anita said looking concerned. She paced around the small room and then turned to me,

"I think there's some stuff I should tell you. You should know what you're getting into. I am so grateful for your help but I feel responsible for your involvement. I don't want you to get hurt too.

Oh, I don't know. Maybe you shouldn't be involved, Abby. I'm scared. I just want to disappear."

"You don't know me, Anita. I don't give up on things easily, especially if someone needs help. But, you're right. I think we should take a few minutes to talk. Those cops were acting strange. I'm beginning to think there's something more than just gang stuff going on here."

Anita sat on a chair looking at me strangely. "It's funny you said that because I was going to tell you about something I remembered that might be important. I told you I didn't know those guys at the house the night of the murder, but I'm thinking they may have been connected to something that happened before."

I noticed her shaking was getting worse, so I interrupted her. "Hold on a sec. Before we get into this, I think we should take care of our stomachs. I'm starving from all my riding today and I bet you haven't eaten for a while." I stood up and motioned to my trusty blender. "How about I whip us up another Abby Faria Special?"

To her credit, she didn't make a face. "I'm not really hungry, coming down and everything, but I suppose you're right. I should eat and something healthy is best." She stood up. "Can I help?"

I nodded, and together we whipped up a reasonably noxious brew, which we downed giggling at each other's green moustaches. It was our first moment of unguarded fun together, and the anxiety fell away. Maybe we could become friends in a better future. Then, as we finished, the mood shifted again and we turned to the task at hand. I took Anita's glass and placed it with mine in the sink.

"I'll get to those later. You ready to tell me the whole story now? We could stay up here or talk downstairs."

"Here is fine," Anita said as she sat down again on the rickety kitchen chair. I sat down on the couch opposite her.

Chapter 14

Her story poured out.

"I was born to a farming family in Czechoslovakia. The farm wasn't doing so well and my parents thought life might be better in the city, so we moved to an industrial town where Dad and Mom got jobs in a factory. My three brothers and I were left at home with our older sister. My job was to help an old neighbour who had once been a civil servant. You know, running errands, making him lunch, reading to him — that kind of stuff. Nice old guy. He taught me English in return. He said I was a really quick learner." She smiled at the memory.

"When Dad got sick and couldn't work anymore, it was up to Mom to support us all. She was always tired, always angry. Sometimes I thought she didn't even like me much but maybe it was just that she was so tired. She had a foreman who kept himself comfortable by running a few sideline businesses, mostly drugs and prostitution. He came home with my mom one day and he said that he liked me and wanted me to live with his family. He said he could teach me more English and also some business skills. One thing led to another and in the end he took me away. I realize now the family more or less sold me to him.

"Of course, he didn't really want to help me at all. He put me on the street to earn money for him. I was pretty and smart so I survived and I learned when to be tough. By the time I was fourteen I was well-established with my own room, and the food was good enough. But then the foreman sold me on, and before I knew it, I was on my way to Toronto. I was kind of excited at first; I thought I could work at a different job here, maybe as a dancer. Not that I had a choice, but I tried to think of it as an opportunity.

"When we came here it was the same old thing only we worked out of a club. I was introduced to this man, Andersen, in the nightclub in the west end. He was so nice at first; he said that with my brains and ability with English, I'd be perfect for a job he had available in Kensington Market."

Anita stopped speaking, seemingly lost in her own thoughts, but my antennae were on full alert. Could this be the same Andersen I'd seen dining with Johnson? I gently pressed her to go on.

"So that's how you ended up here. But what did this Andersen fellow have to do with Dan Burnett?"

"Well, he introduced me to Dan. As I told you before, I thought at first that Dan was my boyfriend. He asked me to move in and everything. But eventually I figured out I was just being used, like always. Andersen already supplied Dan's little business with women and drugs but Dan wanted to be a partner."

I listened in horrified fascination as the story unfolded. For a while Andersen had been happy enough to let Dan do him favours, deal his drugs and duke it out with the other small-time dealers in the area. Then he started hiring Dan to set fire to buildings in the Market. Anita was losing favour by then because she was too heavily into heroin. She explained that there had always been an endless supply of girls in the house, but when Sonya appeared on the scene things changed.

"Now I wonder if maybe Andersen was planning to get rid of Dan. I think maybe the murder was planned and that Sonya was being put in his place," Anita continued.

"At the time I thought she was just Dan's pet worker. He sent her on the street as well, and she and I were friendly. Even though it looked like she was replacing me, I didn't hate her or anything. She was nice to me. It was Dan I started to hate," said Anita disdainfully. "He thought he was king and that everything was coming to him on a platter. Still, to die like that," she shuddered. "A few days before Dan was murdered I told Sonya I wanted to get out. If only I had just left right then, I wouldn't have been there when …" Anita stopped and pressed her hands over her eyes. I went over and gave her a hug.

"Are you alright?" I asked lamely, knowing full well that she wasn't. She nodded bravely, unresisting as I led her over to the couch to sit by me.

"Well, maybe they wouldn't have let me go anyway," she continued. "I get the feeling they were planning to pin this murder on me."

Inside my stomach churned and my heart ached for Anita. Anger boiled at how badly she had been treated. I calmed myself, putting my arms around her shoulders comfortingly.

"What a life you've had. I'm amazed that you are still so sane. You must have been scared witless just living like that from day to day. It's no wonder you needed the drugs to cope."

"There's more," she said, taking a deep breath before she plunged on. "About a week ago, Dan was all uptight, rushing around the house, yelling at us, making sure things were cleaned up. That was usually the sign that the big guys were coming over, so I went to my hiding place as soon as I could. There was a pantry next to the kitchen with a large cupboard at the top. I used this safe spot any time there was a police raid, or Dan was angry or I was coming down from a harsh trip.

"Then I heard people at the door and the next thing I knew they'd come into the kitchen. The only voices I recognized were Dan's and Andersen's. They were arguing; something about a fire Dan hadn't been paid for. Andersen was telling him they couldn't sell yet without looking conspicuous, and he'd have to wait for his money until the investigation cooled down.

"After I heard them leave the kitchen, I hopped down from my spot and crept out to have a look. Dan was at the front door shaking Andersen's hand. There was another man too, who I already knew. I actually had to … well … be with him a couple of times." She made a face. "He's a fat policeman. I think he works for Andersen, some kind of enforcer, a bodyguard or something. I don't like him."

As I listened wide-eyed, something clicked. Maybe the "fat policeman" was my new pal, the angry cop, Joe. Maybe this fellow Andersen was the one who sent the cops to my door and maybe he was the one who had made that little phone call. This sent a shiver down my spine. If that was the case, Andersen was too close for our safety. I had to get Anita out of my place fast.

· 100 ·

Her face was drawn and she was twitching again, clearly close to exhaustion, but she looked determined to go on even though she was obviously agitated by the memories. I decided not to interrupt as she started to speak again.

"Anyway, they were all smiles and handshakes, and once the men had left, Dan seemed very happy. He even smiled at me, which he hadn't done for a while. I remember he said 'Things are looking up, Anita. Soon, I won't have to waste my time taking care of you girls. I'm heading for better things.' I went out to work, pathetically thinking he would like me more if I turned a few tricks that night, and I came home with good cash, feeling hopeful. I was shattered when I came in to find Dan all over Sonya. And I felt betrayed when Sonya told him to get me out of there. He gave me a dirty look and came over and pulled at my arm, half-dragging me up to my room.

"He checked my money pouch and took out all the cash. That cheered him up a bit, seeing that I was still useful. He pulled a bag of heroin out of his pocket, took my works, you know my drug stuff, off the desk and helped me get ready to shoot up. He told me Sonya meant nothing, he was just working her into the house routine. After he helped me find a vein he pushed in the needle. I remember him talking quietly as I drifted off. It was one of the last times he bothered to speak nicely to me."

I couldn't say much at the end of Anita's monologue. Thoughts raced around in my head. I was angry at the world for her plight. Here I had been all along living right around the corner from her sordid life, and knowing nothing. So much for my rosy view of the community.

Would I have been able to do anything to help her if I had known what was going on? Probably not. Could I help her now? I was certainly going to try. Anyway, this was getting personal. If this was the same Andersen I had seen with Johnson and they had designs on my Market, then I was going to step up to the plate. Besides, Johnson had messed big time with my father years ago. Maybe this time a Faria could teach him a lesson.

First things first, I had to get Anita out of my place. Even though I didn't know for sure if I could trust him, I was going to have to see if Beano could help me get Anita into a rehab centre. He was the only person I knew who had the right connections. I roused myself.

"I don't know what to say, Anita. I'm so sorry. It's amazing you aren't more hardened after all this. And don't worry about my getting involved. There's no way I would back out now. In fact, you've given me some very useful information."

Suddenly I noticed that Anita was wearing blue jeans and a matching turtleneck that fit. She had draped a down vest over her chair. A yellow bandana held down her abundant black curls.

"Oh," I said, chagrined, "I guess Maria found you some more suitable clothes. I screwed up there too. Sorry. I get so carried away with one thing that I forget another."

"It's okay, Abby. You've both been very good to me. I hope that someday I'll be able to pay you back."

I shook my head. "Never mind that. It'll be enough to see you safe and clean." I stood up. "Now, maybe we should move on. What do you think?"

She stood up too. "I'm ready," she said resolutely, pulling on the vest.

"Wait, Anita. I think we'd better cover you up a bit more. Don't want anyone to recognize you as we go through the Market."

"Okay," she nodded.

I pulled a hoodie off the hook by the door and held it out to her. "Here, and pull the hood up so your face is hidden a bit."

"Let's go," she said. "I'm getting restless."

As we headed out the back door Anita said a tearful goodbye to Maria, the two hugging like long lost friends. We all knew that the next few days would be an ordeal for Anita.

"Let's walk the long way around," I said as we started out. "That way we're less likely to be seen by people we know."

She nodded silently, clearly nervous about what would happen next. Once out on Spadina we walked to College and back down Augusta from the top. I hoped nobody was following us — I didn't see anyone or have the skin prickles that usually signal someone's eyes are boring into my back.

"Here we are," I said as we approached The Squeaky Wheel. I led

Anita down a lane beside the shop so that we could go in the back way and punched in the lock code, which I know from the days I open the shop for them.

I could see Alice out at the front so I said to Anita, "I'll check things out and be right back. Okay?"

She nodded. "I hope he can help."

"Me too," I said patting her icy hand.

I walked to the front of the empty shop. Alice looked up, startled.

"Oh Abby, you just about gave me a heart attack. Why the back way?"

"Sorry Alice," I lowered my voice. "I brought Anita." Alice's eyes widened. "I was hoping Beano was able to set up rehab for her."

"Do you think it's safe? Did anyone see you?"

"I don't think we have much choice. I had to move her from my place. I had a visit from the police today. I don't think they know where she is yet but I don't want to take any chances." Alice's eyes widened even further.

"No shit. You don't want to fool around with the police."

"Alice, has anyone talked with you or Beano? I got a phone threat today."

"No! Abby, that's serious!"

"Don't I know it! I just can't figure out who would have said something about Anita and me. Oh, and Alice, I haven't told Anita about the call so please don't mention it."

"This makes me real nervous, Abby."

I nodded, "I'm trying to stay cool right now for Anita's sake. Where's Beano, Alice? Did he say he'd help?"

She frowned. "Something's bugging him. He's quieter than usual but he did say he was going over to the centre. Beano found out this morning that they have done some work with Vietnamese illegals before, so they have links with some kind of safe house rehab system already."

"You know what, Alice, don't tell me too much. The less I know, the better, in case anyone questions me … I hope Beano's okay though. He's not getting into drugs himself again, is he?"

Just then Beano entered the store so Alice couldn't answer my question.

"Hello Beano, any good news? Anita's here in the back. I had to get her away from my place."

"You're in luck, or rather, she is," he said smiling. "I've got everything set up. Can't tell you where. Their policy is, the less people know the better."

"That's just what Abby suggested," said Alice.

"Great minds think alike," Beano said

"And fools seldom differ," she shot back, "no offence, Abby."

"You could be right, Alice."

"So," said Beano rubbing his hands together, "where's the patient?"

"Out back. I'm glad you're here to help her. She needs someone who understands what she is going through — she's getting a little jumpy. It's been more than two days." He looked concerned and started out back to see Anita. I followed. I was still nervous about him, but at this point I had nowhere else to turn.

Anita cowered when Beano first walked in. He is a little larger than life with his tall muscular body, dark skin and big smile. However, his behaviour was above reproach. "Hello," he said gently, "I'm Beano. You've been having quite a hard go of it I hear." She nodded timidly as he went on.

"You were lucky to hook up with Abby. She's one in a million. Anyway, she asked me to help set up some rehab for you. Looks like you could use it … I've been down that road, you know. You're in for a rough few days but then you should be okay provided you can stay away from the stuff. We've got a place set up that will be safe. Nobody will know who you are and, if they do figure it out, they won't tell anyone."

She was shaking as she listened but she kept nodding, which I hoped was a good sign.

"Well, gal, we have to go right away so you're going to have to say goodbye to Ab, here. You might be able to see her in a few days, depending on how things go. But right now, she's not even going to know where you are."

I kept quiet, but I didn't like the idea of not knowing whether I was delivering Anita into the wrong hands. Silently I resolved to follow them. Smiling on the outside, I tried for cool and upbeat.

"It's going to be fine, Anita. You're a survivor. This will seem easy compared to some of the stuff you've gone through." I didn't believe it, but I'm a good liar. "C'mon, girl, let's have a hug and off you go."

She clung pretty tightly as she whispered, "Thank you, Abby. I'll miss you, but I'll do my best for you and Maria and her kids."

"And yourself," I said as I extricated myself. "Good luck. Stick to your guns and maybe I'll be able to see you in two or three days."

She smiled through tears as Beano took her hand. She didn't look much like a tough hooker at the moment. I fervently hoped she would get through it okay. I knew the first withdrawal was a big step, but just a first step. I hoped she would get the chance to go the distance without being caught by the police or by Andersen and his gang. I hoped Beano was on the up and up and that I wasn't sending Anita into more trouble. And I fervently hoped that he was not flirting with drugs again himself. He had once told me that the dance with heroin was a dance for life.

As he escorted Anita out of the back of the store, I darted up front and said a hurried goodbye to Alice, who was talking to a customer.

"See you soon, Alice. I'm going to borrow this one if that's okay." I held up a magazine. "Tell Beano thanks, and that I'll call tomorrow or Sunday."

"See you Ab. Take it easy."

I looked around as I came out the door. Beano and Anita were walking toward the community centre. When they reached the corner of College and Augusta I set out sedately behind, hoping that they wouldn't notice me. The sidewalk was busy enough that I could blend in.

The two didn't stop or talk to anyone and no one seemed to be watching them. I arrived at the corner in time to see Beano lead Anita in through the side door of the centre. I'd seen people going in and out of that door, but never realized it was a rehab clinic. It was a well-kept secret. I decided to hang around a bit to see what happened next. I walked a little past the clinic door and stood safely out of view but with a good line of sight if Beano did as he was supposed to, which was to get right back to The Squeaky Wheel.

After an interminable five minutes I was rewarded for my patience. Beano emerged and walked calmly back the way he came. Breathing a sigh of relief I relaxed. I had done all that I could. I gave Beano a head start and then headed back home through the Market.

Chapter 15

It was four o'clock on a lovely Friday afternoon and the Market was getting busy with a mix of locals and 'tourists' coming through to stock up for the weekend. Saturday would be the busiest day — most folks would be off work and out to enjoy the local colours and flavours. I retraced my steps of the day before and was happy to see that the demo posters hadn't been covered over yet. It had been a while since I had had a good coffee so I was tempted to drop in at Overdrive for a brew.

But fatigue won over addiction: an early and much deserved rest was what I needed most. I stopped in at the bakery instead and grabbed a couple of kaiser buns and some cream cheese and salmon spread for a no hassle snack in the evening. Next I crossed the street to the corner fruit and vegetable shop for a box of non-organic pesticide-laden strawberries, a few bananas and two pears. I had everything I needed for a self-contained and quiet evening.

Most of the fish had left their icy bed and Maria was cleaning up the store. She would stay open until all the fresh stock was gone, then head home to rest up for tomorrow, the busiest day of the week. I walked into the front of the store.

"Hey, Maria. How were things today? Did you cope okay until Irene got here?"

"Oh sure, it was all fine. We had a huge single sale for a restaurant so everything was gone pretty quickly. Just some snapper and frozen stock left."

She looked at me carefully. "Are you alright? You look tired."

"I am tired. But good news — Anita's gone for rehab in a safehouse. But I'm still feeling uneasy. I don't know who to trust any more."

"She'll be okay," Maria said firmly. "She's a survivor."

"True." I looked at Maria. "She told me that she shared her story with you too."

"Yes, it was almost unbelievable. You hear about those things but it doesn't quite seem real until it stares you in the face. I'm glad you are helping her, Abby," she said, her eyes serious. "But be careful. Those people are dangerous. Maybe you should figure out a way to get the police involved without getting her into trouble."

"I'm not sure I trust the cops, Maria, but I have another idea. I'm going to see if Liam O'Casey can help her out."

"That's a great idea," she enthused. "He has some clout, and he was good to your dad. Let me know what happens, will you?" She looked at my meagre purchases.

"I suppose that's your dinner ... Look, why don't you come to our place tonight? Frank could drive you home later. It might do you good to have a break."

"Thanks for the offer, Maria, but I'm whacked out. I'm just going to take it easy, read, listen to some music, stuff like that. Mother is taking me to lunch tomorrow so I want to be well rested for that plus I have to work again next week and I have some, er, research to do with Sparky this weekend. So, thanks again, but I'm going to take a rain check."

"Sounds nice to me, actually. Maybe sometime, you can go home and feed the family and I'll stay the night at your place."

I laughed, "They'd starve or have to drink one of my brews. I have a better idea. Have Frank deal with the kids so you and I can have a sleepover sometime. That would be fun."

"I don't know if I could bring myself to do it, Abby. But you're right, it would probably be good for me."

I gave Maria a quick kiss. "Thanks for all your help. I don't know where I'd be without you. You are my touchstone. Say 'hi' to the family."

Before calling O'Casey, I decided to tidy up a bit. I took my stuff upstairs in two trips. Over the past days, bits and pieces had been accumulating in the downstairs room. First, I dumped all the non-recyclable detritus I could find into a big garbage bag. Anita's bloodied clothes were still neatly piled in a corner of my bathroom closet. I gingerly picked them up and double-bagged them, resolved to dump the offending items somewhere far away on my Saturday morning ride. I was glad the police hadn't decided they wanted to look around my place. That would have been awkward.

I washed my hands three times, feeling a bit like Lady Macbeth, and then, deciding that was enough cleaning for one day, I sat down to call O'Casey. It was fortuitous, I thought to myself, that I had bumped into him on Tuesday night. I smiled. I don't think he knew what he was getting into when he gave me his card.

He answered the phone after three rings. "O'Casey," he said brusquely into the phone.

"Hello again, Mr. O'Casey. It's me, Abby Faria calling. I hope I'm not disturbing you."

"Oh, hello Abby. No, you're not disturbing me. Hold on a minute." He must have put his hand over the phone because I could hear him talking in a muffled voice and then he came back on the line. "I was just saying goodbye to a client. You're lucky to catch me here; usually I try to knock off a little early on a Friday. Now, what can I do for you, Abby? Isn't it funny — I don't see you for years and then all these coincidences," he laughed lightly.

"I know," I said. "I was just thinking something like that myself, how you might be regretting giving me your card."

"Not at all, not at all," he said. "It's like the old days. By the way, about that development angle; I spoke with Johnson briefly about it last night. I couldn't think of a way to bring the discussion around to property in Kensington without getting his suspicions up, but I did ask if he was working on any major projects these days and he said he was just at the beginning stages of a major coup. It's not much I'm afraid, but if he's truly at the beginning, we'll have time to organize a strategy for your group. I'll get someone here to keep digging. How's that?" he asked sounding quite pleased with himself.

"That's wonderful sir," I said, not letting on that I was already at work with Sparky trying to do my own digging. "Thanks for your help."

"My pleasure dear. I love that old Market too! Wouldn't do for just anybody to come along and make a mess of its charms, now, would it?"

"My sentiments exactly." Time to change topics. "Um, Liam, do you remember last night that I said I wanted to talk to you about a friend who was here illegally?"

He answered affably, "Why, yes my dear. If it's legal help you need, I'm pretty busy right now, but I may be able to turn it over to one of my junior lawyers for some pro bono work."

"That would be great, but I'd really appreciate it if you could talk to my friend first. Let me tell you a little about her situation."

O'Casey said, "Okay, I have a few minutes now. Why don't you fill me in?"

I took a breath and recounted some bits of Anita's story, just enough to give him the basics but not every detail. I kept out the addiction and the rehab but I did explain why she was afraid to go to the police. What I really wanted was to see if he could do anything about her status.

"So what do you think, sir? Is there anything you can suggest?"

"You're right Abby. This girl does need our help. Is she with you now?"

"No sir, not just at the moment."

"Well, I think you should bring her to see me first thing on Monday morning. I'll arrange to have one of my junior lawyers with me. Meanwhile, I'll give the situation some thought over the weekend and we'll see what we can come up with. Do you think you can keep her safe until then?"

I breathed a sigh of relief. "I'm sure I can figure something out," I said. "Thank you so much. I wasn't sure how I was going to help her. What time would you like us there on Monday?"

"Let me see," he said, "I have an appointment at nine but I could come in early. How does seven-thirty sound? Can you make that?"

"For sure, Liam. I am so grateful."

"A pleasure my dear. Be careful over the weekend. I'm going out of town so you won't be able to reach me. I'll see you Monday. Goodbye Abby. And," he chuckled, "try to avoid picking up any more problems.

"I'll be careful. Thanks again." I rang off, more than relieved to have planned the next step for Anita. In fact, with O'Casey on our side, I was suddenly optimistic for her.

As I waited for the water to heat up again, I read the bike magazine from cover to cover, ripping out an ad for a contest to win a new road bike. You never know, I might be the lucky one in a million and the odds were way better than the lotteries.

The late fall sun cast long shades of yellow over the room. I'd closed the windows as the weather was turning colder but I could still hear the faint beat of reggae from up the street.

I felt a little less vulnerable now that Anita was safely away and we had a plan in place for her with O'Casey. I wondered how she was doing in the throes of withdrawal. Were the people helping her being kind? Would she weather the process well? I hoped that she was in good hands.

I thought about her future as I sat there in my darkening apartment. It still might not be very rosy with people like Andersen at large. In a bizarre way, this murder might be the best thing that ever happened to her if it got her out from under his thumb.

Finally I had a bite to eat and then immersed myself in the shower. The hot water prickled my exhausted flesh. My brain was too worn with fatigue to be stimulated so I just lost myself in the wonderful heat. My eyes were closing as I towelled off and brushed my teeth. A quick survey of my messy bed reminded me I'd have to get to the laundry sometime soon. I reluctantly set my alarm for six-thirty; my only solace was that I would at least get a long sleep since it was only eight o'clock. Without further ado, I crashed.

Chapter 16

As usual, I opened my eyes exactly fifteen minutes before the alarm was due to go off. Pre-empting the unholy noise, I deactivated it and rolled out of bed. With ten hours of sleep under my belt, I was feeling great. I decided to get in a quick and hard joyride and then reward myself with a visit to Overdrive and, of course, a shower. Dressing with uncharacteristic alacrity I grabbed the bag of Anita's clothes and stuffed it in my backpack. My thrill of the morning was deciding which bike to ride.

My brand new roadie, the Cervello, won. I was planning to stick to the Lakeshore bike trail so there wasn't too much danger of its getting banged up. This bike was not yet fully paid for but I couldn't wait any longer. I wanted to get in a ride or two on it before the snows, and thus the salt, sidelined my baby for the rest of the season.

I filled my water bottle with filtered water and ate a banana. Breakfast could wait; eating too much before a hard ride would upset my digestion. So with bike, pack and helmet, I made my way down the stairs. Irene was out front already chipping the ice in preparation for a busy Saturday, so I just quietly slid out the back door.

It was a lovely morning. The exercise quickly dispelled the cold and my bike gloves cut most of the wind on my hands so I was comfortable. The fair-weather riders weren't out so I had the Lakeshore trail almost to myself and was able to get up to a good speed. The wind whipped my face as I inhaled deeply.

What a great life I had. The only thing that might have topped it off would have been a good cycling partner, someone who shared my love of speed. Alice was good for it once in a while but she was usually busy with Beano. No, I needed a cycling buddy who could offer a challenge and a thrill. Too bad men didn't seem to come as a perfect package, with all the necessary attributes in one. But then again, maybe I wouldn't always want to share the freedom of the ride. I could be very contrary.

When I reached my first destination, the old Cherry Street extension, I stopped. Opening my pack, I took out the bag of clothes and pitched it accurately into a garbage can about six feet to my right. With my mind clear and a load off, I turned to ride back west.

There was still the odd swan in the shallows of the lake. They always look serene against the cool blue water as they glide along, in stark contrast to the cars, which flash by unceasingly day and night on Lakeshore Boulevard. The traffic was comparatively sparse that early in the morning, which meant that I wasn't polluting my lungs too much as I rode along the trail. I was going about fifty clicks, and passed a few cars on the down hills. It was a great way to start the day!

On my return through the city, I had to be better behaved, watching out for my precious bike. I decided to drop it off at home before going for my coffee to avoid risking theft, although I would have enjoyed showing her off at Overdrive. It was around eight o'clock so the stores were almost ready to open but real business had not yet begun. The shopkeepers were either out shooting the breeze with their neighbours or inside counting out the day's float. There was a quiet air of expectancy. It was a lovely cool fall day and business would be good.

I raced around the corner of Baldwin onto Kensington, not anticipating any action other than the odd stationary delivery truck. Still reasonably quick but alert, hands in position over my brakes, I turned into the lane and stopped by my door.

I hadn't paid any attention to the car parked face forward further up the lane. Savvy Marketers often use that spot as a free parking space. I leaned my bike against my body and looked for my keys. When I heard the squeal of tires, I looked up disbelievingly as the car barrelled toward me. How could anyone drive so fast in the confines of the Market? With a lurch of the heart, I realized the car wasn't going to slow down.

My choices weren't pretty. It was me or the bike — a tough decision to make in a split second. Deciding to save my own skin,

I sacrificed the bike, letting it go as I leapt back into the doorway, closing my eyes. To my surprise there was no sickening crunch as the car whizzed by. Instead I heard a loud bang as the bike fell against the side of the car. I did not escape unscathed because the bike bounced back at me and I received a healthy wallop across my outstretched arms. Sprawled back against the door, the bike on top of me, I heard the car tires squeal again. It took off and I lay there stunned until Maria wrenched the door open exclaiming,

"Holy shit, Abby! What happened? Are you okay? I thought I heard tires squealing." She knelt down hurriedly and helped me lift the battered bike off.

I looked at it and cried, "Oh, Maria, my beautiful bike!"

"Jesus, Abby, you could have been killed and you cry about your bike! You're really crazy. Come on, can you get up?"

"I'm okay, I think," I said flexing my arms. "Nothing's broken." I looked at my bike again. "On me, at least."

"Let's get you inside, Abby," she said, helping me up. She led me into the back room and sat me down on my couch. "You might have a concussion, Abby. Shall I call an ambulance? I'm going to get some ice."

"No. No ambulance," I said as firmly as I could. "I'm sure I'll be okay. I'm just a little stunned. But I really think I'm going to be fine."

She nodded but looked doubtful. "You wait here while I get the ice."

While Maria was gone, I checked my various moving parts. Other than my sore arms and a throbbing in my chest, I seemed fine. But I was mad as hell. How could someone be so irresponsible? What did they hope to gain, driving down the lane so fast? Didn't they see me? Then it began to dawn on my slow mind that perhaps this was not just some stupid, idiotic behaviour. Maybe it had been intentional! That made me even madder. What were they trying to do, kill me? Or just scare me? And who the hell were they?

Maria came back with the ice. I guess she had been thinking the same way.

"This isn't good, Abby. You could have been killed. Why would someone do that? You've got to be more careful," she said pressing the huge ice pack against my arms.

"I know, I know, Maria, I'm not sure what brought this on. Thank God Anita's not here. Anyway, for what it's worth, I don't think they were trying to kill me. Maim me, yes, but not kill me. I think it was just a warning, a threat."

"I'm worried for you, Abby. You sure you don't want to go to the police?"

"Not yet, Maria. I want to get Anita in to see O'Casey first. Then we'll see."

She didn't look pleased but she did agree, "Okay, Abby, provided there are no more warnings like this."

"Right then," I said, crossing my toes. "Listen, Maria, when Mom gets here, please don't let her know what's going on. I don't want to worry her."

"Okay, but if something else happens, the deal's off. I'm scared for you, Abby. Someone has already been killed."

"You don't have to tell me that," I said getting up cautiously and handing back the ice.

"Maria, I'm going to Overdrive. I need some time to calm down. I'll be back in a bit." I gave her arm a squeeze. "Thanks for the ice and don't worry. I'll be okay."

She shook her head as we walked through the store. "Not worry? Abby, just to know you is to worry about you."

I made my way gingerly to Overdrive. Outside the corner vegetable stores were baskets overflowing with a colourful array of apples, squash and cabbages. An outside speaker in front of one store belted out Spanish salsa music. The house on Kensington Place still had yellow tape decoratively festooned over the porch, but I noticed the doorway was clear. Presumably Sonya was back in residence. I would have liked to pay her a visit but my friend Joe the portly policeman, this time in plainclothes, was still lounging around the entrance to the lane. Was he working overtime for Andersen, the police or both? I wondered.

Even though the Market proper was only just starting to come alive with customers, Overdrive was packed with groggy early birds looking for their caffeine fix and zombie parents who needed a hit and an outing to placate the angels for a while. Mario and Veronica were both behind the counter pumping out coffees and light breakfasts, obviously too busy to chat. I wasn't really in the mood anyway, my pleasant high from the ride destroyed by the demise of my bike and my own aches and pains. I had a strange spaced-out feeling and wondered if mild shock was setting in. I took two mushroom turnovers and a double cappuccino to a single chair at the back of the two-room café.

I thought about my bike; I was pretty sure the frame was salvageable although its beautiful paint job was trashed and I was going to have to replace some components. Beano and Alice were going to freak when they saw it. I decided to drag it in for a post mortem the next day. The repair work would have to be added to my never-ending bike bill. I had still not fully paid the $6000 I owed for it. There was no point reporting the 'accident,' and as for insurance, the premium on bikes had made getting insurance pointless. I was sure that this had been another warning but for what — helping Anita? I was obviously too close to something. I just had to figure out what. I wasn't going to stop now. I was seriously angry and wanted to get whoever was responsible, wherever it led.

As I stared at the bottom of my coffee cup, Mario, taking advantage of a lull in customer traffic, came by as he collected dirty dishes and wiped down empty tables.

"Why so glum, Abby? You look like your boyfriend just dumped you. I always told you I was a better choice."

"Nothing as easy as that, bud," I responded, a little cheered by his banter. "My best bike just got on the injured list."

"Not your new Cervello? That *is* serious. Were you hit, Abby? I can't believe you would take that beauty for a ride in traffic."

"No, I was out for a fast jaunt on the Lakeshore. It was a fantastic ride!"

I decided to downplay the malevolence of the attack. I was sure the felons had no clue that the bike was so precious.

"Someone sideswiped me and then took off. The frame looks okay, but the rest ..."

"That really sucks," he said shaking his head in sympathy.

Absurdly, my eyes started to prickle with tears. I got up hurriedly in an attempt to hide my emotion. "Well, I've got to go get cleaned up. Mother is coming to take me out."

"That sounds like fun," he said, looking dubious. Mario knows that my mom and I have our ups and downs.

"Tell you what, Ab," he said, eyeing my averted face as we walked to the front of the café. "Have a Mario Special on me in sympathy for your loss. That'll rev you up." He carefully stepped over an imp who was driving his toy cars on the floor. Some people think of this place as their living room.

"I'll take you up on that, old friend," I said gratefully. "You know I'd never pass up one of your special efforts." The special proved to be a powerful and decadent double espresso with whipped cream and chocolate shavings on top. As Mario handed me the drink in a milkshake-sized glass mug, he said,

"Just bring the cup back next time you're in. I can't bear the thought of my creation in a take-out cup. And Abby," he gave my arm a sympathetic squeeze, "take it easy. Forget about the bike for a bit and take care of yourself, sweetheart."

Any more of this good treatment and I'd start bawling my eyes out then and there. But he was right. It would take a while to recover, my sore arms serving as a nagging reminder. As I sipped and walked I decided to step over to the cheese shop for the promised breakfast tasting special. It was busy in there; the front and back counter both had customers lined up. I waited at the front where Sarah was busy giving out samples and selling chunks of cheese.

"Hello my friend. Been to Overdrive, I see," she said approvingly. She recognized the signature mug. They are liberally spread throughout the Market waiting to be taken back and refilled.

"Hi Sarah, have you got any of that spiced Gouda you promised me?"

"For sure. Hey, and try a bit of this too." She cut me a piece of havarti and passed it over. I popped it in my mouth as she cut a piece of brie and held it out temptingly on the end of the knife. This was going to be my second breakfast, I saw.

"Delicious as usual," I said. She passed me a taster of the promised Gouda, which is when I protested.

"That's got to be the last one, Sarah. You've got other customers and I'm stuffed." I rolled the last piece of cheese in my mouth, "Mmm, it's good though. I'll take a chunk of that for later tonight."

She took a piece, already wrapped, out of the glass fronted fridge.

"Here you go. It's on the house. Hope you have a nice wine to go with it."

That reminded me that I had promised to see Roger tonight. Perhaps I would make the supreme sacrifice and share the cheese with him. He was sure to have a passable bottle of wine. I insisted on paying for the cheese and then finally took my leave, much to the relief of the people waiting impatiently behind me.

Maria was already hard at work when I got back to Neptune's, so I sketched a wave, gave a little okay sign with my thumb and forefinger and went around to the back. I gave the downstairs room a miss, as I wasn't ready yet to confront the full extent of the damage to my bike. Instead, I headed for the shower to prepare for Arabella Sr.

She arrived on the dot of twelve. I was sitting out front waiting for her. My mother is so punctual I can set my watch to her movements. Sometimes I wonder if she arrives early for appointments then waits around the corner so she can show up exactly on time. More likely the world moves in tune with Arabella's notion of precision. Smart, quick and effervescent, she is interested in health and always exploring the latest trends. She grasps most of them quickly, but just as quickly tires of them. As a result, Arabella appears to hop like a bird from one interest to the next. But whatever she does, she does with impeccable style.

Some things have rubbed off on me but, in general, we follow different paths. I am a little too basic, and a lot too sloppy. Arabella and I love and respect each other, but learned long ago not to intervene in each other's lives. As a result, sadly, we haven't a lot to say to each other in general. We are both pretty sensitive too — our outer veneer belying a vulnerable inner-thinking self. That's probably why we can't spend much time together at one sitting. We seem to peel away each other's layers without intending to. And then I start to squirm, and Mother brooks very little of my self-protective back talk.

When her sleek BMW rolled up in front of the shop I hopped in before the cars behind her could start honking. Mother, around whom the world revolves, was not worried a bit. She idled long enough to greet me.

"Hello Abby, darling." She kissed me daintily on the cheek while giving me the once-over with her steely eye. I felt as if she could tell everything that was going on just by looking at me. I hugged my arms to me defensively, hoping she didn't see me wince.

"So, where to, Mom?"

"I thought we would visit the Vegetarian Emporium for lunch," she said as she directed her attention to Saturday driving. She navigated smoothly through the Market and up Spadina to Dupont. Fortunately, the Emporium is located within what I consider to be my part of town so I could safely avoid a nosebleed.

We could have spent a great deal of time looking for a parking spot but even the sea parts for my mother, and she snagged a choice spot immediately in front of the restaurant. I had mostly kept quiet as she drove but habit kicked in and I grumbled, "Why don't you get a hybrid, at least? You know how much these cars contribute to smog pollution."

"Oh Abby, can't you get off your high horse for a few minutes so we can enjoy lunch?"

I knew that in the name of peace and goodwill I had better shut up so I murmured a contrite and uncharacteristic, "You're right. I'm sorry."

My mother raised her eyebrows but said nothing. She didn't usually win that easily.

I am always happy to visit the Vegetarian Emporium. Amanda, the proprietor, is a genius with simple foods and serves only organic vegetarian meals. Her concoctions prove that healthy can also be delicious. She can take the same stuff I throw in a blender and magically make it into a nectar of the gods.

I continued trying to hide my aches and pains while Mom chatted away about her latest health discoveries. Fortunately, she was off the talk about parasites that had made eating so difficult last time. Now it was health through chakra awareness.

"You can even eat dirt and be healthy," she was saying authoritatively as the waitress arrived to take our order.

Neither of us chose dirt. I ordered an Artemis shake and a Mercury's Delight, while Mother, in her usual way, prefaced her order — fresh orange-pineapple juice, herbed broccoli soup and tofu steak — with the statement that she wasn't very hungry. I guess her high metabolism helps her maintain her diminutive figure. I inherited my father's body shape. Tall and full figured, as they say. I have been consoling myself lately with the reminder that Marilyn Monroe was a size sixteen.

The food was excellent, as usual, and my mother's steady stream of chatter was soothing. I ate and listened, lulled by her comforting voice. But once she had told me all about her latest endeavours, the inevitable happened. She asked about my life.

"So, how are things with you, Abby? How was your date with Roger?"

Looking up in surprise, I said, "How did you know about that?"

She looked pleased, as she always does when she thinks she has something over me. I'm just a little paranoid around such an omniscient mother.

"I was talking to your sister the other day. She told me that Bell had dressed you up for the event. So? Was it fun? I'm sure that with Bell helping you looked quite glamorous. She's very gifted."

"That's true. She took this gorgeous skirt and top she'd made and added a few of my things — she made me look like a fashion maven."

"I would have liked to have seen you dressed up, Abby. I'll bet you were beautiful. Was Roger pleased?"

Mother has met Roger once and was quite taken with him. I think she likes the idea of someone being able to support me in the style she's accustomed to.

"I believe so," I said, trying to ignore her unspoken criticism on my usual choice of style. "We had fun. By the way, Mom, I saw Liam O'Casey at the restaurant. He sends his regards. In fact, I saw him at a meeting a couple of days ago in the Market too. He's still supporting the fight against gentrification."

Her eyes grew alert.

"I haven't seen him for quite a while. How is dear Liam? You know, we had a fling one time, just after I divorced your father. Just think, he could have been your stepfather," she laughed.

I put down my fork and swallowed carefully. Fatherly he may seem in some ways, but I remembered his roving eyes and his series of 'trophy' wives.

"He's a good guy, Mom, but I'm glad you didn't marry him. He's got quite a reputation as a womanizer."

"Yes dear, but he was a change of pace, all charm and style — a welcome change after your dad with all his earnest political antics. Liam even helped arrange a good stock investor for my portfolio. It's because of him that I decided to sell my mother's old place on College Street and had the broker parlay the money into my independent living.

"In the end, though, I knew it wasn't a good idea to hook up long term with Liam. I was beginning to enjoy my independence. Besides, I still loved your crazy father. He was just a tad too difficult, what with all his protesting and that time he spent in jail. I was very grateful to Liam for trying to help him and for sticking by me through the whole thing. He behaved like a gentleman."

Her comments about my father surprised me. "I didn't know you still loved Dad."

She looked a little sad, "I did then. Now, it's changed. As I said, I'm enjoying myself."

"You know, I still admire some of what Dad did. Look how he stood up to that bastard Johnson."

She tutted disapprovingly at my language before exclaiming bitterly, "And what did it get him? A jail term, a broken family ... and the condo on St. Clair got built anyway. He's got commitment, that's true, but surely there could have been more effective ways to stop that kind of development." She paused for a moment, delicately sipping her soup off the spoon.

"You know, Johnson must be very absorbed with his business.

When I was in that bridge group, I met his wife, Bitsy. Now there was an unhappy woman. She was smart and played amazing bridge, but she was so bored. It looked like she had everything: money, a lovely house, a successful husband. But she felt left out.

"She was well-intentioned too, always trying to get people to support one good cause or another. I remember thinking at the time that she could have been a good influence on Johnson's business, if he only let her get involved. You know, Abby, I might want you to marry well but no matter what, don't give up your mind or your independence. We had it all wrong in those days."

I was touched by my mother's frank disclosure. We had never talked like this before. There must be something to this chakra stuff.

"Don't worry, Mom. If anything, my penchant for independence will keep me from ever marrying. I'll probably still be a courier when I'm sixty."

She shuddered, "I certainly hope not. A perfectly good university education, wasted."

I decided not to react to that comment either, but mother's talk about Bitsy Johnson had given me an idea.

"Mom, you said Bitsy Johnson is interested in good works. Do you think she would be willing to support the bike program at the community centre? It's really good for the kids."

"Perhaps, dear. Would you like me to ask her?"

"No, that's alright. It might be better if one of the more presentable kids went round to talk to her about the program. Do you think she'd be okay with that? It might make their plight seem more immediate."

She seemed to think for a moment. "Good idea, Abby. Just make sure you don't send someone who will case her house while he's at it."

"Of course not. Where did you say she lives?"

"I didn't, but she lives on Cramden Road in Forest Hill. I don't remember the exact number. Just tell them it's the largest white colonial house on the street, about four or five doors east of Bathurst."

"Thanks Mom. And I should probably keep the family name out

of this. I don't want to alienate Mrs. Johnson."

"Don't worry about it, Abby. I'm not sure she was even aware of all that mess with your dad. She certainly never said anything about it to me when introduced. I think Johnson keeps her well out of the business unless he can use her in a social setting. I would never have put up with that but, as I said, we had it all wrong and many women in those days didn't know there were other options."

We had finished our lunch and, since there was a lineup for tables, the waitress was beginning to hover. I was ready to go, thrilled with the info my mother had so willingly shared, and anxious to act on it.

"Well, Mom, that was a great lunch as usual. Amanda sure can cook. Thanks for taking me out."

"It's been my pleasure, Abigail," she said as she paid the bill. "We should do this more often. Maybe we can include Joan next time."

I quietly gulped; two family members at once might be too much outside of major holidays. My sister is a corporate lawyer, not a profession I aspire to — but then, she doesn't think too much of my lifestyle either. We have to choose our words very carefully when we spend time together. I shouldn't really criticize — she is successful in what she does, and has produced a lovely creative daughter. We just don't have too much in common except that we are both somewhat insecure in a brash way. I wasn't about to get into this with my mother after such a relaxed lunch. I decided to take her advice and stay off my high horse.

"That's an idea. I'll let you know when I have time."

We drove back to the Market in silence. As she drove slowly through the Saturday crowds on Baldwin, Arabella finally said, "I heard about the murder in the Market. It sounds terrible. Did you know the man?"

I had been hoping we would be able to give that whole subject a miss. There was no need to worry my mother. "No, Mom, I didn't know him, but the house is just around the corner. Apparently it had something to do with drugs." I shrugged. "It seems to have quieted down pretty quickly although I don't think they've arrested anyone yet."

"Hmm," mother said as she pulled in front of Maria's shop. "I'm glad you're not involved. Be careful Abby. This city is getting dangerous."

"I'm careful, but this could have happened anywhere, you know. The Market is usually pretty safe."

Maria came out of the store to the car with a plastic bag. "Hello, Arabella, how are you? I hope you had a nice lunch." She proferred the bag. "Here is a nice fresh red snapper for your dinner."

"Why thank you, Maria." Mother took the bag as I got out of the car. "You're looking well. How is your family?"

Maria smiled, "They're just fine. We will have to have you over soon. The children are very fond of you."

"That would be lovely."

Maria gave a little wave and went back into the busy shop.

"Thanks again for lunch, Mom. I'll be in touch soon. I really had a nice time." I leaned over and gave her a quick hug through the car window.

Mother smiled as she kissed me on the cheek, "I did too, Abby. Take care of yourself, especially on those bikes."

I didn't let on that that piece of advice was too late. I just waved goodbye as she drove smartly away. It had been an amazing lunch, no rancour, no anxiety. Maybe our relationship was maturing.

Chapter 17

What I had purposely avoided telling my mother was that I was planning to visit the Johnson household myself — that very afternoon. I decided that a disguise would stand me in good stead. I wanted to look like I fit into the posh neighbourhood, and my usual biking clothes just wouldn't do it.

I dug through the back of my closet to find the stuff my mom had once given me — nice silk blouse, conservative tweed skirt and jacket, the dreaded pantyhose, low-heeled, suitable shoes. Then I poked around way in the back and pulled out a makeup kit my sister had once given me for Christmas in the hopes that I'd actually use it. After I had set myself up as what I hoped looked like a Rosedale matron, I put on my one treasured item from my grandmother: a string of real pearls.

From my chest of drawers I retrieved four brochures for the bike workshop. I actually do have to fundraise to keep it going and it would be a nice irony if Johnson unwittingly footed some of the bill. The fun part was deciding which of my two cruiser bikes I would ride — the refurbished antique or the new Raleigh. I decided that in Forest Hill the antique would be under-appreciated, and thus settled on the Raleigh. It *is* pretty cool; lightweight with an enclosed gear hub, and painted forest green with lime green trim. That baby completed my disguise. I took the bike on the subway, to avoid working up a sweat on the way uphill to Cramden Road.

It was four o'clock by the time I rode past number 38, to drop a brochure into the mail slot at number 40, just in case anyone was watching. Then I rode up the driveway to number 35, which was truly the largest colonial-style white house on the whole street. It looked like the Johnsons had presidential aspirations.

I prayed that the society matron was home alone, and that I could bluster my way in. I wanted to work on Bitsy's obvious philanthropic tendencies. The bell, a classy muted three-tone job, echoed through the hall. Bitsy herself answered the door. It must have been the maid's day off.

"Hello dear," she said. "Can I help you?" I sure hoped so.

"Good afternoon, ma'am. Are you the lady of the house?" I said in my most melodic and cheerful of tones.

"Why, yes I am," she said. "And you are?…"

"Madeline Brisset," I said, handing her one of my Bikeworks brochures. "I'm wondering if I can have a little of your time this afternoon. I'm fundraising for a program we run for street kids downtown."

"Well, perhaps I have a little time," she said. "Won't you come in … umm …"

"Madeline," I said, crossing the threshold.

"I can't help feeling that we've met before," said Bitsy.

"I don't believe so, unless you've seen me in the area," I lied. She must have remembered my face from seeing me, in my other disguise, at the restaurant the other night. Mother was right. This woman was sharp.

"I've just made myself some coffee," said Bitsy, dispelling my assumption that she was indolent, as well as rich. "Would you like a cup?"

"That would be lovely," I responded in my best effusive-yet-gracious tone.

"Just make yourself comfortable in the sitting room while I pour the coffee." She pointed toward the room on the right and smiled. I was beginning to regret any harm that might come to her by exposing her husband's corporate skulduggery.

"You know, I wouldn't be doing this if it weren't for my desire to help the underprivileged," I said confidingly, delicate demi-tasse in hand, as we sat side by side on a plush couch in Bitsy's well-appointed sitting room. All the furniture was upholstered in a tasteful floral pattern and the oak surfaces of the coffee and side tables gleamed with a high maintenance polish. On the main coffee table sat a large flower arrangement in colours chosen to accent the upholstery. It was a designer's dream and had likely been featured in *Better Living* or whatever the other ten percent reads these days.

"I know just what you mean," she said comfortingly, rousing me from my speculations. "I am grateful I have the wherewithal to help others. It's one of the virtues of my position, I suppose."

"Oh?" I said encouragingly, leaving room for her to elaborate.

"Yes," she said. "I have inherited a little wealth from my family. We have a long history of sharing what we have. My husband does well, too. He develops properties. Condominiums appear to be the thing these days. He helps with donations when he can also."

"That must make you very happy," I said gushingly.

"Yes, I suppose," she said. "But I do wish we could do more for the homeless and the youth living in the streets. So let me take a look at your brochure. Perhaps I can get my neighbour's wife, Emma, interested too. Lars Andersen is my husband's business associate. David is always asking me to be friendly with Emma."

I was amazed at how talkative Bitsy was. Perhaps she was lonely or perhaps door-to-door charity workers are the equivalent of housewives' bartenders — an anonymous, safe pair of ears. It was disarming and I was regretting the fact that I was beginning to like Bitsy.

I didn't know if I would find out anything that was worthwhile. She didn't seem to be involved in her husband's more shady dealings. In fact, she seemed blissfully unaware that what he was doing exacerbated the problems of the homeless. She probably thought condos were affordable, as they were many steps down from her lifestyle. I continued to pump her, anyway, seeing how easy it was to get information.

"It's nice of you to help your husband," I said.

"I suppose, although the Andersens can be annoying. They are from Eastern Europe, you know, they aren't really part of our circle." Thank goodness Bitsy revealed some prejudice. It brought things back into balance.

"I'm sure you try," I said mollifyingly.

"Hmm," she said, lost in her own thoughts as she leafed through the brochure. "David does spend a lot of time with Andersen. He says it's business. They are playing golf at the club all weekend — some kind of best-of-three rivalry to celebrate a business deal. That Roselawn Golf and Country Club is beginning to seem like his second home. Emma doesn't seem to mind. She just begs me to arrange more bridge games for the girls. But really I'm getting tired of that game," she sighed. "I much rather my volunteer work at the hospital and the art gallery."

It sounded like our Bitsy was a golf widow.

"Your husband is a lucky man," I said kindly. "I hope he appreciates all you do."

"Yes, well," she said in a more business-like tone. "Shall I write you a cheque?" I could see that the comfortable little scene was coming to a close and I put down my empty coffee cup with some regret.

"That would be wonderful," I said honestly. "Just make it out to Bikeworks. I'm sure your donation will be very helpful," I gushed as she handed me a cheque for a very generous one hundred dollars. "Should I send the tax receipt to this address?"

"That will be fine," Bitsy said as she walked me back to the door.

"You have a nice-looking bicycle," she said, and once again I warmed to her, fantasizing about friendship under different circumstances. Anyone who admires my wheels can't be all bad.

"I used to ride quite a lot when I was younger," she said. "Perhaps I should take it up again. It might be more fun than going to the gym with Emma."

"This is a comfortable cruiser," I said. "It's more efficient for this kind of work than getting in and out of a car or walking up all these long driveways. Well, thank you for supporting our cause, Mrs. … Johnson," I said, glancing at the name on the cheque, feigning unfamiliarity with her last name.

"I'm glad to have helped those children," she said warmly.

"Oh my," I said, glancing at my watch. "Look at the time. I guess that I'm done for today." And with that we parted company.

Either Bitsy was a consummate actress or she knew very little about the nature of her husband's business; whichever, she had unwittingly helped me. Anthony Bellini, the pro at Roselawn Country Club was, believe it or not, an old friend. Although ultra-respectable at work, he had once been a punk rock musician of some promise. He had been a neighbourhood friend until his parents moved to the suburbs, and we had kept in touch. The inklings of a plan were taking shape. Maybe Tony could help me get a lead on Johnson and Co.

Tony could still be cajoled occasionally into donning his old grunge gear and letting loose at some choice downtown club. I hoped he'd think our old friendship worth a favour or, failing that, perhaps a little bribe. Maybe I could think up a good trade. I'd give him a call when I got home.

Meanwhile I made the best of my ride down the hill on Bathurst Street. It was late enough in the day that the traffic was going mostly the other way. As I picked up speed on my cruiser, I revelled in the relief of the refreshing ride after my mother's stuffy car. As I felt the wind run through my respectable clothing I could think of nothing better than the joy of a bike ride on a cool fall afternoon.

The Market had pretty well wound down business by the time I wheeled myself back to Neptune's. A few tourists were still wandering around but most of the folks hanging out were locals. I didn't expect a second dose of trouble in one day but decided to err on the side of caution. Dismounting before entering my lane, I looked carefully around before walking my bike to the door. I breathed a sigh of relief as it closed firmly behind me. The fresh ride had taken the ache out of my arms and I was feeling pretty good about my bit of amateur sleuthing.

Drawing on the stored energy, I hoisted my cruiser upstairs and then went back down to face the poor wrecked Cervello. I took a deep breath and walked into the office room. My beaten up baby lay on its side against the couch. I gave it a quick once-over and started a mental list of parts I'd probably need. I wasn't looking forward to Beano's reaction the next day — he's never pretty when it comes to injured bikes. I could see that I needed at least a new handlebar and one pedal, and both wheels retrued, but it seemed miraculously intact overall so maybe he wouldn't be too hard on me. Of course, it depended a little on his overall mood, which, as Alice had said, wasn't too great lately.

Once I had that painful business out of the way, I headed back upstairs. I was starting to flag from my exertions but I still had to call Tony and Sparky before I scooted up to Roger's. I wondered if Rog still wanted me to visit. I hadn't heard from him since our dinner. Maybe I'd call him too, just to make sure. Then I noticed the answering machine was blinking again. I was nervous about checking messages after the nasty threat of the other day, but I held my breath and pressed play, hoping for innocent messages from friends.

"Hey Abby," my niece's voice rang out. "I'm going to need my clothes back for school. Hope it all went well. If you don't plan to be in on Monday morning, leave it all in a bag with Maria, not too close to the fish, mind you, and I'll get them from her. See you soon."

Well, she had that all worked out. I was lucky to have such a sweet niece.

The next message was from Sparky. "Hi, Abby. I see you planted the worm. I've been looking over Johnson's files and I've found some fascinating stuff. Call me, if you get this before seven. I'm going out with a cracker I met at the last 2600.com meeting. I want to pump him for some new ideas. Those boys don't get a chance to talk to females about computers very often; makes them kind of cute and eager to share. I just hope I don't end up at McDonald's watching him override the order window." She laughed as she rang off.

Sparky had once described a date with a guy who showed her how he could use an old cordless phone to override the order window frequency at a fast food drive through. He used the phone to make obnoxious catcalls at the female order servers. Needless to say that was her last date with him.

As if in response to my earlier thoughts, the last message was from Roger. "Hiya, babe. I was short a few items when I was doing my laundry. Would you like to come over and make an exchange? Remember, I'm holding these clothes hostage. Seriously, Abby, I had a great time the other night and I miss you. If you're still free tonight, give me a call. I'll throw in pizza and a video."

Not exactly gourmet, but cozy, nonetheless, I thought as I dialled

Roger.

"Hey there. It's me."

"Hi, Abby," he said. "Did you get my message?"

"Yeah, that's why I'm calling. Is the invitation still open?"

"Absolutely." He was always so eager. "Are you coming now?"

"Well," I said, "give me an hour or two. But I have to work tomorrow," I added, "so I can't stay too late."

"No problem Abby. See you soon."

The thought of curling up with my comfortable puppy-dog guy was appealing. I figured that the visit merited another shower. I could hang around home in my sweat-bound body, but a beau deserved a minimum of sweat, at least to begin with ...

But before getting ready, I had to finish my calls. I started with Tony at the golf course. A voice answered on the second ring: "Pro Shop."

"Hi. I'm looking for Tony Bellini."

"Sorry, he's out retrieving a late group from the course. He should be back shortly after seven o'clock. Would you like to leave a message?"

"Yes please. Ask him to call Abigail as soon as he can." I left my number.

"Abigail huh? Sure thing," the casually efficient disembodied voice said and then hung up.

Next I dialled Sparky, hoping she was still in. I needed to borrow another helpful device. Usually her dates start late given that she lives in another zone on the reverse clock, so I was in luck.

"Hi, Ab." Of course Sparky would have call display, I thought.

"Hey Sparky! I got your message. I know tonight's out but I was wondering if you could do me another big favour?"

"Sure, Ab. What's up?"

"You know that little recording device you showed me once, the one that a client gave you?"

"Aha! So now you're looking for spy gadgets, huh?"

"You got it. Do you think I could borrow it for tomorrow night?"

"Sure Ab, can you come pick it up after my date? You'll need a little lesson on how to use it. I should be home by around one. Is that too much past your bedtime?"

"I can handle it, thanks. But I won't be able to stay long to talk about the Johnson stuff. Can I drop by again tomorrow? By then I might have something interesting for us on the recorder too."

"You devious thing you. You're wasting your time being a courier. Anytime after midnight should be fine tomorrow night, or should I say, Monday morning."

"Okay, see you later, Sparks. Have fun tonight."

"Oh," she laughed, "he should be good for a giggle."

The main thing left on my agenda before I visited Roger was my delicious shower.

The steaming water flowed over me and reawakened my brain cells. Other than a disastrous start, it had been a good day. All that was left now was connecting with Tony. If he didn't call before I left, I'd phone back and leave Rog's number.

Refreshed, I dressed in a casual version of my off-duty bike wear, quite fashionable in certain riding circles: tight colourful leggings in '60s style, decent T-shirt advertising the Overdrive Coffee Shop and long, loose red cotton sweater. Teeth and hair brushed, some nice clean runners and I was ready. In my haste, I almost forgot Rog's sweats, which were unwashed, I'm afraid. I bid my bikes a fond adieu, promising to return before the sun rose. I tried Tony again, but he was dealing with some customer, so I left another message, asking him to call me at Rog's number after seven. That done, I was ready to go.

I decided to splurge and hailed a cab on Spadina. It had been a busy day and I was tired, and besides, I wasn't going to risk bringing Arabella's clothes home later on a bike. As I strolled into Roger's building the autumn air was cool but still lovely. The longer we put off Toronto's soggy winter, the better.

The doorman buzzed me in right away.

"Good evening, Ms. Abby," he said pleasantly.

"Hi there, Andy. How's the family?" Andy and his wife Anna lived in Portugal Village, not too far from my own digs.

"They're fine. Little Joey is getting to be quite a handful. Not so little either, fourteen years old and going on six feet tall."

"Sounds like a good victim for my bike mechanic's workshop. Send him over to the community centre on Monday. I'll try to straighten him out." I grinned. "See you later, Andy."

"Have a nice evening, Miss Abby," he said, smiling.

It's always dicey taking on a new troublemaker. Sometimes they just exchange lessons in new criminal tactics with the other kids. What we really need are some tough male bike mentors, I thought. I should try to coerce some of my courier pals — maybe Beano, or perhaps Mario. He might have fun playing with bikes and kids again.

My temperature rose correspondingly with the elevator at the prospect of seeing Rog. He must have felt the same way, because I was barely inside the door before we were in full body contact.

Well, I thought, mid-kiss, we might as well get the sex out of the way first so we can relax over dinner. We practically tore each other's clothes off in our enthusiasm. After heatedly exchanged kisses and caresses, Roger fell into his usual attentive routine and I lay back to enjoy it. As Roger wormed his way into my lust-filled heart I became more and more revved up and finally had to get him to let me reciprocate. It was more fun that way. Finally we lay back exhausted.

"That was a nice hello, Abby," Roger said when he regained his composure.

Luckily we were already at the cigarette stage, if we'd been smokers that is, when the phone rang. Roger answered.

"Yes? ... uh ... just a minute." He held the phone out to me. "It's for you," he said, "someone named Tony."

He looked at me questioningly, but I just smiled cryptically and took the phone to the bathroom.

"Hi, Tony," I said. "Thanks for calling."

"What's up?" he said. "I haven't talked to you in a while. Everything okay?"

"Sure, it's been pretty quiet," I lied. "Anyway Tony, I'm calling to ask you a big favour. I'm not sure if I'll be able to repay you anytime soon but if a night with me at a club will help convince you, you're on."

"Let me hear it. What can you possibly have in mind?"

"Well, here's the thing. Do you know these men, Johnson or Andersen, who play golf there?"

"Do I? The question is, what's it to you? That guy Andersen, in particular, likes to make a big show of himself. He's pretty unpopular and always bossing the caddies around."

"Well, if you must know, I think Andersen has been making himself unpopular down here too. I know it's a lot to ask," I continued, "but I want to get some dirt on him, and maybe on Johnson too. I think you can help me do that."

"It would be a pleasure but I have to be careful, you know," he said. "I don't want to lose my job." He paused before he said thoughtfully, "On the other hand, it would be a favour to the club if he couldn't harass our caddies anymore. So, what can I do for you?"

"Well, first off, can you go around with the guys, offer to help them with their game or something and keep your ears open for anything interesting?"

"Sure, but I don't think they will say much around me."

"Maybe not, although you'd be surprised how invisible us lowly workers can seem to businessmen. When are they scheduled to play?"

"I think they tee off at one o'clock."

"Cool. And Tony," I said in my most winsome voice. "Can I set up a little taping device at their dinner table? I could bring it up in time for their dinner — say six-thirty or so?"

"That might be going a little too far, Abby. I could really lose my job for a stunt like that."

"I know it's asking a lot. But you'll see, I can be a master of discretion. No one will even know that we're doing it. Where's the daredevil I once knew?"

He was silent for what seemed like an eternity but finally he said, "Okay, okay, Abby, but you have to stay here at the club until they're finished their dinner and then you have to make good right away and check out the Queen Street scene with me afterwards."

"I can handle that, but it won't be really hopping on a Sunday night."

"That's okay. I'm slowing down a bit myself these days. It'll probably be just my speed. Just come prepared. I'll take care of the caddying and you can do the taping. It'd be a good idea if you came in the employee entrance when you arrive." He explained how to find my way around and secured my agreement to the deal.

"Sounds good. You're a peach. I'll see you tomorrow." I exhaled in relief when he had hung up. I hadn't been sure he would go for it.

When the phone and I exited the bathroom, Roger repeated his questioning look.

"Sorry Rog — business," I smiled. My stomach growled, reminding me that we had moved straight to dessert. "Hey Rog, I'm hungry — did you mention pizza? Any lying around, getting cold?"

He chuckled. "I'm way ahead of you. One pizza coming right up." He trotted to the kitchen with me on his heels and, true to form, removed two chilled wine glasses and a bottle of Chardonnay from the fridge. Some slightly crusty pizza emerged from the oven.

Back in bed, we balanced our plates on our laps and munched while the city twinkled below us. I tried to enjoy the pleasant interlude but I was getting edgy, in a hurry to get back on the trail. So, when Roger showed signs that he was ready for a second dessert, I said as diplomatically as I could, "Down boy. We both need to work tomorrow and there's a few things I have to take care of tonight." He complied like a good boy, but I had to work hard to ignore his puppy-dog eyes while I got ready to make my exit. Before my resolve could weaken I collected Bell's clothes, gave Roger a quick peck on the cheek and a pat on the head and was out the door.

It was a few minutes to one when I knocked on Sparky's door. I was tired and my bed was beckoning so I silently prayed she was in. Sparky answered on my second knock, blinking under the streetlight that shone in on her.

"Oh, hiya, Abby," Sparky smiled owlishly from the doorway. "Come on in."

She keeps the place dark. Night and day are all the same to Sparky. I guess it makes sense; she graduated to computers after a brief fling with the goth lifestyle, so darkness still reigns. While my eyes adjusted to the lack of adequate light, I followed her through the warren of computer paraphernalia.

In the heart of her space was a long table loaded with three computers, a printer, other computer related things foreign to my eyes and of course, in this virtual age, numerous piles of various colours of paper, the ultimate irony of the supposed paperless era. To the side were a cot, a hot plate and a small bar fridge. Sparky usually keeps food and dust religiously away from her electronic loves; thus she rarely cooks. She is tall and gangly, yet seems to move fluidly through her cramped space. As she folded herself into a chair, she pulled up its rickety partner for me.

"Let's get down to business." She pulled the minuscule recorder from a small leather case. "Here's the little baby," she said. "Be nice to it and it will reward you with about three hours of clandestine recording."

"Perfect. Show me how it works."

"It's pretty simple really," Sparky said. She showed me all the bells and whistles and how to position it so it would pick up best.

"Just make sure it's within four feet of whoever you're recording and you should have no problems."

"This is so great, Sparky," I said, giving her a quick hug. "Gotta go now. I've got to get some sleep."

"You never were very stationary, Abby."

"I guess you're right — I'm the queen of the road."

Just then, the pile of blankets on Sparky's bed started to move. What appeared to be little more than a pair of skinny arms, with a pale face and short red and green tufts of hair, sat up in a skimpy T-shirt. The arms writhed with tattoos of snakes and lizards. He looked a little disoriented as he rubbed his eyes and blinked at me. My face reddened as I realized that Sparky was not alone.

"Oh, Sparky," I blurted. "I'm sorry, I didn't realize you had ... er ... company." She followed my gaze.

"Oh hi Reg," she said. "Abby, this is Reg, a fellow cracker." And what else? ...

He got up, fumbling a bit as he tried to put on some wire-frame glasses.

"Hi," he said briefly, sitting down at a vacant computer, immediately focussed on shifting screens and bits of data. Apparently, they were well matched.

I told Sparky I'd be in touch soon and left the two to the glow of their computers while I homed in on my solitary bed.

Chapter 18

I awoke feeling peaceful and relaxed; at least until a luxurious stretch turned into pain as I felt the bruises along the backs of my arms. Then, memory rushed in and with it a desire to tend to my wounded bike. I gently reminded myself there was no hurry. Beano and Alice don't open until twelve on Sunday and I sure wasn't going to bother them this early. Instead, I took the time to enjoy my ten-minute shower. Then I put on an old Eurythmics CD, whipped up a Faria Special and poked around dusting my bikes and tightening the odd brake cable.

When I had avoided the massive laundry pile for as long as I could, I sighed.

"Okay, okay. I hear you," I said to the festering basket. I grabbed a bag and my ecological laundry soap disks, stuffed the load in a bag and stomped down the stairs to the laundromat located conveniently across from Overdrive. After depositing my dank pile in an oversized washer, I strolled over to my favourite café.

"Fancy seeing you here, Ab," laughed Veronica. She was looking relaxed leaning on the counter, only a few people resting with their coffees in the 'living room.'

"You could keep this place solvent all by yourself with your high-class coffee habits." She turned serious. "How are you? Mario told me about your accident."

"I'm fine. The bike didn't do so well but at least it wasn't totalled. We were both lucky."

"Thank God. We don't want to lose our best customer."

"Very funny," I said drily. "I don't want to bother you, but if it's not too much trouble could you please make me a big cappuccino so I can indulge in this high-class establishment and wait for my clothes to finish washing in the high-class laundromat across the street?"

"Right away, ma'am," she said with another laugh. "Feeling feisty today, are we?"

"I'm just feeling rested for a change. It's been a busy week what with the excitement around the murder and all the deking in and out between cars the last few days." I didn't bother to mention all my extra-curricular activities especially since someone had already leaked enough to get the criminal minds on my case.

Veronica handed me a frothy double cappuccino in another glass mug. "By the way, Mario said to remind you to return any others you have. We're running low on glasses. Too many folks in the Market are collecting these. Every so often we have to call them all back in."

"Sure makes the coffee better, Ronnie." I held up the mug in a salute. "Thanks for this. I'll go switch the load into the dryer and then I'll wander home and grab my collection of your mugs. See you shortly."

"Thanks ma'am." She doffed an imaginary cap. "We sure appreciate yer business."

As I walked home I noticed that the questionable cop was not at his usual post and the yellow tape was no longer decorating the house down the lane. I made a mental note to ask Veronica if she had the scoop on recent goings on.

"Four down and about fifty to go. Thanks Ab," Veronica said as I presented her with four reasonably clean glasses.

"Hey, it looks pretty quiet over there," I said, indicating the house. "Have you heard anything lately? Have they caught anyone?"

"As a matter of fact, I heard through the grapevine that the police picked up four guys on Thursday based on some fingerprints they found at the crime scene. But apparently they all conveniently had alibis so they've been released."

"So what does the grapevine say — are they the ones or not?"

"Probably, but I haven't heard," she said shaking her head. "Nobody's talking much. Strangely enough, business still seems to be flowing in and out of that house. Either the police are blind or they're lying in wait for someone else." Or at least one officer is dirty, I thought privately.

"I think folks are a little nervous," she said interrupting my thoughts. "It's one thing to know who has done what. It's another to be wondering what's going on while guilty people walk around with impunity."

"Now you're making me nervous too, Veronica," I said quietly. "I'd better move on before you scare me away for good."

"No chance of that with Mario's coffee on sale here! Hey, thanks for the glasses. Could you put out the word on your travels that we've issued a recall?"

"Sure thing. Bye again."

I picked up my clothes from the dryer and walked them home. Once I'd folded my laundry, put it away and tidied my bedroom, I figured that was good enough. I am a haphazard house cleaner at best. My mother and the sainted Maria gave up long ago trying to teach me to clean properly. I guess they love me anyway because they still visit occasionally even though there are large dust bunnies living in the corners.

I got out a few crackers for the delicious spiced Gouda and sat in my kitchen killing time till Beano's opened. Fifteen minutes later, at about eleven forty-five, I'd had enough of waiting. It was still cold out so I put my down vest over my bike jacket and went downstairs to collect the patient.

As I half wheeled, half carried the scratched black and red beauty up to The Squeaky Wheel I got a running commentary from the Market regulars on the state of my once-pristine bike. The ever-present Jeff, beer in hand, lounged against the railing in front of Stan's.

"Hey Abby. Nice roadkill. I thought you took better care of your babies."

I glared at him, not bothering to answer.

Next it was Adam, a former community centre brat. "Whoa Abby. After all those lectures about bike safety ..."

To this annoying quip I retorted, "What is it about the Market today? Everybody is a smartass."

Talita, standing outside hawking her fragrant, mouth-watering empanadas, overheard us.

"Don't listen to him, Abby. He should know better than to be so rude." She wagged her finger at Adam who just winked. "After all Abby did for you … Instead of making fun, why don't you help her?"

He put a contrite look on his face and said, "Sorry Abby. Talita's right. You must be mortified showing everyone what you did!" He laughed as he lifted the featherlight bike up and hooked it onto his right arm.

"Here, I'll take the credit for this bang-up job for a while."

I looked at Talita. "Good work friend. You got this young ingrate to do something useful." I took Adam's other arm.

"I'll just hold on and make sure that this bike gets where we want it to go. Not that I don't trust you, Adam," I said, winking right back at him and feeling like we were a little more even.

"Smart move," said Talita. "See you later."

Once we were out of Talita's earshot, Adam turned to me, "I'm sorry, Abby," he said more sincerely. "It must really hurt to have this beauty damaged. What happened?"

"Let's just say that it was a very unfortunate accident. I have finished weeping, but Beano is going to have a fit. This was his showpiece."

We arrived at The Squeaky Wheel, at which point Adam handed me back the Cervello.

"I'm not staying for this," he said. "With my luck, old Bean will blame me. I didn't do so good when he hired me last fall."

"Coward," I said, sniffing the aroma coming from his jacket. "Lay off the dope so early in the day and you might do better at wrenching. You're talented with bikes. Shame to waste it."

"Sure thing, Abby," he said, rolling his eyes. He looked up as Beano opened the door of his shop and said a hasty, "Whoops, gotta go! Good luck, Ab!"

Beano walked over to me with a shocked look. "Whoa, Abby, what happened?" He surveyed the damage. "I sure hope you put whoever did this into traction. It's bike murder!"

"Oh, I'm so sorry, Beano. I know you love this bike. I know you warned me to take extra special care of it." I was jabbering on as if it was his bike, which, in way, it was. He had put it together. We had shared in its genesis. And I still hadn't finished paying for it.

Silently, Beano eyed the victim as I carried it cradled in my arms to the shop. As he opened the door for me he called to Alice who was working in the back room.

"Drop everything! We have an emergency."

Alice rushed out. Seeing the bike in Beano's arms, she exclaimed, "Oh Abby, your bike." She was clearly more normal than the rest of us because she turned to me immediately and asked, "Are you alright? Did you get hurt?"

Beano hit his head with his palm and looked me over, "I'm sorry, Ab. I got carried away looking at the damage. I didn't even think to ask you. But after all, you are standing upright."

"It's okay Beano," I said patting his shoulder, "I understand completely. It was my first reaction too."

I looked at the broken bike sadly. "I went for a great ride by the Lakeshore early yesterday morning. She rode beautifully, you guys. Smooth, sleek and fast. Just perfect. I got home fine and then," it all spilled out of me angrily, "some assholes decided they wanted to ram me in my lane. It was me or the bike, I had a hard time choosing, but in the end I sacrificed her."

"Oh Abby! I can't believe it!" Alice eyes were wide with horror.

"Yeah, and it was no accident. They were waiting for me," I said grimly. "Someone is upset with something I'm doing." I turned to Beano who was standing there with his mouth open.

"Beano, please tell me Anita is still safe."

He snapped his mouth shut and then said, "Yeah, Ab. I spoke with the leader of her support group this morning. She is coming through the worst of the withdrawal already. She should be ready to move on to planning lifestyle changes tomorrow. That's the big thing — staying off the stuff."

"I don't want to ruin her chances of recovery, Beano, but this thing is getting overheated. I want her to see a lawyer before one side or another catches her. Can I take her to an appointment tomorrow morning?"

He pursed his lips, "Don't know, Ab. It's out of my hands now. I'll ask this afternoon and get back to you, say, around four o'clock. How's that?"

I was still wondering if Beano was being straight with me but I didn't know how to ask. Instead I said, "Do you think you could arrange for me to speak with her some time today or tonight? I'd like to talk with her — see for myself how she sounds."

"All I can do is ask," he said. "It's up to Anita and the experts."

"Fair enough, Beano. Now," I said as I turned back to the bike. "I looked her over and I think she's salvageable. I'm broken-hearted over the scratched frame though."

As Beano turned aside for another tool I thought I heard him say, under his breath, "... mad too. I didn't think they'd go so far," but I couldn't be sure. Maybe I was being paranoid.

Alice spoke up. "It's going to cost you, Ab, but I think we can fix it up, right Beano?"

"Of course. Abby, we'll go over it carefully and give you a tally in a day or two. I want to take some time on the assessment, make sure there's no cracks in the carbon fibre. That would be serious."

I nodded my agreement. "That's fine. Take all the time you need, I'm going to have to work for quite a while just to finish paying for the original, let alone the new parts."

"No sweat, take your time," Alice said.

"You are the greatest. I don't know what I'd do without your help with Anita and I know that no one else could treat my bikes with such care."

They looked pleased. "We love you, Abby," Alice said. "Besides, you're our single best customer."

"I've heard that already once today at Overdrive," I said ruefully. "Am I such a spendthrift?"

"Maybe, but that's part of your charm," laughed Beano. He rubbed his hands together. "Okay, let's get back to work, Alice. I want to find us some time to look this baby over later. Hey, Ab, you can work off some of your debt closer to Christmas, if you like. We'll have lots of next year's bikes to assemble for spring. What do you say?"

"Sounds great, Beano. It gets a bit rough doing deliveries in the deep slush. I'll welcome the change ... Okay guys, I'm going to get out of your hair for a while. I'll call or check in around four. Take your time with the bike. I'll relax knowing it's safe here."

Alice headed for the back room while Beano was already back to work replacing stock on the parts wall. "No problem, Ab. Talk to you later."

I left the shop with mixed feelings. Anita seemed to be in good hands if I could rely on Beano's information. I still had that niggling feeling that something wasn't quite right. I hoped I would be allowed to take her to the appointment with O'Casey in the morning and I'd feel a lot better if I got to speak to her today.

I had three hours to kill before I would hear back from Beano so I decided that the best thing I could do to occupy my mind was to go for another ride. Not wanting to risk my Bianchi, I grabbed my old standby, the no-nonsense Trek. It had warmed up outside since the morning so I opted for my light windproof riding jacket. I decided to just do a little loop to High Park and back. On such a lovely fall day, there would be pedestrians everywhere so I would have to take it easy. I'd save the harder effort for the evening's ride up the Don Valley to the golf club.

I stuck to the side streets, enjoying the last of the colours before the dismal grey of winter. The trees were ripe with a wild array of yellows and reds. The drying leaves on the road crackled as I rode over them, their musty-sweet smell emanating upward. I inhaled deeply, feeling myself unwind as I rode slowly through the neighbourhoods along the way.

High Park was as full as I'd expected. People were enjoying the last of the warmth before they were forced to bundle up and face winter. As I swooped down to Grenadier Pond, the sun reflected off Lake Ontario beyond the expressway bordering the park. Even the sight of cars whizzing by couldn't dispel my feelings of goodwill. Picnickers sat around a park table, while swans and ducks paddled around the pond and children threw them bits of stale bread.

The bread and my now-growling stomach reminded me that it was time for a mid-afternoon snack. I found a bench in the sun and got two vegetable empanadas out of my saddlebag. I'd picked them up on my walk back home from Beano's. Talita had thoughtfully wrapped them in foil and then in a towel so they were still a little warm. I washed the remaining crumbs down with water from my hydration pack and sat back to soak up a few of the sun's last warming rays of the year. It was hard to believe there was evil in the world when all I could hear was the sound of childrens' laughter, the pleasant hum of people's conversations and the screech of the seagulls overhead. Almost completely relaxed I headed back home around three-thirty.

The streets were more packed as I rode carefully along College through Little Italy. This is an area that serves the local Italian and Portuguese population by day with lots of homey espresso bars, bakeries and chi-chi restaurants interspersed amongst the usual hardware stores, dollar marts, grocery stores and laundromats. At night however, it becomes a haven for young club-goers. There is more of a traffic jam at one in the morning along College than there is during the normal five o'clock rush hour.

The one bonus about Sunday riding is that everyone is a bit more relaxed than usual. Even I didn't feel the need to yell at dopey drivers. We were all very polite and I arrived back in Kensington Market fully intact. There, too, it was heavy going. The Market is open seven days a week with the odd exception, the major difference on Sundays being that the urgency to buy and move on is diminished. People meander from store to store, making more leisurely purchases and just lolling around.

I waved at the Rastas as I rode by; their soothing reggae fit the Market mood perfectly. I looked warily up my lane but there appeared to be no menace lurking so I bravely rode in. It was going to take a while before I could relax again about going up that lane.

When I had safely stowed my bike and my pack inside, I sat down to phone Beano.

Alice answered, "Squeaky Wheel, how can I help you?"

"Hey Alice, it's Abby."

"Oh, hi Ab, I'm with a customer. Hang on, Beano'll just be a minute." She put down the receiver with a clatter. I could hear people talking with Beano in the background. His voice grew louder, and I heard him say, "I'll be just a moment," and then he spoke into the receiver.

"Hi, Abby, it's really busy so I've got to be quick but here's the scoop." He lowered his voice a little. "I spoke to the folks. They say our friend is doing very well and that the worst of the worst is past. She's resting a lot and they've got her eating regularly to build up her strength. They say she's tough. Anyway, grab a pen. You can call her tonight to arrange your little rendezvous. They're willing to spring her for a while but do recommend she comes back if she can later. She's not completely out of the woods yet." He recited a number to me, which I jotted on my palm.

"Fantastic, Beano. Thanks again for taking the time to do this. I know she appreciates it too."

"I know," he said. "She told me as much. I spoke to her too, sounds okay. Said to say hi and she's looking forward to talking to you tonight. Oh, and I'm sorry about your accident." There was more noise in the background. "Gotta go now, Ab."

"Thanks Beano."

I sat back, confused. Yes, I was going to speak with Anita but what did Beano mean, he was sorry for the accident. Was this just some off-the-cuff well-meaning comment or did he have something to do with it? Just when I thought things were going smoothly, he had to mess with my head.

Well, tonight I would focus on trying to get some incriminating material on Johnson and Andersen. I had about an hour before my ride up the Don Valley trail to see Tony and, although that would likely produce a new layer of sweat, I couldn't resist a shower now anyway.

As I enjoyed the heat of the spray, I decided that the most pressing question was which bike I should ride in the evening. Figuring the risk was minimal, I decided to take my second-best one. I thought sadly about the empty hook where my injured Cervello should have been hanging but decided it wouldn't have wanted me to mourn its loss too long. It would have wanted me to be happy riding its best friend. So, after I had dried and dressed I lifted down the gleaming Celeste Blue Classic Bianchi and leaned it against the wall near the door. I safety-checked it and smiled. It was going to be a fine trip.

CHAPTER 19

THE EVENING RIDE UP THE DON VALLEY TRAIL WAS BRACING AND beautiful. The fall colours were still brilliant against the last rays of the sun. I really moved, a wonderful release after the slower ride earlier in the day. Even so, I got to the club with just moments to spare. After I had triple-locked my bike I went in the staff entrance as Tony had directed.

"I thought you'd never get here," Tony said nervously as he hustled me into the kitchen. "I'm not good at this spy stuff." He pointed at a small arrangement of flowers.

"Can you be quick and plant the thing somewhere in that? Johnson and Andersen are just about done in the bar. I want to get this on the table before they come in."

"Okay Tony, relax. Thanks for thinking ahead though." I tucked my little listening device out of sight amongst the flowers and Tony whisked the bouquet out to the table.

After that all we could do was wait. I was itching to ask him if he had heard anything, but we couldn't talk in front of the kitchen guys. As we whiled away the time hanging in a corner of the kitchen I asked Tony if there was a phone I could use. He took me to the empty staff lunchroom.

"You can dial direct from here," he said. "After hours, this line stops going through the main switchboard. Take your time. I'll wait for you in the kitchen."

I called Anita using the smudged number on my hand.

"Hello," a woman's voice said warily.

"Hi, this is Abby Faria. Could I please speak to Anita? I think she's expecting my call."

"Oh, yes, hello Ms. Faria. Beano said you would call. Just a moment. I'll get her." She put down the receiver. I could her heels click on a floor as she walked away.

About half a minute later, Anita came on the line, her voice sounding a little tentative.

"Hello? Abby, is that you?"

"Hi, Anita. How're you doing? Was it awful?"

Her voice got a little stronger. "I'm okay now. It was pretty rough yesterday and last night. I wasn't very nice to these people but they stuck by me. They were firm when I freaked and kind when I let them be. I'm so glad I was here. I don't think I could have done it on my own."

"Well, I'm glad to hear your voice. They say you're tough and that you did well."

"They're just being nice," she said. "I think they saw the worst of me. I'm making an effort now though to make up for it. Abby," she said, her voice growing more serious, "I had this memory flashback when I was thrashing around last night. I don't know if it will help or not but it's related to the work I did for Andersen."

I held my breath. "What is it, Anita?"

"When I was working in the club, Andersen made me be the 'girl-friend' for this man named Johnson. Andersen said that he wanted Johnson to owe him and that I should do anything he wanted. It was pretty gross. That man is totally pathetic, likes young girls to make him feel like he is a bad boy."

I bit my judgemental lip and let her continue.

"I won't go into details, Abby, but I had to become a regular girl for that man. I didn't like it much, but I felt kind of sorry for him too. I think Andersen was trying to make him help out with some kind of property deal in Kensington."

"So what happened?"

"Johnson got tired of me and took up with Sonya. She was better at being mean. Andersen said that with Sonya taking care of Johnson, he wanted me to help work on someone else but by that time I was too fucked up on drugs to be much use that way. So I just ended up working on the street most of the time. In some ways that was better," she said sadly. "It was mindless." There was a short silence, and then she continued.

"The point is, I overheard some of the people who are looking after me here talking about someone called Johnson, that he is a big developer and that he has bought a couple of flophouses on Jarvis. They said he is going to build a condo there but that would mean more homeless this winter. It made me wonder about the property in Kensington Market."

Oho, this was getting interesting! But she was starting to sound tired and agitated and the last thing I wanted was to get her worked up so I stopped her.

"Anita, it's okay. Don't think about that right now. You can tell it all to Mr. O'Casey, the lawyer, tomorrow."

"Oh yes, Beano said you wanted to tell me about something you set up."

"Um, yeah. O'Casey's an old friend of the family. I think he can help you with your legal status."

"Abby, I'm a bit nervous about this. He's a lawyer — can you be sure he won't say anything to the police? I just went through this withdrawal thing. I don't want to blow it."

"I'm pretty sure it's okay, Anita. I'll be there with you. He's a good man."

"Okay, if you say so. You've helped me so much already."

I explained what I had planned. "Can you meet me at seven o'clock tomorrow morning outside the Museum subway station? We can walk to his office together from there."

"Hold on a minute," Anita said. "I'll check if it's okay."

While I waited I looked idly around the room. Hanging on hooks were waitress uniforms and white kitchen workers' clothes. The waitress uniforms looked like old French maid costumes. Kind of degrading for serving old fuddy-duds at the club. And did these fuddy-duds get some kind of kinky thrill from being waited on by young women in those clothes? My musings were interrupted by Anita's return to the phone.

"Hi Abby, I'm back. It's all set. Someone will drop me there at seven o'clock. I'll see you then. And, Abby?"

"Yes?"

"Thanks for listening. I needed to get that off my chest."

"No problem. Now try not to worry. I'm sure everything will be fine. Just keep on track tonight. You've done a great job so far from the sound of it."

"Thanks. I can't believe how completely my life has changed in just one week. It seems like a weird fairy tale."

"Yeah, like Snow White meets the Big Bad Wolf." We both laughed. "Goodnight Anita. I'll see you tomorrow."

"Bye Abby," I hoped for her sake that it really was going to be like a fairy tale and she would live happily ever after. My experience had taught me otherwise but I was willing to be proved wrong.

When I had found my way back to the kitchen I saw Tony chatting with some of the staff as they nibbled tray remains from a cocktail party that was in full swing in a large private room. He picked up the next returning half-full tray and we settled into a corner of the kitchen to wait.

We talked about bikes, the goth and punk scene and the very little I knew about golf. As the clock ticked slowly towards ten I got a little restless again. I'm not very good at sitting still waiting for things to happen.

"Have they gone yet, Tony?" I asked, walking to the door and peering through the small circular window into the dining room.

"Come back here, Abby," he said nervously. "I'll go check." He left the room.

Tony was back in two minutes, smiling and carrying a tray of flower arrangements. He set them down and brought one over to me.

"You can take out your toy. They're just leaving and Mr. J. doesn't look very happy. They've been arguing all day. Are they married or what?"

"You don't think much of marriage do you, Tony?"

He shrugged. "You know me, always ready to play the field. I don't want to be someone's pecking post; I guess I'm sort of like you that way, Ab." He stood up. "Are you ready to party?"

"There won't be much action on Queen Street tonight but we might still catch the kitchen open at Toscana."

"Spoilsport," he said. "I'm going out to change in the car." He handed me his cell phone. "Call Toscana, order us a couple of pizzas, then we'll check out the Chameleon Sex Club, okay?"

I complied. After all, he had done me a big favour and I had some time to kill before I went to see Sparky.

Tony was true to his word. He had changed into tight black pants with silver studs, holey runners and a black sweatshirt that said, "Death Starts Here." He had gelled his neat, wavy hair into vertical black tufts and was ready to go in his Sid Vicious look. He was a little too healthy to pull it off to perfection but what the heck, no one would notice in the dark.

"Looking good, Tony. Do they know your alter ego at work?"

"Nah," he smiled. "I keep a change of clothes in my car for just such an occasion though." We loaded my beautiful Bianchi onto his carrier at the back of the car.

"Nice wheels," he said.

"Be careful with that. I've already damaged one honey this week."

"I won't ask how," he said. He knew my lifestyle well enough. "But I do know you have one or two more lying around."

Conversation was out of the question in the car, as Tony's music blasted out our eardrums. We were slipping into two bar stools at Toscana thirty-nine minutes later. The proprietors kindly allowed me to lock my bike on the back patio so I could relax as we ate.

"So tell me," I finally said, as he tucked into his pizza. "How'd it go on the course?"

"One thing was obvious," Tony said between chews. "Johnson was not happy and Andersen seemed to be enjoying the situation. He was needling the guy constantly. He must have a hold on him to keep him around when Johnson obviously would've rather been elsewhere. But if they were talking business at all, they didn't say anything around me."

He took another few bites of pizza and continued. "They seemed to be arguing all through dinner. Actually, Johnson was more heated — Andersen was just eating, laughing and sitting back. That's about all I can tell you but I think that you have what is closest to a fly on the wall in that little machine there. Hope it's useful. Oh, another thing. Johnson paid for everything today, course fee, equipment, caddies and dinner. Seems a bit masochistic to pay for your own mistreatment."

From what I had just heard from Anita, he seemed to be good at masochism, I thought.

"Thanks a lot, Tony. Well worth the price of this dinner, at least," I said paying the bill. It looked like we were closing the place, so I suggested we move on. "Great," he said, rubbing his hands together. "I haven't been on Queen for a while."

The man had stamina, I had to give him that. The Chameleon was open and hopping. I like punk more than goth, but this place had created a kind of fusion; styles change rapidly down on Queen Street West. Anyway, the music was intense and in stark contrast to the mellow reggae in the Market. It's not possible that I am losing my edge, surely not. Maybe it was just the intensity of the day's activity. But as my head pounded in protest at the loud pulsating music, I thought that maybe I'd start a new movement: soft punk.

Fortunately for me, an alluring pale-faced beauty caught Tony's eye. She was your classic goth, vampire-style, long, revealing black gown, suitably wraithlike, liberal mascara, eyeliner, black lipstick and pure white face paint. I'm sure Tony was intrigued by the contradictions. This vibrant death was quite a nice alternative to the heavily painted matrons, the walking dead, that I'd seen on my rare forays to country clubs and other such places.

Once Tony was chatting to the young goth, I was able to slip away. After the dark club, the semi-crisp Toronto air was refreshing, but not enough so to make me want to linger in that neighbourhood. A couple of street folk were tucked up for the night in sleeping bags on the corner of Queen and Bathurst in the doorway of the former bank building. It probably wasn't cold enough to kill them yet, but the concrete couldn't be that comfortable.

Judging by the number of empty bottles on the sidewalk it looked like these fellows had numbed their discomfort with booze. This was not choice real estate, but for the homeless, this spot was probably prime; good for panhandling, sheltered, not too unfriendly. I rescued my triple-locked bike again and, as the bell tolled twelve-thirty, I wheeled my Bianchi into Sparky's darkened abode.

As we navigated our way to the table by the glow of computers I asked, "Is it morning or bedtime for you?"

"I don't half know sometimes Ab," she said, yawning. "You're up awfully late for a morning courier yourself."

I yawned back. "Yeah, I've had a few too many nights without much sleep lately although I managed to stock up a bit yesterday." I looked at the bed, "No other visitors lurking around?"

She laughed and shook her head.

"Had a good gabfest with the nerd tonight though, quite a fount of cracker knowledge. I sent him on his way a while ago. We girls need some time to play." Miraculously she found a box of cookies and some iced tea amongst her computer paraphernalia. As she chewed on a cookie, she said, "So, who's first?"

I put up my hand. "Me, me!"

I flipped on the recorder and we settled down to listen. At first they just talked about the golf game, Andersen jovial, Johnson monosyllabic as food and drinks were ordered. Andersen's self-satisfied voice ordered roast beef and an expensive red wine — all very exciting. I fast-forwarded the tape every few seconds until we got to a bit where Andersen's voice had become more business-like. Finally it looked like we were getting to the juicy bits.

"You've had a few days to think about my proposition, don't you think it's time to sign these papers?" There was the sound of rustling paper as he continued, "As I explained earlier, these will give me a thirty percent share in the development firm, not much considering you will continue to receive certain perks and I will remain silent about your, let us say, predilections, and about the Kensington deal. I'm sure you don't want your lovely wife to know about your 'dates' and rather questionable behaviour." Aha! We could add blackmail to the list of Andersen's sins, I thought.

To this, Johnson prevaricated. "Look, it's true I always wanted to find a way into the Market, but arson? Murder? I may have been pretty hard on those anti-development protesters in the past and maybe I've allowed it to get too heavy-handed at times, but I can't play by your rules Andersen. You're way over my line."

"Come on Johnson, don't be a sore loser. You have never had any illusions about propriety. You did whatever suited you at the time. You just can't handle the fact that I have you out-leveraged."

To that Johnson spat out, "You are a pig."

Andersen laughed, "I'll give you until tomorrow night."

I snapped off the tape. "What do you think Sparks?"

"That now it all makes sense. When I was nosing around in my computer networks and chatting with some other crackers online, I found out a few interesting things. Johnson has bought land from a company run by a man named Andersen. I couldn't figure out exactly how Andersen's company is structured but I bet if I dug long and hard enough, I could get there. Anyway I decided to check on this Andersen person. That's where it got interesting.

"He's not a Canadian citizen, but Johnson was his character witness or sponsor or something for his residential status. Also, from what I've dug up so far, it looks like he has set up an impressive network under various names and numbers through which he moves money that is not all accounted for. And finally, he has been buying small numbers of shares for Johnson's company through these different businesses, so that his company owns just over twenty percent of Johnson's, on paper at least. It's all printed out here," she said, handing some papers to me.

I could have kissed Sparky but refrained, remembering her name and all the electricity in the room.

"Wow, Sparky, you're brilliant. I don't know how to thank you." She looked pleased but she wasn't finished yet.

Her eyes sparkled as she rubbed her hands together. "Maybe we can interfere here. I know of a really cool cracking game we can pull off with stocks. I've been wanting to try this for real ever since I heard about it. But I'll need you to do the legwork."

"I'm in," I said. "If it works, I promise I'll be your slave forever. So, explain your trick to this layperson and tell me what I need to do."

"Okay. Didn't you tell me that this Bitsy feels left out of her husband's affairs? Well, why don't we give her a few shares to play with and see what she can do to help poor Johnson out of his development illness?"

"Sounds good so far, Sparks."

"So here's how it goes. While I was checking up on him I noticed that Johnson's shares are cross-listed both in the New York Stock Exchange and the Toronto Stock Exchange. I can set up two new accounts at different brokerage firms and then I simultaneously enter two sale and purchase records. Then I short both accounts at the same time. The software gets confused and essentially the shares disappear in cyberspace." She glowed with excitement just talking about this devious internet sleight of hand.

"Okay, I think I'm following you Sparky, but what about the paper shares? Don't they still exist?"

"Yeah, but that's where you come in. Let's assume that Johnson faces the music as told and transfers the shares to Andersen's lawyer tomorrow morning. Who just happens to be their courier?" she said triumphantly. "You figure out a way to remove about a fifth of the certificates en route and we'll hold on to them or, perhaps we'll give them to Bitsy or maybe some local neighbourhood group … Nah, they'll be safer with Bitsy. Johnson won't be in a position to ask too many questions if she turns up with them. And she'll have enough stock to tip a proxy fight if it comes to that. You don't mind contributing to a little meaningful petty larceny do you?"

"I'm with you Sparks. You're a genius! Can you do all that tonight?"

"No, I'll wait till the exchanges are open tomorrow but don't worry. I *know* it will work."

"It's a go then but one last question, Sparky: do you think Andersen has wind of your nosing around? I don't want him alerted."

She looked mildly offended, her nose crinkling, making her glasses ride up above her eyes. Then she shrugged and they slid down.

"No way, Abby. I'm good at covering my tracks. Lots of practice with the Anarchists and some of the local eco groups."

"Good," I said, "I'm going home to get my beauty sleep!"

I grabbed my bike. "This is very exciting, Sparks. I'll call you tomorrow."

Chapter 20

Six o'clock came far too fast. My eyelids were glued so tightly shut that I had to feel my way to the alarm and grope my way to the shower. I knew that this level of exhaustion would only respond to shock treatment so I clenched my teeth and turned on the cold tap. My eyes were wide open soon enough and I reverted thankfully to hot. Thus revived, I emerged to face the new day.

I had almost an hour before I had to meet Anita. Deciding that it would be wise to project a business-like attitude at O'Casey's, I moved my nose ring to my ear, brushed my short hair into a sedate style, and put together an outfit somewhere between my Forest Hill disguise and my regular courier clothes — short dress, a respectable jacket and clean black leggings so I could still ride my bike.

I hopped onto my Trek and decided to hit a tiny traditional java joint in Little Italy on the way. I was likely to be anonymous there, and could collect my thoughts before meeting Anita. With a double espresso, a glass of spring water and two chocolate almond biscotti, I sat and watched the early morning traffic roll by.

I was hoping that I could get O'Casey by myself for a few minutes to brief him and to make a few suggestions. If his junior lawyer came along, maybe I could foist Anita onto him for a few minutes. I still couldn't make up my mind what to tell him and what to leave out. Nothing would surprise him, I'm sure, seeing as he had dealt with my father's shenanigans during the so-called illegal protests. However, I decided that I would leave out all the details of Johnson's involvement and how I found out about them.

O'Casey was a lawyer, after all, and I had a feeling Sparky and I had broken a few laws. For sure he wouldn't be thrilled to hear about my break and enter or my bugging of a private conversation, and it might confuse the issue with Anita. As my thoughts moved in that direction I realized that maybe I shouldn't bother trying to talk to O'Casey alone. Anita's story was compelling enough and I had a plan that might help catch Andersen just using Anita and his bought cop.

As I pedalled my bike up to the Museum subway stop, I wondered how Anita and O'Casey would take to each other. I hoped he wouldn't hit on her, given her fragile state. And what would they think of my plan? Would Anita be willing to take such a risk?

She was there trying to look inconspicuous, which was tough for someone so tall. Someone had lent her clothes again and this time she looked good, if a little haggard. She looked more like twenty-five than nineteen in a tight grey pantsuit and elegant but serviceable black flats. She was leaning her elbow on the edge of the metal subway entrance, her knuckles in her mouth belying her studied expression of calm. She looked relieved to see me.

"Hi, Abby," she said. "I wasn't sure you would come."

"Of course I would, Anita. I'm in for the long haul. But listen, did you check to see if anyone saw you leave, or followed you here?"

"I don't think anyone followed me," she said. "The people at the house are pretty careful. I think they do this kind of thing with illegals often."

"Okay," I said as we started walking. "Let's go see the lawyer. Simply tell him what you told me."

"I'm nervous, Abby. I don't want to make any mistakes."

"You'll be fine," I reassured her. "You've got a winning way about you. By the way, Anita," I said. "I have an idea I want to run past him after you're done. It might involve some risk on your part." I filled her in on what I had in mind. "Are you in?"

She nodded, and we finished walking the two blocks to O'Casey's office. His firm was located in one of those converted Victorian town houses, very posh but low-key, a nice departure from the grey steel offices in the downtown high-rises. The old man himself arrived at the same time, so he ushered us in.

"It's a little early for my receptionist, I'm afraid," he said. His office was in what might have been the giant drawing room of the former house. It was pretty impressive: wooden panelling, tall modern windows, large oak desk, a few signed photos from celebrities on one wall, his credentials on another, strategically placed next to what was probably an original Miró painting.

To one side of the room was a pleasant seating arrangement around a fireplace, probably very much like what might have been there eighty years ago. The other trappings of business — filing cabinets and computer hutches — were wood panelled and thus quite unobtrusive, old world charm at its best. Coffee and pastries were laid out on a silver service on the table.

"Oh, I see Juaneva has set up coffee for us." It turned out that the junior lawyer was an attractive black woman. So much for my stereotypes. O'Casey introduced her as Juaneva Martin. She seemed quite reserved as she shook our hands solemnly. I wondered idly if a male junior lawyer would have been expected to set out coffee. Did she resent it?

After introductions had been completed, we sat around the coffee table and I suggested that Anita tell her story. O'Casey sat back to listen while Ms. Martin took notes. Neither interrupted, but Juaneva looked sympathetic. Sometimes O'Casey appeared to be dozing, but I assumed he was concentrating. At one point in her recitation, he excused himself and left the room, returning in a few minutes. When Anita finished, O'Casey turned to her.

"Would you mind going with Juaneva in the next room? She is going to type up a little summary and go over it with you. If you are in agreement, you can sign it." Anita looked at me.

"It's okay. You can trust these people."

O'Casey smiled reassuringly. "We won't do anything without discussing it with you."

She went off without demur. I had to keep reminding myself that she was young, despite her experience.

Once they were gone, we sat in silence until O'Casey said, "Quite a life, hmm?"

"Hard to believe," was my intelligent reply.

He continued, "When I left the room, I placed a call to a friend of mine in immigration. I asked whether they would be willing to support someone's refugee claim in exchange for eyewitness evidence in the Kensington murder case. He was noncommittal, but said it was possible. I think Anita has a reasonable chance as a refugee anyway, but Andersen will be a problem for her as long as he is around, so if we can get him put away, we kill two birds with one stone."

"I know," I said. "I've been thinking about that and I have an idea. It will involve Anita's cooperation and sweet-talking the cops." I laid out my plan. "What do you think?" I asked when I finished.

"You must have learned devious plotting from your father ... but it might work. I have a friend in the police chief's office who can be discreet. Maybe we can spread a net to scare your bad cop into doing some good. Once we have the backing of the police, we can request that particular officer come along as he's already involved in the investigation. I'll get him into my office and set things straight by this afternoon. We'll take care of the details. Do you have a place in mind for your, um, idea to take place?"

"I was thinking about down by the hockey stadium tonight when people are arriving for the game. It's public enough that we can blend in and yet it would appeal to Andersen as the crowd would provide anonymity."

"Good idea," he said. We turned to small talk while we waited for Anita and Juaneva to return, O'Casey asking a little about couriering, and me getting my two cents worth with innocent questions about his young new wife.

When Anita returned, we outlined the plan to her. She agreed without hesitation.

"It's risky," I said. "Are you sure?"

"I am very sure," she said. "I'd be happy to give him a taste of his own medicine and I am definitely ready to do anything it takes to get him put away." She still seemed a little down. Would Anita get a chance to be young yet? I harboured few illusions, but she was plucky, very tough and a survivor. I had heard her chatting with Juaneva in the hallway. It was an unlikely combination, the taciturn Juaneva and the street-hardened Anita. With everything settled, O'Casey and I both looked at our watches.

"Well, my friends," he said. "I'm afraid I have another appointment. Anita, Juaneva will work out the details with you for this evening, but in the meantime we need to keep you safe. I want you to stay here for the day. There's a little room upstairs where you'll be comfortable." He rubbed his hands together. "This might be fun," he said. "Like the old days, a little intrigue. Juaneva will take care of you for now; you are in very competent hands."

I thanked O'Casey again and said I would talk to him later. We shook hands and he asked me to leave my number for him with his receptionist on my way out.

Already Juaneva was looking protective as she ushered the young woman out. The best way she could help Anita for tonight would be to take good care of details. I hoped she would.

Before she left, I asked Martin to speak with me in private for a moment.

"Thanks for taking Anita on. She seems to have really connected with you."

"It's my job, Ms. Faria," she said formally and then she softened, "but that young girl deserves much better. I intend to make sure things are well planned for tonight."

"I'm sure you will. I can see that you have taken to her. What I wanted to tell you is that she has just come through heroin withdrawal. She might be a little depressed and antsy as the day goes on."

"It's alright, Ms. Faria, she already told me. Maybe that's the connection. I have some experience trying to help my sister kick it. I'll stick by Anita until she goes with Mr. O'Casey. Don't worry, I won't tell Mr. O'Casey about the drugs unless it becomes necessary. It may distract him from the immediate issue."

We shook hands and Juaneva Martin gave me her card in case I wanted to call in the afternoon. As we re-entered the reception area I finally felt at ease with the situation. Anita would be safe, at least for the day.

"Anita," I said as she looked up. "I'll see you tonight. I've got to get to work and I have some things to take care of this afternoon. I'll try to reach you on O'Casey's line before you go tonight but if I can't, don't worry. You're in good hands. Just do what they tell you and it will all be fine."

"Okay, Abby. And thank you." It was a far cry from our first meeting.

It was already nine o'clock. I had some important couriering to do and I didn't want anyone to scoop my pickups so I hopped on my bike and pedalled furiously to Johnson's. I wasn't due until nine-thirty but I was hoping to get there before they expected me. A lot of my plans hinged on timing and a good dose of luck.

When I got to the developer's office I asked the snooty receptionist if I could speak with Johnson.

"And why would he want to see you?" she asked protectively as she looked down her nose at me, the lowly courier.

I kept my cool.

"Not that it's any of your business," I said sweetly. "Just tell him I have some information about a Mr. Andersen that he might like to hear. Believe me, he'll want to see me," I said, sounding more sure then I felt.

"Alright," she said grudgingly as she stood with exaggerated slowness.

As soon as she left I took my customary place on the corner of her desk. That's when I hit pay dirt. On the desk were the composite parts of my package, all nicely laid out and not yet sealed away. A lovely blue plastic envelope, conveniently labelled "Shares" sat in the middle of the array. Checking that no one was about, I hurriedly unwound the string that held the flap down, slid out the folder within and grabbed about a fifth of the stack of beautiful crisp certificates. I surreptitiously shoved them into my satchel, slid the folder back into the envelope and looped the flap down again.

It's unbelievable how easy, and yet scary, it is to steal something. I was perspiring and my heart was beating staccato by the time our friend sauntered back. I was hoping that to her I just looked annoyingly innocent.

She looked pleased with herself.

"Mr. Johnson says he can't see you right now but that he will meet you at the King and Strachan site at three-thirty this afternoon. Just go down to the sales office, they'll find him for you." She looked like she wanted to stick out her tongue and say: *So there, you're not so important.*

Instead she said, "Now if you'll just wait a moment, I'll pack all this up and you can be on your way." She picked up the plastic envelope, a brown paper envelope and a CD and put them all in the courier bag, which she sealed and passed over to me dismissively.

"Thanks, and have a great day," I said, hoping I wouldn't have to deal with her again for a while.

I ran the package over to Smythe, Blondin etc., and then did a series of normal runs until one-thirty when I was informed that the courier manna had run out for the day and I could retire. That suited me fine. It gave me time to run the swiped shares over to Sparky's for safekeeping. They had been burning a guilty hole in my bag and I was happy to be rid of them.

Sparky answered the door sleepily, took them and gave me a wink.

"I took care of the other part this morning. Smooth as silk. I'll just count these and make sure we have 'disappeared' the right number, and if we're a little off, I'll just shift some back or forth. Then I'm back to bed. We'll have to figure out how to get them to Bitsy eventually. Talk to you later my fellow female felon." When she closed the door I felt pounds lighter.

I had time for a quick bite, my stomach, as usual, reminding me it was lunch time, so I hopped over to Queen Street in search of a fast meal. Being a creature of habit, I stopped again at Toscana for a perfect cappuccino and a roasted veggie sandwich on toasted foccacia bread. I sank my teeth into a satisfying mix of crusty herbed bread, tender smoky eggplant, green peppers and tart sun-dried tomatoes. Olive oil dribbled decadently onto the plate.

My heavenly delight ended when I realized that the place was busy and waiting customers were pointedly eyeing my spot. It was just as well that I was in a hurry. Having coffeed up so much already, I decided that a second cappuccino to go would be overkill, so I packed up and skipped out, ready to beard the lion. Or so I thought.

Land that used to be filled with factories and warehouses just north of the lakeshore has slowly given way to development. The area where I was meeting Johnson had been empty for a while as the developers waited for property values to creep up, but the ads for affordable townhouses were already pushing it in the papers.

I entered the sales office where pictures of the potential "homes" were displayed on the walls; interior views were available on little computers. I had been wondering how they could sell such low cost housing and here I found my answer. What looked like lovely little townhouses on the outside actually concealed at least three stacked residences within. Aha! Condos in disguise. No wonder the kinky condo king is in on this.

A salesperson approached me, asking if I needed any help. I said I had an appointment with Johnson.

"Oh," she said, looking disappointed. Mondays must be slow, I thought. "I think he's down in the planning office."

She pointed out the window at a rectangular trailer next to the building site. There were signs of construction: a few workers, a substantial hole in the ground and a cement truck that was pouring foundations.

"Thanks," I said, but another couple walking in the door had already captured her attention.

Chapter 21

Roadways and streetlights were already in, so obedient citizen that I am, I followed them to the trailer. I walked up the steel risers and knocked on the door. I heard some movement within and then Johnson himself opened the door.

"Ms. Faria?" he asked.

"Yes sir, Mr. Johnson."

He seemed almost nervous. "Come in," he said, holding the door open. Inside was a small room set up with a drafting table laden with plans, a few chairs, a work table and an area to the side where a desk stood with a computer and telephone. There was another door which led perhaps to a kitchen or a washroom.

Johnson looked to be in pretty good shape. He must visit the gym as well as play golf, I thought, wondering if he did his business deals on the course. His face showed his age, however; anxious wrinkles around his eyes, greying temples, a bit of a drinker's nose, red and veined. He might have a reputation as a confident businessman but he didn't look too imposing to me.

"What can I do for you?" said Johnson, sitting on one of the chairs. He was actually sweating though it was a cool day.

"Well, Mr. Johnson," I said, starting to bluster to cover my nervousness. "I was hoping that we could help each other actually."

"Is that so? And how could you help me?"

"You might want to hear what I have to say about a man named Andersen. I am under the impression that you have become a reluctant associate of his. While I don't agree with what you do, sir, either publicly or privately, I think I can provide some information that might help you deal with Andersen."

"Now, Ms. Faria, I've heard of you and have had dealings in the past with your famous father," he said, clearly a little angry but trying to maintain his cool. "Why would you want to help me?"

"Well, for two reasons sir. One, while I completely detest your development schemes in low-rent areas, I hate what Andersen does even more. And two, I think you can help me out too."

"Why would I want to do that?" he asked, avoiding my eyes and picking at the arms of his chair. He was asking the right questions but his heart didn't seem to be in it. I carried on nonetheless, ignoring the skin prickles on my back and arms.

"Frankly, Mr. Johnson, what I know about your activities could cause you some difficulty if it became public knowledge. Also sir, your generous wife might be shocked by your business decisions and your sexual tastes." It bothered me to hear myself sounding a bit like Andersen had when he threatened Johnson the night before.

Johnson paled.

"I don't know what you are talking about. I love my wife," he spluttered. "Leave her out of all this." The man seemed to be less and less like the ruthless businessman who had my father jailed but I went on gamely.

"I'd like to believe you, and I also prefer to leave her out of it, Mr. Johnson. But now let me tell you what I know and what I want from you. I think you will find that I can be quite reasonable. I know that you recently acquired properties in Kensington Market that were quickly turned over by Andersen for a very low price. Those properties became available in the first place under suspicious circumstances. I know, sir, that Mr. Andersen also arranges liaisons for you with very young women. Those two facts could cause some scandal if made public but what you probably don't realize sir," I took a dramatic pause, "is that Andersen has recently bought over twenty percent more of your business and stands to take control."

To this last bit, Johnson reacted with shock and anger. "Impossible!" Then his shoulders caved in as realization hit. "But that means he owns the company now. What am I going to do?"

At that moment, there was a sudden commotion in the adjoining room. I had committed a cardinal sin ignoring my instincts, in this case crawling skin at Johnson's anxiety. I had assumed we were alone and had been very reckless to not check more carefully. Before I had time to move, the door flew open and Andersen and two thugs emerged. I gasped in horror.

Andersen smiled broadly at the hapless Johnson.

"That is a very good question, David."

One thug pointed a gun at my midriff; the other man took up a position at the outer door. My haste and foolish overconfidence had put me in grave danger. To top it all off I found myself nearly speechless.

"Well, well, Ms. Faria," said Andersen. "So I finally meet you in the flesh. You, my dear, have caused me a great deal of trouble in a short time but you have just run out of luck."

"Don't be silly, Mr. Andersen, you'd never get away with doing anything to me. You don't think I would have come here without telling anyone, do you?"

"Ah, but that is exactly what I think. You see, I have done some research as well, and it is common knowledge that you are a loner, an independent."

"Just what do you think you are going to do, Andersen?" Now I was the one who was sweating while I desperately tried to activate my sluggish brain. "I can't just disappear. People will ask questions."

"True, but by the time they find you, you will have had a little accident, along with Mr. Johnson here."

Johnson blustered, "Now look here, you can't do that."

"Yes, David, you have used up your usefulness also. It's too bad, I would have liked you to see me take over your business. But my plans have changed. Oh, don't worry, I'm still moving ahead with those shares Ms. Faria very kindly delivered this morning, only now I have a new partner, one that would surprise you if you knew, but I'm afraid you never will." He laughed ghoulishly.

I was holding my tongue, thinking furiously how to extricate myself while Andersen continued, obviously enjoying himself.

"The way I see it, Ms. Faria here will have been blackmailing you or confronting you, whatever, when you got angry and knocked her out. Then, tonight you will try to make Ms. Faria a part of the foundation. Unfortunately, you will slip in too and drown in the cement."

This was just too surreal.

"You can't do this to me, people will ask questions," Johnson said, stealing my line.

"Yes, maybe," said Andersen. "But you see, you were distraught about losing your business so you were not rational. I won't even figure into all of this except as a savvy arms-length business partner."

My heart was beating triple time but I had a sinking feeling he was right. He could do away with us and no one would make the connection. What did I care anyway? I'd be dead. It wouldn't help me if Andersen was nailed for it.

With the cold logic that comes when you are scared to death, I found myself listing my regrets. If only I hadn't been so sure I could coerce Johnson. If only I had let O'Casey into this part of the scheme. My only solace was that if the rest went according to plan, at least Andersen would not go scot-free. I wondered if he had heard from Anita yet.

For the second time today, I received a small gift. Somewhere a cell phone rang and one of the thugs answered.

"Hello." He listened and then said, "Just a minute."

He handed the phone to Andersen. "For you, boss. Anita — says she has some kind of deal."

Andersen lifted the phone to his ear.

"Hello my dear. So, you've finally surfaced. I was worried about you," he purred. "Oh really? Yes, I'm interested. Can you trust this person? Tonight? Yes, I think I can arrange that. Where? Okay. Eight o'clock. Okay. Alone?" He winked at me. "No problem. See you soon Anita. Good work and welcome back. I'm glad you're alright." He hung up, but looked thoughtful for a few seconds. "Hmm," he said, smiling.

He snapped out of his reverie and became businesslike again.

"Taylor, put those two out of commission until tonight. We'll come back when it's dark to finish this job. I have something to arrange, a little deal with Anita. Make sure they're secure, but no mess and no signs of force, except perhaps for Johnson's knock on Ms. Faria's head."

"What's this?" he said, taking the papers that I still held in my hands. They were the printouts of Sparky's computer searches and stapled on top was a wish list of demands I had intended to make of Johnson. Fortunately, Andersen looked only at the top sheet and laughed. "Aren't we a goody two-shoes, all these nice little projects? Here," he said, handing them to the silent Johnson. "These will be useful as evidence for your tragic reaction to Ms. Faria's blackmail."

He smiled at me. "You'll be seen as just another misguided reformer, Ms. Faria, like your father. Only you're going to miss the jail part."

Over his shoulder he said to Johnson, "Maybe you'd like to include those in your will." With that he left, still laughing.

The two henchmen began to make preparations. They marched us into the windowless back room amidst loud protestations by Johnson, who feverishly clutched my list. Idly, I noticed a counter with a sink on one side and a Formica table with condiments and empty beer bottles on the opposite side.

The one called Taylor was pouring liquid onto a cloth. "I'll do you a special favour and put you out before I crack you on the head," he said. "But, either way, of course, you'll have an awful headache if you wake up before we take care of you tonight." I tried to hold my breath as he shoved the cloth into my face, but eventually the sickly smell overcame me and I sank, at least temporarily, below the sea of consciousness.

He was right. Complete exhaustion and a nasty crack on the head might have been enough to keep me sleeping forever if it hadn't been for the incessant bumping. It started as a dream in which a stunningly handsome young man kept nudging me as we waited in line for something; the Pearly Gates, maybe? At first it was kind of nice, and then he got downright annoying and I became more and more frustrated with my inability to get him to stop.

As I gradually came to painful consciousness, I would have happily gone back under to that irritating young man. My head didn't ache: it pounded. Each nudge created a crescendo of exquisite pain. As I tried to shift away from whatever was bumping me I came to the unfortunate realization that I was trussed and gagged. My wrists and ankles were tied and looped together so there was no chance of swinging my arms under my legs to the front. I was going to remain very uncomfortable and I had no choice, I would have to open my eyes.

I blinked them open only to find myself in darkness anyway. We were still in the room at the back of the trailer, I guessed, remembering that it was windowless. The nudging continued. It felt like an elbow, pointy and sharp. I mumbled, "Stop that!" which came out "Mmmm mmmm." The bumping ceased.

"Ms. Faria," came Johnson's voice, hardly one I ever thought I would welcome. Hadn't he been gagged?

"Mmmm," I mumbled again, working on a whole new language of intonation. My eyes were getting used to the dark, and I could make out a faint crack of light at what must have been the door but I couldn't tell if it was daylight or a streetlight. I wondered how much time we had until the others returned.

"Ms. Faria ... I worked my gag off but I can't untie myself, I'm afraid. Are you tied up as well?"

"Mmmmm," I mumbled, hoping it sounded like a "yes."

He continued, "How about we have a go at these knots?"

Well, Johnson wasn't a quitter, I had to give him that.

"If we get back to back we can try to find each other's hands."

"Mmmm," I assented.

His suggestion made sense, or at least, I couldn't think of anything else to do, and since the thought of becoming part of some condo foundation didn't appeal to me I painfully rolled and inched my way to Johnson's hands.

"Well done," he said.

Faint praise indeed. I was sweating. That had been harder work than a ten-kilometre bike race. I lay panting, already exhausted and low on hope.

Johnson squeezed my hand. My opinion of him was softening. Perhaps he was a victim himself when he was young. I started imagining his childhood of abuse, which accounted for his predilection for nasty sex with young women, and his need to be a barracuda in business. Maybe, I thought, he would have been quite sweet in another life.

Anyway, he clearly wanted to live another day so maybe he was having a different epiphany than I had planned for him. I hoped he would survive long enough for it to bear fruit. While I rested, he pushed and pulled and poked and, as I slowly recovered my wits, I helped him.

"Damn," he exclaimed. "These godawful knots are too tight. We need to find something to cut the ropes with."

"Mmmm?" I said encouragingly, hoping he'd somehow magically understand that I was getting tired of making monosyllabic responses and needed my tongue more than my hands at the moment.

Johnson read my mind. "I think we should do something about that gag first. This one-way conversation is pissing me off."

"Mmmm," I agreed.

"See if you can wriggle down so that your head is by my hands. I might be able to push the gag down at least."

We did a little sideways dance and when my gag made contact with his hands he was indeed able to push it down without groping my face too much. "How's that?" he asked.

I licked my lips and said a breathy, "Great, thanks."

My head ached from all the movement but I knew we had to keep moving.

"Okay, Mr. Johnson. What's next?"

"There were some bottles on the table. If we could knock them off and break them, we could use the glass to cut the ropes. Why don't we each roll a different way and see what we come across?"

"Sounds like a plan," I replied, moaning as I started the arduous process of rolling with legs and arms trussed. Unfortunately for me the pain was only to increase when I hit pay dirt; the side of my already aching head made contact with the leg of a table.

I groaned again as I called out, "I've found the table."

"Well done," came his distant response.

"I'm going to try and break a bottle," I said. "You'd better stay away. No point in us both risking a severed artery."

"Good thinking," he said, sounding suspiciously relieved.

"Okay, here goes." I readjusted my position so my feet could hook the table leg and I rocked and rolled as if Elvis himself were overseeing the proceedings. I heard one or two thumps as things fell over and kept up the action, hoping something would roll off in my general direction. Again, I was more than successful; two bottles smashed on the floor around me, and a third rolled off to the side. As I turned my head to start groping for shards, I was rewarded with one in my cheek.

"Shit!" I yelped.

"Are you alright?" I heard from a worried Mr. J.

"Yeah, I'm okay. Just maimed. Listen, I'm going to grope around and try to find a decent piece of glass. Don't come too close. There's glass all over."

I didn't manage to avoid all the glass and was quite cut up by the time I eventually found a good-sized piece that I could hold between my fingers. As I rolled back to my cellmate I wished I had listened closer to my mother's lecture on Buddhist pain control. I could've used some of it right then.

I lay still for a moment, panting from exertion, my head swimming from pain and dizziness. "Um, Mr. Johnson," I said, giving him a jab with my feet to let him know where I was.

"Listen, I'm going to roll over now so you can take the glass. I'm spent, so you'll have to try the cutting."

"Okay, here I come," he said.

I rolled over, we wiggled a bit more, my hands met his and we made the exchange successfully.

"Okay," he said. "I'm going to start with the ropes from your hands to your legs. That might be enough to loosen them all but, if not, at least you'll be a little more comfortable."

He was pretty good with the backhanded cutting and after a few misses and curses on his part the taut rope snapped and my body straightened correspondingly. That just added to my aches and pains, but he was right, I was able to wiggle my wrists loose and suffer some more as the blood flowed into new places. "Ohhh," I groaned.

"Are you okay?" Johnson asked again.

"No, but you were right. I think I can get loose now. Give me a second." I finished wiggling my hands free and bent over to loosen my feet. "Okay, I'm free." I gently moved my aching fingers. Okay, most of the pain was around my wrists where I had ground in God knows how many shards of glass. Good thing I couldn't see them or I might swoon. I'd try to pick them out as soon as I could see.

"Hold on a sec," I said through gritted teeth. We were ever so polite. I leaned over to undo my leg bindings. It took a little while — my stomach churned as each jolt of pain rushed through me.

The best way for me to cope was to talk, to keep my mind off the pain. "I'm going to make my way to the light switch. It'll be easier to help you once we can see."

"Okay, but can you hurry up? I don't want to be that bastard Andersen's latest victim."

My ankles were freed so I rubbed some feeling back into them and then very carefully made my way blindly to the door, arms outstretched in front so I wouldn't bump into anything. It had been quiet so I assumed that our captors had left, but, just in case they'd left a guard, I didn't want to attract attention by turning a light on. I opened the door a crack and heard only the welcome hum of night time traffic.

The ambient city light helped me locate the light switch. I closed the door again, shoved my sweater against the crack, turned on the light and our cell bloomed into stark reality. I glanced at my watch — six forty-five. Not much time until Andersen's meeting with Anita. After what had just happened I wanted to be in on that, to see Andersen get his. But first I guessed I should untruss Johnson, so to speak.

He blinked up at me, "Good idea," he said nodding to the sweater at the door. "Hurry, please … I want to get out of this hellhole. If I get out of this alive I'm going to have this near coffin of a trailer taken away and burned."

I held up my cut and bleeding wrists, "This is not going to be a picnic. I'm going as fast as I can so keep your pants on. I'll get us out of here. I promise."

"Well," he said abruptly, more like the Johnson I had expected, "If you hadn't come here in the first place, we wouldn't be in this predicament."

"Hold on buddy, I know my methods may not have been perfect but Andersen and his thugs would have dealt with you one way or another eventually." I worked doggedly at his knots. He had sustained some cuts on his hands so the ropes were a little slippery. I tried not to look at the wretched mess of my wrists or to move my head too quickly, in order not to jar what was left of my brain. Johnson was starting to piss me off but I tried to keep my cool.

"Um, this being a construction site and all, you wouldn't have a first aid kit around, would you?

He nodded. "In the front room. We'll grab it on our way out."

As I fumbled around with his knots, I said, "What do you know about predicaments anyway? You put my father in jail and didn't care what that did to my family. And what about all those people who end up on the street as you happily condo-ize and uglify the city? I ought to take off right now and leave you to rot. You're just lucky I can't bring myself to condone murder — not like you and Andersen."

He was silent for a minute, probably realizing that he had been acting like an asshole. I had almost finished his wrists when he said,

"I know that it looks that way Abby, but I wasn't the one who sent your father to jail."

"Yeah, right. Of course you were. You had him charged."

"Not me. Look, just get me out of here. Things aren't quite what they seem, but it's all irrelevant if Andersen and his men come back and find us here."

"Okay," I said "but it better be good."

At that point his wrists came free.

"Finally," he said. He leaned over to untie his feet while I staggered to the door.

He was with me in a matter of thirty or so interminable seconds. I turned out the light, picked up sweater and opened the door. The cool night air was reviving as we rushed outside.

"I left my bike behind that building," I said, heading for the sales office. "I hope it's still there. Come with me and tell me about my dad."

"Okay, but do you think you can ride with your wrists like that?

You should really go to the hospital."

"You're probably right but it will just have to wait. Just bring along that first aid kit. I'll wrap them up for now."

"Suit yourself. I'm going straight home. Bitsy'll get the doctor over to my house. You can come too, I owe you that much at least."

We made it to my bike unscathed.

"Thanks for the offer, Dave. But I'll give it a pass." I opened the kit and took out two bandages. "Here, help me bind my wrists up and tell me what you meant about my father and jail."

After Johnson wrapped the cloths around my wrists, he secured them with some tape.

Then he dropped the bombshell.

"It was O'Casey."

"No way. You're lying! He *defended* my dad. In fact, he helped the whole family, even made sure we were well provided for!" But even as I was saying this I was having a sinking feeling that it was all starting to make sense.

"It might look that way but you see, Abby, O'Casey has always had shares in the company," Johnson interrupted bitterly. "He has been a silent partner for years and wanted it kept that way. He didn't want to spoil his public image as a crusader for the people."

"Oh my God," I said, the wheels starting to turn sickeningly.

"Yes," Johnson continued, "It was great at first. O'Casey is a legal whiz; I practically owe my whole success to his know-how. And the success made me feel independent from Bitsy. I felt like I was finally supporting her. You see, she was wealthy when we married. I wanted to prove I could do it on my own. Only I wasn't really; I totally depended on O'Casey. I was willing to go along with his excesses and build the business, even let your father go to jail. But after that, all I wanted was to get rid of O'Casey — he was going too far."

"Is that why you hooked up with Andersen?" He nodded as he started shivering. It looked like he was starting to go into shock. "I think, Mr. Johnson, that you traded the frying pan for the fire." I realized now why O'Casey liked the idea of setting up Andersen. Johnson must have been way easier to control. I didn't tell Johnson this. I wanted to keep him on track.

He hung his head. "I see that now. I've fucked up royally." He sighed. "I'm going home to my wife. I think it's past time that she and I have a talk."

"I'm happy to hear you say that sir," I thought about the gift of shares sitting at Sparky's. "It might go better than you think. My mother has met her and says she is very smart. Maybe she'll help you if you give her a chance."

He shook his head, "I hope you're right, but I'm not very optimistic. Right now I have to say I'd like to make amends all round. I'm even sorry about your dad, although he was a bit of a pain."

I looked at his hands. They looked better than mine but he still bled from several deep cuts he must have got while sawing through my ropes. Then I saw sticking out of his breast pocket the papers I had brought earlier. There was my wish list, a little worse for wear. That gave me an idea. "Listen, Dave, if you still feel that way later, take a look at that list I gave you. It might give you some ideas."

He looked curiously at the papers in his pocket as if he wondered how they got there. "I'll do that," he said, shaking even more. It was time to get this man home. I didn't want him to die of exposure even though it would be a fitting end to someone who had made so many homeless. I carefully unlocked my bike.

"Let's go Dave. I'll walk you to the street and find you a cab." He came along docilely as I said, "You know, a lot of this is bound to come out. It's only a suggestion but you might want to get yourself a good lawyer, one who is not friends with O'Casey." The man nodded again as he shuffled slowly out to the street.

I privately thought to myself, once Andersen is out of the way, I'm going to find a way to get O'Casey, the bastard. He probably screwed my dad around so he could try and get his hands on my mother. And to think that I'd admired him, the slimeball.

I flagged a cab for Johnson and helped him into the car. "Good luck." I said. "It's been interesting." He sat back and closed his eyes in response. I gave the cabbie the Forest Hill address and told him to make sure that Johnson got inside safely.

After Johnson left I thought I should try O'Casey's line to make sure everything was still on track. I warned myself not to let on to him, if he should answer, how much I hated him at the moment. I wanted the man to help get Andersen out of the picture and to get Anita somewhere safe before I found a way to set the dogs on him. I found a pay phone at the corner of King and Strachan and hoped I'd catch them before they left. Although I had told Anita not to worry if I didn't call, I didn't want her to think I had abandoned her.

Someone finally picked up but I was startled by the sound of a mechanical, gravelly voice saying, "Mr. O'Casey's line. Oh ... hold on a minute ..."

After a second or two, the receptionist's normal voice came on the line.

"Sorry, there was some kind of interference. I've switched over to my line. Who's calling?"

That distorted voice — it set off a clamour of alarm bells in my head. It was just like the voice of the threatening phone message. Appalled at the implications, I struggled to sound normal as I explained who I was and asked if O'Casey was still in.

"You just missed them, Ms. Faria. They left a few minutes ago."

"Did they leave any message for me?"

"Miss Anita asked if you had called but Mr. O'Casey said not to worry, you were probably tied up and that you knew she would be okay with him."

"Okay ... uh ... thanks for letting me know.

"Okay Ms. Faria. Goodbye."

"Thanks again," I said, and hung up.

I stood there in delayed shock while my mind processed the fact that O'Casey had a voice-altering device on his phone. Finally a second realization hit.

Oh my God! They're going to hurt Anita!

CHAPTER 22

As I FEVERISHLY DUG IN MY POCKET FOR A SECOND QUARTER, I thought, You idiot! Of course he knew you were tied up. He's in cahoots with Andersen and I just gave them Anita on a silver platter. And here I was, thinking Beano was up to something. How could I have been so stupid?

It made perfect sense. Andersen and O'Casey fit together. They both were devious crooks with no compunction about hurting people. I finally found the quarter and dialled Sparky's number.

"Please, please be there and pick up," I prayed as the phone rang.

My prayers were answered as her sleepy voice said, "This had better be good."

"Sparky, it's me Abby. Don't talk, just listen. I don't have much time. Something has gone terribly wrong. I can't explain but please, call the cops, the RCMP, anyone you can and tell them anything that will get them to the front of the ACC just past the viaduct! Tell them to be fast. It's supposed to go down at eight o'clock. Do whatever you can to convince them. If worse comes to worst make a bomb threat or a gun call. I'm heading down there now myself to see what I can do." I waited to make sure she understood how imperative this was.

She didn't respond for a second, but when she spoke her voice was alert and serious.

"Okay Abby, gotcha. Be careful. I'll get someone there, don't worry."

I hopped gingerly back on my bike. Adrenalin pumped through my veins and dulled the pain a little. There was a steady stream of traffic both ways, but I could hardly focus on the cars. It was an excruciating ride, what with waves of dizziness, and wrists that throbbed mercilessly. I wobbled dangerously out into the road once or twice to a cacophony of honks from enraged drivers. I blocked them out of my consciousness, concentrating completely on keeping upright. They probably thought I was drunk or stoned.

"Please let me get there in time," I prayed in a continuous mantra as I mentally kicked myself. I had assumed that O'Casey and Martin had covered all the details because I had witnessed the receiving end of Anita's call to Andersen. She was to have hooked Andersen telling him she had set up a large drug deal and I had thought I was seeing him go for it. She had told him she had a new customer who was interested in being assured a steady supply of high quality heroin, and willing to pay well for it.

The plan was for O'Casey to have pulled in Joe, the sour cop, and to have read the riot act to him. He was going to give Joe a chance to redeem himself in exchange for holding his tongue. Joe was to double-cross Andersen, witnessing the deal and then assisting in the arrest.

O'Casey had said he was going to get his friend in the upper echelons of the RCMP narcotics squad act as the prospective client. It was all very risky and Anita would be in peril if anything went wrong.

Now I realized that I had helped set her up as the victim in a bigger game than I had ever imagined. I had virtually signed her over to Andersen and his new partner. Nobody was going to be there to protect Anita; no police, no immigration officers. O'Casey wouldn't have called them!

The "deal" was supposed to go down near the entrance to the hockey arena, the ACC. It was south of the tunnel just under the Gardiner Expressway, a suitably chaotic and noisy place for a supposedly anonymous drug deal. You can get into the ACC underground from the train station, but I had wanted a nice public outside location.

There was no time to ditch my bike. I rode down the underpass on the opposite side of the road. I could hear sirens in the background, which could mean anything in Toronto. Please let those be for us, I thought. Please don't let me too late. As I emerged from the other side of the underpass, I saw O'Casey leaning against the guardrail looking intently across the street. He didn't see me. Of course, he wasn't even expecting me because he thought I was still safely tied up in Johnson's trailer.

First things first, I thought, adrenalin filling in where brain cells should be, good for quick action and lots of extra strength. I wanted him out of commission fast and quietly so he couldn't alert Andersen that I was there. I had to try to rescue Anita without O'Casey's interference. I quietly laid down my bike in the shadows and grabbed the courier's best tool for self-defence. I hoped O'Casey wouldn't give me a reason to swing my lock, as I had more than one axe to grind.

As I came up behind him, he must have sensed something because he turned around, eyes widening when he recognized me.

"Hello, Liam, I got here as soon as I could. How is the set up going? Is Anita alright?"

"What the …" he spluttered, and then he seemed to regain his composure, the crafty bastard.

"Why, hello, Abby. I'm glad you made it," he said smiling. He leaned on the railing again. I guess he thought I would just watch the little scene in dismay and accept that there had been a mistake made along the way.

I didn't really have time to let him play out that scenario. I was sure he knew I had been trapped by Andersen and I was sure he was there to watch the sad end of Anita, just another heroin addict either gunned down or given an overdose or spirited away to God knew where. There was no way I was going to let that happen. I didn't really relish hurting him but I didn't know how else to preempt him at short notice.

So I made as if to lean and watch too, but instead I lifted my lock and brought it down in as controlled a way as I could on one side of his head. He made no sound as the lock made contact, but slumped over the railing. I lifted him carefully under the arms and dragged him to the grassy verge. His head rolled loosely but he was still breathing and there was only a little blood. I hoped he would stay put until I got to Anita.

On autopilot, I locked my bike to a pole with the freshly bloodstained lock and carefully made my way across the road in the shadows of the underpass. Dodging cars to a chorus of honks, I must have looked like some maniac trying to get herself killed. I made it across with my life, the effort hyping me up again.

I could see Anita huddled just away from the doors, talking to a man, the supposed client. Nowhere did I see Andersen or his henchmen. I hoped they'd gotten cold feet and I could whisk her away from there before he arrived. I started to move forward out of the shadows but just then spotted Andersen approaching from the other end of the street.

His two henchmen and the bad cop flanked him. I prayed that Sparky had managed to convince the authorities to appear. Since I didn't see any backup I decided that the element of surprise was my best weapon. I started to approach Anita as well. She was expecting Andersen but not me. I got to her a little ahead of the others. She looked understandably confused.

"What are you doing here, Abby?" she hissed. "You're going to mess things up."

"Get behind me now, Anita," I said quickly. "Plans have changed."

Andersen stopped in confusion when he recognized me.

"Good evening, Mr. Andersen," I said evenly.

Chapter 23

His reaction was instant, and devastatingly effective. What had I been thinking? The man was a professional killer, I never stood a chance. Before I could move a finger, he had my arm in a vice grip and a gun to my head. So much for my tough girl image. Just as Andersen made his move, four or five plainclothes officers materialized out of nowhere, guns drawn. "Nobody move," one of them yelled. It was the standard hostage scene — *Don't move, or she gets it* kind of thing. I guess I'm lucky everybody froze.

At this point, Joe must have realized that, unless he did a quick shift, his goose was cooked. He pulled out his gun as well and shouted, "Andersen! Let her go. It's all over. You'll only make things worse."

Andersen didn't seem convinced, but maybe he was thinking twice about committing murder with a pack of cops as witnesses. He shifted his grip on me as Joe started to move.

"Joe! What the hell are you doing?" he spat.

Joe kept moving in. "It's done. You can't get away," he said.

"Don't come any closer." Andersen's voice was dangerously low. I felt his body tense.

Maybe Joe knew that it was now or never to prove himself a good cop. He closed in, holding out his hand for the gun like a father to his delinquent son. I felt the pressure ease from my head, but not the grip on my arm. But Andersen didn't hand the gun to Joe. He levelled it at him.

I saw my moment, and reflex took over as I yelled and threw my weight against Andersen's gun arm. I heard shots and screams; maybe some were mine because I felt a searing jolt to my shoulder. Then it all went black. I fell back — down into an inky blackness where pain had no hold.

I'm not sure how long I trod water down there. Occasionally I must have come up for air — I dimly remember flashing lights, worried faces looking down at me, sirens, an attractive pair of male eyes above a sterile mask, the odd shot of pain.

They must have drugged me well, because the next time I surfaced, this time in a hospital bed, I felt no pain. It was very white after all that blackness. Next to me sat my mother. It was strangely pleasant to see her. She was meditating or sleeping, and I couldn't seem to talk anyway so I just slipped a little less deeply down into a peaceful, drugged slumber.

My injuries were not life-threatening, I was just completely exhausted. When I finally awoke properly, they told me I'd slept for two days. My mother stayed by my side for the first day, but once I had surfaced long enough to say, "Hi Mom, I'm fine, nice to see you," or something like that, the nurse convinced her to go home for her own much-needed sleep. Roger found out I was there — from an account in the newspaper, he said — and came to visit after I regained consciousness. I wasn't very good company and neither was he. He said something about my being too fond of trouble and shuffled out awkwardly mumbling something about seeing me later. As he left I caught a glimpse of a uniformed policeman outside the door. Shit, I thought, wondering if he was protecting me or protecting the rest of the world *from* me.

Early on that third morning, the attractive eyes arrived without the surgical mask, but with a very pleasant bedside manner, to give me the medical details on what had happened to me. I was beginning to take an interest in my surroundings and was registering a dull throbbing from various locations in my body. My wrists were nicely bound in white tape, and my arm was taped from wrist to shoulder. My upper body was wrapped like a mummy and I could feel a turban-like bandage on my head.

"You had a nasty bump on your head and several cuts to your arms and wrists. You were pretty bloody from the bullet that hit your upper shoulder, but very lucky actually: no bones impacted and little muscular damage. We've immobilized your arm for the time being. With some time to heal and a little physio you'll be good as new."

Dr. Jaeger went on, "Your wrists were badly cut, I'm afraid. We took out almost twenty slivers of glass, and salved the wound extensively. We'll see how it looks after your dressing is changed. How did you damage them so badly? It must have happened prior to the shooting."

Memory flooded back. "You don't want to know," I said.

He raised his eyebrows at me, but when I didn't elaborate, he shrugged and continued, "Anyway you're a lot better off than the other three they brought in that night."

Oh my God, I thought. What happened to Anita? Maybe it was a case of temporary amnesia: I had forgotten all about her.

"Doctor?" I said anxiously, my gaze held by his mesmerizing eyes. "What other three?"

"The ones that came in with you. There was a young woman who was seriously injured with a gunshot wound in her upper chest. She had internal bleeding, a collapsed lung and severe shock. Good thing she's young and a fighter. She's still in intensive care, not completely out of danger, but stable. We were lucky."

I closed my eyes and said a silent prayer of thanks to numerous gods.

"Can I see her?" I asked.

"Not yet," he said. "Don't want to risk infection. But she's receiving the best of medical attention, and some protective lawyer is standing in for next of kin."

"What lawyer?" I asked, suddenly in a cold sweat as I remembered about O'Casey.

"I believe they are calling her 'Bulldog Martin.' She's pretty tough, keeping everyone at bay."

Not O'Casey then. I breathed another sigh of relief, unable to believe that Juaneva would have been involved in anything nefarious.

"Doctor, you said two others came in. Who were they?"

He looked doubtful.

"I will leave that for Ms. Martin to explain." With that, the doctor made an efficient and very graceful exit before I could think of any way to scrounge another minute or two of those beautiful baby blue eyes.

Oh dear, I thought. Maybe I murdered O'Casey. That's why Doc's not telling me anything. And that would explain the police officer at my door.

Interrupting my thoughts, an efficient nurse came in, disconnected me from the IV and helped me out of bed. The going was tough. I was bedsore, achy and still tightly bound at the upper chest and shoulders, but I knew I should start the rest of me moving before rigor mortis set in. The nurse assisted me through my morning ablutions and helped me back into bed, where I lay longing for a tall cappuccino.

I promptly dozed off, exhausted from the rigours of the morning's exercise, but woke with a start when Juaneva arrived, looking tired and overworked.

"You're looking much better," she said. "I'm sorry that I don't have much time to visit but I imagine you want to know what happened."

"What about Andersen? Is he talking?"

"He's in jail for murder. He killed that police officer O'Casey had called in."

I stared. "Joe's dead?"

"Yes," she nodded. "Shot twice by Andersen before the other police got to him. Andersen went for Anita too but his shot went wide. My guess is that our friend Joe took advantage of Andersen's public aggression to try to silence him. You were caught in the crossfire. But, as with any police shooting, the Special Investigations Unit has to do a thorough investigation. They are going to ask you some tough questions. Once you and I have sorted things out, I'll let them see you. Don't worry, I won't let them badger you as long as you cooperate with me."

I nodded, and then I had an anxious thought. "Juaneva? What

about O'Casey? Is he … okay?"

"He's in a coma," she said. "I'm still coming to terms with that one. They expect him to recover but the one thing Andersen has said to the police is that O'Casey was his partner. Maybe he thinks that by fingering O'Casey he'll get leniency, but that's unlikely."

"Juaneva, it's true about O'Casey. He and Andersen were working together. When I phoned your office that evening just before the setup, the receptionist said there was interference on the line but I think it was a voice distortion machine. I had received a threatening call with the same distortion earlier in the week. I put two and two together and when I saw O'Casey at the ACC I had to stop him from alerting Andersen. I hit him, Juaneva, with my bike lock. I wasn't trying to kill him but I had to stop him somehow. Who knows what would have happened to Anita?"

I stopped talking abruptly and put my hand to my mouth in shock. "Oh no!"

"What's wrong?" said Juaneva in alarm.

"My bike. It's been there for three days. It's bound to be gone. Or seriously stripped. Not another one!"

She rolled her eyes. "Is that all," she said. "Don't worry. The police took it for evidence. At least we can explain now how your lock has O'Casey's blood on it. I don't imagine, given the circumstances, the police will be pushing for assault charges. And you'll get your bike back eventually."

"Oh my God, I'm so relieved. You've set my mind at rest. Look, O'Casey's into a lot more dirty stuff than you could ever imagine. If he wakes up before I can fill you in, promise me you won't tell him anything or listen to anything he tells you, and don't let the police near him either. We need to plan out a strategy to protect Anita and make him accountable for what he has done."

She looked at me warily but nodded. "Okay. I'm going to trust you for now on this. Not much change recently in his condition anyway. Doctors are hopeful though." She patted my knee, the one safe place to touch. "I'll talk to you later."

My next visitor was Roger again. I could tell that he was still uncomfortable.

"What's wrong, Rog?"

"I don't know, Abby," he said almost squirming. "I guess I just don't like hospitals."

"I know. Neither do I." I didn't press him. I was tired again and ready for an uninterrupted nap. He left a short while later with only a light kiss. I'd learned to trust my instincts, and they told me that his distance was more than temporary. Maybe my days with Roger were at an end. The fact that I lived a little wild seemed to have lost its allure. It had been fun with him for a while but in the long run, he probably wanted a nice, staid, upwardly mobile, professional wife. I felt sad, but who was I fooling? It had never been a relationship destined for permanence.

Later that evening Juaneva returned; she got right down to business.

"Now, if I am going to advise you, I need to know how this all happened. I learned some from Anita on Monday but," she indicated my wrists, "there are obviously pieces missing."

So I told Juaneva the whole story. I detailed what I had discovered about Johnson and Andersen's business dealings and Andersen's hold on Johnson. While I told her about the little shares finagle, carefully keeping Sparky's name out of it, Juaneva was shaking her head but did not interrupt. When I described how I had set up a meeting with Johnson and the horrifying consequences of that, her eyes widened, she pursed her lips and she shook her head again.

"When I realized that we were trapped," I said. "I was regretting not letting O'Casey in on my plan. I thought we were toast and he could have saved us if he'd known about it."

I continued on, describing how Johnson and I had managed to extricate ourselves and how I had called O'Casey's line to check in. Then I stopped for a moment and looked Juaneva straight in the eye.

"This is where things began to fall into place and I realized that I had made a terrible mistake taking Anita to O'Casey. Remember that I knew O'Casey because he defended my father when he was fighting developers like Johnson? I had always thought of O'Casey as a hero, and so did my dad. He held him up as an example, a rich man standing up for the poor working people ..."

Juaneva nodded. "Go on."

"Well it turns out that was all just a lie. He was in on Johnson's plans all along, both when he was supposedly defending my dad and now with Anita. In fact, Johnson told me that O'Casey was his silent partner, and masterminded most of his business dealings.

"And listen, Juaneva," I said, anxious that she believe me. "Something he said to his assistant, that I was 'tied up', shows that he was part of the attempt to put me away permanently. It wouldn't have made any difference if I'd had let O'Casey know about my plan to see Johnson except that maybe I would have clued in sooner. As it is, I was almost too late. Anita could have been disappeared back to Eastern Europe, sold elsewhere or worse. O'Casey's been getting away with this for a long time. No wonder he, the wonder lawyer, couldn't keep my dad out of jail. He didn't want to! O'Casey wanted my father out of the way because Dad was actually being effective. It was the perfect cover, human rights lawyer with a social conscience by day, developer's friend by night.

"If I hadn't caught on, Anita might have been badly hurt. Think about it Juaneva, why were there no cops, no immigration people, no RCMP officers? Of course O'Casey wouldn't tell you what he was really up to."

Juaneva interrupted for the first time.

"I don't know what to think but we're going to need proof of all this if it's true. Andersen's squealing but we don't want him to get a deal. I think Johnson is our best bet — now I see why his lawyer has been trying to contact me. But we'll need evidence that will stand up in court."

"I know," I said. "I've been thinking. I bet if we got my computer friend on to it, we would find an electronic trail that shows that O'Casey is tied to many of Johnson's and Andersen's dealings."

She stood up and began to pace. "To think that I trusted that man. I wonder how many other times I have hurt someone without knowing it. That's not why I became a lawyer. I chose to work for O'Casey precisely because of his humane reputation."

She looked pretty pissed.

"Okay," she said. "I'm going straight to work on this. I'll draw up some plans for different scenarios. At least O'Casey taught me some things well," she muttered.

"I'm glad of one thing," she went on. "Anita was wired. I insisted on it. O'Casey probably agreed just for my sake, thinking he would get rid of it when he dealt with Anita. I'm sure he didn't realize that it would serve to incriminate him. The tape was voice activated and I remember O'Casey reaffirming that he had everything set up and that Anita would be well protected. He said that he had called the police. We were going to get Andersen cold. The recorder would have caught all that, so now this will serve to link O'Casey to Andersen because of course he didn't call the police. There was no friend from the RCMP — nothing. I better track down that tape." Juaneva said, agitated. "I was so busy concentrating on keeping an eye on Anita's condition that I forgot completely about it. I'm going to make sure it's safe now."

"That was pretty swift thinking about the wire, Juaneva," I said as my eyes started to droop. I was feeling pretty tired and worn. I had finally gotten the whole thing off my chest and I was very relieved to see that "Bulldog Martin" was going to help me out.

"Juaneva. I'm sorry but I'm feeling pretty bagged. Can the rest wait until tomorrow?"

She got up. "Of course. I'm sure that this was tough for you but I had to know the details. I really like Anita. She has struggled so hard and has been ground down long enough. I'm determined to help her out of this mess so I guess that makes us friends, Abby. I'll do what I can to help you too. Have a good rest. You'll have to speak to the police tomorrow before you're discharged. Your doctor says you'll probably be well enough to go home.

Chapter 24

Juaneva brokered a satisfactory visit with the police on Friday. I had signed a prepared statement. She spoke and I did as she had told me: nodded my head and kept my mouth shut.

The nice doctor brought me two bike magazines as a goodbye present.

"I gather we share a penchant for bikes. I thought I'd give you these to look at during your first days of recuperation. There are some hot new bikes in there and one or two good articles on the trails in BC."

He was drop-dead gorgeous, sweet, competent, no wedding ring and a biker to boot!

"So, you're a bike enthusiast?" I said, ever so nonchalantly.

"Whenever I get some time off, I hit the trails."

"I've never been a big mountain bike rider," I mused. "Maybe I'll try it out once I recover. Thanks Doc. You've been great."

I was trying to remain disinterested. After all, I wasn't likely to see him again. I certainly wasn't planning on any more harrowing adventures that would require renewed medical assistance.

"You should be fine if you take it easy with those wounds." He wrote some scribbles on a pad.

"Here is the number for physio. The doctor in charge there will take over your care. Enjoy the magazines."

As he got up, I saluted with my free arm. "Will do. Thanks again." I was sad to see him go. What a lovely bedside manner.

Juaneva came in around noon.

"I hear you'll be leaving today. Congratulations."

"Thanks. I'm chomping at the bit, though I guess it'll be a tough go for a while."

"I'll be in touch about the case. The police seem satisfied at the moment with your part in it all. Don't forget to follow up on the search for hard evidence with your computer friend." She paused and seemed to be trying to find her words.

"From what I've heard from Anita and some of your friends who came by, you're quite the hound when it comes to uncovering and following up on clues. If you're interested I might be able to use you in some investigations. After all, you won't be able to earn a living riding for a while."

I laughed as I exclaimed, "What a concept, being hired to be nosy."

"One thing is absolutely necessary though. You have to be completely open with me and stick to what I ask you to do."

"I think I can try to do that. I'd be thrilled to work for you!"

"Okay then. I'm negotiating with another firm that heard I am getting out of O'Casey's. Once things are settled and they agree to my terms, I'll let you know what I need for this case. You can start with the computer stuff right away, though. It will take a while for this case to wend its way through the system to court." She got up to leave. "I'm sure I'll see you here when you come to visit Anita anyway."

"They said I can see her Monday if her condition continues to improve. Thanks Juaneva. I'm your slave."

"I hope so. Be prepared for hard work."

My mother came to pick me up near the end of the day in her sporty BMW and drove me the short distance back to Kensington in style. I took all the cards from well-wishers and three of the flower arrangements; one for Maria, one for Arabella and one for me. I sent the rest on for Anita with a message to get well soon. My mother was attentive and helpful even though it was tough being so dependent. When we got to my place she delivered me to the front door into Maria's welcoming arms. As I turned to thank Arabella, she interrupted,

"Abby, I'm going to park the car and then I'm coming back," she said seriously. "We have to talk."

Uh oh, I thought. I must be really in for it if Arabella was actually using the parking lot and venturing into my place.

Maria interrupted any further musing. She had carried in the flowers and now was back for me.

"Don't stand out here in the cold, Abby. We want you to stay well." She frowned, "Are you sure you don't want to stay with us or your mom for at least the weekend?"

"Thanks, Maria, but I'll be fine." I said as we walked into the busy shop. She opened a path ahead through the customers to prevent my being bumped. I still was pretty sore, although the doctor's prognosis was that I would heal well.

"Make way for the patient," Maria announced to the crowd. "The Kensington hero has returned!"

"Oh Maria," I exclaimed, embarrassed as people began applauding and whistling. "You know I'm not one for the spotlight."

She shrugged and smiled, "That's too bad, Abby. We're happy you and Anita are alive. You're too irresponsible when it comes to your own safety, but you did a good thing bringing those guys down. We're allowed to be proud of you."

It was a long speech for Maria. I decided to accept with good grace.

"Okay, okay, but can we go upstairs now? I'm worn out."

It was true; I was tired from the trip back. It was frustrating to have to go so slowly. I was glad to be out of the hospital but I knew I wasn't going to be a very good patient, even if I was taking care of myself.

"Maria," I said as we started up the stairs, "one of those flower arrangements is for you. Could you bring the other, the one you sent me, up to my place when you get a chance? I left the rest for Anita." I stopped on my threshold and caught my breath.

"I should have known that you and Arabella wouldn't be able to resist," I said as I walked in. The place sparkled. The fruit bowl was full, the eight remaining bikes had ribbons festooned on them, and a homemade *Welcome Home* sign was pinned to my wall.

"It looks lovely, Maria! Did the kids make that sign?" She nodded. "Tell them it made me feel better right away," I said. Maybe the painkillers were making me sweet and gracious. I made a mental note to get off them as soon as possible.

Arabella came in carrying two cappuccinos and Maria said, "Now your mom's here I'm going back down to work. I'll check back later, okay? Oh, by the way," she said turning to me again, "Sparky called and insisted that I tell you that she has couriered the package to Bitsy. I'm sure you understand her cryptic message better than I do," Maria said drily, shaking her head.

I nodded, glad that Sparky had taken the initiative. I made a mental note to call her the next day to thank her and pass on Juaneva's proposal. Sparky and I would go from fellow felons to partners in search of justice. It felt good.

"That's great news, Maria. Thanks."

"No problem. See you later."

"Come up after you close the store."

She gave me a thumbs-up and closed the door behind her.

I turned to Arabella, "Hey, Mom," I said. "I guess you had fun fixing up my place. You did a, um, good job."

"Thanks, darling. I know you don't like people messing with your space but we thought that you might make an exception this time. Not that you had much choice," she laughed. "Now, before we talk, I want to help you get settled in. Are you exhausted? Do you want to go straight to bed?"

"I am tired but I think I'll sit up for a while." I picked up one of the coffees. "Thank you so much for this. I have been dying for an Overdrive coffee."

Mother walked to the little fridge and pulled out a small platter of fresh vegetables with three different dips in the centre.

"Make yourself comfortable, Abby," she fussed. "I picked this up from the Emporium. I knew you'd need a hit of fresh food after the hospital."

"Such treatment!" I exclaimed, munching veggies and sipping gratefully at the coffee. "But Mom, you've got me worried. What do you want to talk to me about?"

"Down to brass tacks right away as usual, Abby. It must mean you're well on the way to recovery," my mother commented with a wry smile. Then she turned serious again.

"It's time we have a talk about Liam O'Casey. There are some things you need to know."

"You too Mom. He's not what we thought."

"I gathered that you figured that out, dear, from the little that the press have revealed."

"Are you telling me that you knew he's a crook and kept it to yourself?"

"That's just it, Abby. I had no idea of his connection to the Market or this man, Andersen. I didn't even know you were nosing around in all this. If I had known you were going to take this girl Anita to him, I would have told you a thing or two. All I knew about was his connection to Johnson many years back."

"But Mom, if you knew about that, why did you continue the myth about him helping Dad?"

"I know it seems strange, dear, but I did it for your dad. It would have crushed him to know that O'Casey had lied and thrown him to the wolves. He was never quite right after that time in jail anyway. And your father always saw himself as the underdog, the people's martyr. I didn't want to be the one to tell him he trusted the wrong guy. I told you I still loved him even though I just couldn't live that way anymore."

I slumped.

"This just bites, Mom. Why did you go out with O'Casey then?"

"I'm not too proud of that, dear, but I had to figure out a way to get his help, to make sure I could provide for you kids. I played along with him. I'm not sure he was even aware that I knew about him and Johnson. I think he tried to make some kind of internal moral peace with himself by helping make sure we could stay on our feet."

"Okay, so we've got the bastard now. What's the problem?"

"Well, first I have to say how sorry I am not to have let you know — I could have been responsible for you being killed. And secondly, I want to ask you and Juaneva Martin to keep quiet about the fact that he betrayed your dad."

"What?" I exclaimed. "But why?"

"Because dear," she said quietly, "it will hurt your father too much should he get wind of all this. He'll never be able to trust anyone again."

I thought for a bit. "I guess you're right — he probably would take it that way. But I don't know if we can suppress this."

"I realize that. I'm just asking you to try. We're all very angry with Liam and he deserves our anger, but let's try to direct it in the most useful way possible."

It peeved me to have to think of this but I realized that my mother had done what she felt she had to do to take care of her family. She had compromised in a way that was unpalatable, but she did it for us. It was all going to take some time for me to digest.

"Now we'd better see to your needs," said Arabella brightly, the conversation obviously over. "I want to make sure that you are well set up for your first weekend on your own, although I'm sure your friends will be over. They were hassling the hospital and Maria all the time asking when you would be home. And Abby, please call me if it's too tough. It's hard for me to let you do this on your own but I know how independent you like to be. Since I love you, I'll have to let you do things your own way."

My eyes filled with tears. "I know you love me, Mom, and I really do appreciate your honesty about the whole thing with O'Casey. It must have been so hard for you back then."

She gave me a gentle hug. "It's okay dear. I may not have done the right thing but I did what I thought was right at the time. I made my own peace with it long ago."

Arabella helped me change into loose sweats, the most practical apparel for the next day or two. She showed me some other treats that she had brought, some fair trade chocolate, Portuguese tarts and a simple power shake mix. Before she left she made me get into bed, well propped up with pillows that had materialized from nowhere. When she had done all I would let her she gave me another hug and kiss and took her leave. She left me with plenty to think about and a larger appreciation of the sacrifices she had made for us.

I soon dozed off. Maria woke me briefly before she left and then I drifted again into a deliciously quiet, uninterrupted sleep.

***

Anita looked amazingly healthy and happy as she and Juaneva served us a delicious vegetable pasta dinner. Although she had been cautioned to take it easy for a while, doctors predicted a full recovery. Juaneva treated her like a good friend; they seemed to flourish in each other's company. In a twist of fate, having to convalesce in the hospital had helped Anita finish her heroin withdrawal. And moving in with Juaneva had helped her remain drug free and optimistic about the future.

I felt a large dollop of contentment as I looked around the table at my assembled friends. Maria, Beano, Alice, Sparky, Anita and Juaneva all seemed similarly content. Sadly, Arabella hadn't been able to make it. She was helping to run a meditation retreat with a new-found guru boyfriend.

Lucky for us Juaneva was an excellent cook; she had been teaching Anita who was, as she phrased it, a willing sponge for any new information. Anita preferred to say that she was not going to blow the chance to start her life over and swore she'd do everything to the fullest.

"Okay, you two," I blurted as we finished the main course. "What about those surprises you mentioned? Were we brought here under false pretences?"

Juaneva laughed.

"Okay, Anita, you win, she waited until dessert."

Anita laughed too, looking like a cat that just found a pint of cream.

"You see, Abby, we had a little bet about how long you could wait. Juaneva thought you wouldn't make it past the appetizer stage. I had a little more faith in you. So I win."

"Anyway," Juaneva interjected. "We're actually waiting for one more guest before we start giving out the goody bags, so to speak."

That piqued my interest even further but before I could say anything else, the doorbell rang. Anita ran over to answer it.

"Come in, come in. We're all in the dining room. You're just in time for dessert."

We looked expectantly toward the doorway. Who was this unexpected guest? When he entered, my heart dropped and soared simultaneously. It was the glorious Dr. Jaeger.

Anita smiled. "Hey, everyone. For those of you who don't know, this is my miracle — Dr. Jaeger. Come on in."

He smiled, "Hello all, just call me Andy. I hope you don't mind my crashing your party." Sparky gave me a knowing wink.

Jaeger turned to me. "I met Anita at the hospital the other day when she was on the floor for a check-up. She suggested I join your celebration after I asked how you were doing, Abby."

I was momentarily speechless. Juaneva brought a chair next to mine and the golden boy sat down, his hand casually resting on the back of my chair. Be still my heart. Maria raised her eyebrows and Sparky winked again. Both had heard all about my fantasy doctor. Beano reached over and shook the doctor's hand. "Glad to meet you, Andy."

I recovered my voice.

"Okay, I've got my present," I said, no longer pretending to be cool. "What about the rest of you?"

Juaneva smiled mysteriously as she served fruit salad and yogurt.

"All in good time, Abby."

I was forced to sit back and accept the wait. At least I had a diversion. Andy turned to me again, while the others politely ignored us, or at least pretended to.

"And how are you, Abby?" He gently lifted my hands and peered at my wrists. "It looks like your wrists are recovering. I guess you haven't had a chance to get out for a ride in this snowy weather."

"I still can't put that much weight on the bad shoulder," I said. "But I have gone to a couple of spinning classes on King Street. They have reclining bikes so I can work my legs and not strain my arms. I'm pretty confident I'll be up to par by spring."

"Sounds good. Where are those classes you go to? Maybe I could join you sometime. We could go for a bite after."

"Do they let doctors out of the hospital for that long?" I teased.

"Only if we're very good," he quipped back. "I could say I was making a house call."

I remembered to be polite. "Oh, and thanks for the magazines. I read them from cover to cover those first few days. I couldn't move much, so it was a great way to let my mind run free." I didn't mention that he himself had figured prominently in my imagination.

"No problem. Did it get you thinking about mountain biking?"

"As a matter of fact, I've been thinking of visiting a friend in BC who runs a bike shop. He's really thrilled with recumbents. Said I should try his and said he'd lend me a bike to try trail riding. I told him I'd see if I can get away in the summer."

Our conversation was cut off as Juaneva rose to speak again.

"Okay, you guys, Anita and I did entice you here with the hint of surprises. It's been fun to watch Abby struggle with the suspense but I think we found the right diversion for her."

Everyone laughed as I reddened. When Andy asked innocently, "Am I missing something here?" the laughter doubled in volume, but he seemed to take it all in good stride.

Juaneva stood up and raised her hands to quiet everyone down. "Anita has the first announcement." All eyes turned to Anita expectantly.

"Hold onto your hats," she paused dramatically. "I have a real job, mentoring at the rehab clinic in the Market." She looked so proud. "I have to thank Beano for recommending me, I am so thrilled at the thought of being able to help other people." We started to applaud but she held up her hand.

"Wait! There's more. In the fall I'm enrolled to study for my high school equivalency and then I'm going to college! I'll be taking Early Childhood Education because I want to work in a daycare," she said triumphantly. Now we clapped wildly and chorused our approval.

When things settled down again, Maria commented, "That's wonderful Anita. You were so good with my kids. They keep asking when you'll come over again. You'll make an excellent daycare worker."

We nodded as Alice stood up and raised her glass, "To Anita," she said.

"To Anita," we all agreed.

Anita smiled with delight. "I want to thank you all for being so helpful and supportive. Two months ago I was a washed-up drug-addicted hooker and now look at me. I particularly want to thank

Juaneva, Maria and Abby for their belief in me. I am so lucky. I think of you all as family."

She turned to Beano, "I also want to thank you Beano for finding me the rehab. I know that was tough for you. Alice told me that it stirred up your memories of addiction and withdrawal."

He nodded. "Well, that's all in the past now. I'm glad to have helped."

We were silent for a moment at these moving declarations until Juaneva spoke up.

"Thanks, Anita, for getting everyone to be quiet."

This broke the tension and we all laughed again.

"Now it's my turn," Juaneva said over the laughter. We quieted down again as she began, "As you know from the news, or from Abby's uncontrollable mouth, the net is closing in on O'Casey, who has recovered well enough to be prosecuted in court. Andersen is still cooperating in the desperate hope that he will have a reduced sentence or avoid deportation. And Johnson seems to have turned over a new leaf. I think this is mostly due to his brush with death and his wife, Bitsy. He is cooperating too and we consider him a helpful witness. Oh, and the police finally broke the alibis of the actual murderers so they are now in custody and busy singing about Andersen's role.

"It turns out that Joe was actually a double agent. He had infiltrated Andersen's organization. The police still aren't sure if he turned bad in there or was just trying to get in deeper to uncover all Andersen's dirty dealings. That's why the police hassled you, Abby. They were afraid you would upset the balance of their investigation and perhaps expose Joe. Now we're working with them to build a solid case, so we should be successful when it comes to court in the spring.

"But," she said, holding up a familiar brown-spotted, crumpled piece of paper, "I have a message from the Johnsons for all of you. Well, essentially it's like a shopping list, with items checked off. It appears that Abby was attempting to lean on Johnson that fated Monday." She looked at me pointedly with raised eyebrows.

"All in a good cause," I said protesting.

Juaneva continued, "Here we go."

"For Abby's computer friend: one iMac computer." Juaneva looked up. "It's in my office, Sparky. I may have trouble letting it go.

"A $10,000 trust fund for Anita's education." A spontaneous cheer broke out.

"Jerry Sifton, the housing activist, has been hired to assist Johnson in his developments in the Market and conduct consultations with the community anti-development group on appropriate construction of mixed housing on the sites in the Market."

"A $2000 infusion of bike parts to the community centre bike workshop, which will be bought from The Squeaky Wheel."

"A $2000 donation to the drug rehab centre in the Market. And, finally," she looked up, smiling, "a Rocky Mountain bike for Abby."

"Alright," said Jaeger with a broad grin, "Now you've no excuses."

"But that wasn't on the list," I protested.

"Well," said Juaneva, "perhaps Johnson decided that you deserved something for your, um, pains. I think it's an appropriate gift."

There was something to being nosy and mouthy after all. How about that! While plumbing the murky depths trying to hook a shark, I had also netted a challenging new job that was right up my alley and a shiny new mountain bike. And, to top it all off, it looked like I might get to enjoy Dr. Andy Jaeger's bedside manner after all. Things were looking up!

More Fine Fiction from Sumach Press ...

- THE BOOK OF MARY
A Novel by Gail Sidonie Sobat

- RIVER REEL
A Novel by Bonnie Laing

- REVISING ROMANCE
A Novel by Melanie Dugan

- ROADS UNRAVELLING
Short Stories by Kathy-Diane Leveille

- GIFTS: POEMS FOR PARENTS
Edited by Rhea Tregebov

- OUTSKIRTS:
WOMEN WRITING FROM SMALL PLACES
Edited by Emily Schultz

- AURAT DURBAR:
WRITINGS BY WOMEN OF SOUTH ASIAN ORIGIN
Edited by Fauzia Rafiq

- CAST A LONG SHADOW
A Novel by Leena Lander

- THE MIDDLE CHILDREN
Short Fiction by Rayda Jacobs

- PENNY MAYBE
A Novel by Kathleen Martin

- THE OTHER SIDE
A Novel by Cynthia Holz

- THE Y CHROMOSOME
Speculative Fiction by Leona Gom

- GRIZZLY LIES
A Mystery Novel by Eileen Coughlan

- JUST MURDER
A Mystery Novel by Jan Rehner
WINNER OF THE 2004 ARTHUR ELLIS AWARD
FOR BEST FIRST CRIME NOVEL

- HATING GLADYS
A Suspense Novel by Leona Gom

- MASTERPIECE OF DECEPTION
An Art Mystery by Judy Lester

- FREEZE FRAME
Mystery Fiction by Leona Gom

Find out more at www.sumachpress.com